3 into 2

Winifred Beresford-Davis

Outskirts Press, Inc.
Denver, Colorado

Outskirts Press, Inc.
http://www.outskirtspress.com

ISBN: 978-1-4327-3079-6

Outskirts Press and the "OP" logo are trademarks belonging to Outskirts Press, Inc.

I want to thank my Lord and Savior, Jesus Christ who is first in my life. I thank you, Lord for inspiration. When there seems to be no more, you open up a well spring and just let it flow. I thank you.

I would love to thank my prayer partners. These ladies motivate and encourage me and each other to live the life God wants us to live. I thank you for the daily prayers and your enthusiasm in discussing the Word.

Of course, my love and appreciation go out to my children, Dawn, Daniel, and Richard and my beautiful grandchildren, Jahstin, Judah, Malik, Medina, Kaitlyn, and Logan. God bless you.

Dedication

This book is dedicated to my school mate and good friend, Janett James. We have been friends for over fifty years. Janett has always encouraged me to "write it down." One day I decided to take her up on it, and to my surprise, the thoughts just kept flowing, so here we are with our first of many. Thanks Janett for your love, prayers, motivation and encourage-ement.

"And you that were sometime alienated and enemies in your mind by wicked works, yet now hath he reconciled. In the body of his flesh through death, to present you holy and unblameable and unreproveable in his sight."

Col.1:20-21, KJV.

CHAPTER 1

"Stop tickling me! Stop it! You're making me pee myself; Oh, Lawd! Stop it Joe!" Lula Mae laughed shrilly as Joe released her.

"Yuh gotta stop doin dat; yuh mek meh laff too much."

"I like to see you laugh, it makes me happy," replied Joe.

"O.K. but yuh know if meh mama hear meh laffing she gon know dat I ain't doin meh work, and she sure gon whip meh behin when she get de chance. I have to hang de wash now."

Lula Mae got up, picked up her basket of clothing and went to hang out the laundry. As she walked with the basket under her right hand, she waved goodbye with her left, and gave Joe a sweet smile.

It was so much fun playing with Joe. He was cool for a white boy. He was a skinny boy with some freckles around his nose. He had brown hair with a little curl in it. Joe was 5 feet tall, and he was 10 years old. I was a skinny Black girl, around 4 feet with short, dark brown hair. My short, tiny braids would not stay flat, but would stick out in all angles on my head; so I would use a head scarf to keep the braids flat. I had dancing eyes, at least that's what my mama told me; I would imagine my eyes dancing around in my head, because I did not understand what dancing eyes were. My mama said, "Yuh jest have pretty eyes, dey smile an dey dance, dat's all."

Well, Joe liked playing with me and we had a lot of fun together. We would get behind one of the houses and sit on the ground and have ourselves a very good time. We would run and play catch, marbles, and hopscotch in the yard.

I don't think his mama liked him playing with me for whenever she comes to the back of the house to sit on the back porch, and if she should see us together she'll say, "What you and that colored gal doing? Come on up and get to your books; and you, Lula Mae run along and find something to do. You got no business hanging round with white folks."

"Yes ma'am."

I would run off to do whatever I was supposed to do.

Years later, whenever Joe came to the back yard where we lived, I would leave what I was doing when I saw Joe, and he and I, would run off to the woods behind the colored folk's huts to play. We had lots of fun as usual. There were times when Joe helped me with my reading as I was not able to go back to the schoolhouse. There was too much work to be done, and they needed help in the big house, so school was eliminated. Joe brought me books and helped me so much that I was reading the books repeatedly, as I had no other books to read.

He said, "I can't keep up with you and these books." He smiled, and said, "I'm glad you like to read; books can take you so much farther than you can go."

Joe looked up at the sky, and raised his hand to drawn an imaginary place, as he spoke, "You can travel, meet important people, learn how to remedy things and lots more just by reading. It's just marvelous."

"I love to read and I love all the people in the books I read about," I said. "Sometimes I would pretend I was the person I was reading about, and make the faces and impressions as I read; you should see me, Joe. I try to imitate the way they talk, look at the pictures in the books and wish I had the clothes to dress like those rich white people. It is so much fun reading. I just love it." I was laughing so hard and Joe began to laugh too.

"Reading does make you happy, and I can hear it in your voice too." He mimicked me, "You sound fabulously well read," and he bowed to the ground when he said it.

"I decided that when I grow up and get married I would name my children all the names in the books I read."

"Really? How many children are you planning to have, Lula? Joe said with a smile, "Remember you have read many, many books." He turned his head to look at me, and was waiting patiently for my reply.

"I might have about ten or twelve," I replied and nodded my head as if I was agreeing with myself.

"Well, good luck to you, twelve is a lot of children," he said, "But if it makes you happy to have twelve, then so be it."

Over a period of time, Joe brought me some old tattered books, one was a dictionary; it started from the letter 'c' and ended at the letter't'. I didn't mind; it was mine and I loved it. I learned a new word everyday, and tried to use it in a sentence, the book gave me an example of how to use the word; so I muttered the sentence under my breath all day long, spelled the word, and wrote it in the air, in the sand, wherever I had the chance to use the new word. So I learned a lot of words, and their meanings. Although I did not understand many of the words and their meanings, the more I read, the more I understood.

Mama found me reading and would scold, "Git yuh hed outta dem books, gyal – dey nut gun do nuttin fo yung black gyals, git de housewuk dun. Yuh keep foolin yousef, yuh nag gon git no job wit dem books or nuttin, so stop de nunsense an do sum wuk."

I did what mama wanted but I will never give up on reading. I got to the point where I was reading about 10 books a month. If I did not get new books I would re-read the ones I liked.

After Joe saw that I could master the books on my own he started to help me with math. This subject also fascinated me and I was an eager learner and Joe liked teaching me. He was a good teacher himself. He was very patient. I loved it when he tried scolding me, "Oh! You made a careless mistake, now you'll have to kiss the teacher."

We both giggled, and I made so many mistakes that we did a lot of pecking on the cheek. I would peck him on the cheek, and I would get right back to work. I did not want anything to interfere with my learning and I did learn a lot from Joe.

As I read more and more, my speech improved. My pronunciation was flawless, however, when I was around the white folks I pretended to speak like all the Blacks on the plantation.

Oh, if things were always so simple. But, we grew up and what a life we led. I continued to work in the home of Mrs. Margaret Kettering, and whenever I got the time and could hide, I read the books Joe brought me. There was a library at his home. One day I took one down with the pretense of cleaning it and Mrs. Kettering came in. "What are you doing with that book?" she yelled.

"Ma'am, it wus dusty, jest wanted to mek it clean, Ma'am" Lula Mae quickly put the book back and continued with her work.

The Ketterings home was the best in Georgia to me. I had not seen many other homes, but everyone said it was a beautiful place to live. There was over ten acres of land. The Big house as we called it was where the White folks lived. It was made of white brick on all sides; there was a sun room, huge kitchen where it seemed all the Negroes worked. There was always so much to do. There was a spacious living room, formal dining room, an office, library and a large back deck. The bedrooms were upstairs, and there were five of them, with four full bathrooms. Mr. Kettering was always having something updated in the house, so the house was beautiful to look at. Further back, about a quarter mile stood other smaller houses for the staff. There were five cottages for us Negroes to live in.

Our house was the second one from the big house. It was a beautiful cottage, with two bedrooms, a small kitchen and a family room. Mr. Kettering had architectural skill and had input on how these houses were built; he was very proud of these houses. Ours was painted pale white on the outside with a blue trim. My dad liked gardening and he planted flowers for all the houses. He also planted a vegetable garden specially for my mom. My little sister, Janie who was two years old, and I were able to water the garden and pick the vegetables with the other children who lived in the other houses.

We were well cared for as Mr. Kettering was Mayor of our small town of Stedmore. Mr. Kettering was a fine old man, very gentle and had wispy grey hair. His face had moles on it and some brown spots. He had many wrinkles and they puckered when he laughed. It was told that Mr. Kettering had lots of children by the colored women on the plantation. We saw many mulatto children running around the yard. They were also treated special by everyone because we all knew that they belonged to Mr. Kettering.

However, Mr. Kettering treated everyone fairly. He visited our cottages in the yard and talked to the men, always asking everyone "Is everything alright here? If not, let Bill here know when you need any help and he will fix things for you."

We all knew to tell Mr. Bill when we needed anything because Mr. Kettering told us this repeatedly.

Mrs. Kettering on the other hand had been different. She was stern, unkind, and real mean. She had light brown hair, a real pointed nose, deep set gray eyes, and she always wore her hair in a bun at the back of her neck. She was medium weight, and around 5 feet 4 inches. She had a nice shape but somehow her breasts were big for her body. Sometimes she would pick them up with her hands and settle them in her bra neatly.

There was sadness about her and she didn't seem to have any close friends. She had one sister that lived far away and would only come to visit on some holidays. This sister was not married and it seemed Mrs. Kettering would make her feel badly about this situation, so she never visited much. Mrs. Kettering was a very lonely woman and because of this and other issues she had, she became a very bitter woman. Nobody wanted to be around her much – not her husband, her children or the servants. She was uncomfortable around the Black women, especially the ones Mr. Kettering was nice to. The problem was he was nice to everybody. He was a politician and always stopped and talked to people. He made you feel as if you were somebody. Even the children on the grounds he would stop and talk to them, he also knew everyone by name, and most of all he listened to whatever they had to say. He also always had candy on him for the children. Everybody loved Mr. Kettering; and so it was a sad day when he died.

CHAPTER 2

Joe and I were great friends, and stayed that way for a long time. Even though he went off to school, whenever he came home I was the first person he came to look for. He talked to me and encouraged me to keep up with my reading and math which he taught me to do. I was good at it and he brought me back books to read whenever he came back. He also helped me with my speech and laughed when I imitated people. He would hold his tummy and roll on the grass laughing so hard I think he would pee himself. He said to me, "One day you might even be an announcer on the radio."

We laughed, and I pretended to be announcing on the radio, "and now for the 6 'clock news. Master Joseph Kettering was seen behind the bushes playing with his colored friend, Miss Lula Mae Jackson."

"That's not exciting enough; you'll have to do better than that," Joe said.

"O.K. Sir," I mimicked. We continued to have fun with each other whenever Joe came home and could spend some time with me.

When Joe was 16 and I 12, He told me that he loved me and wanted to take care of me. I said, "You crazy! What do you want to happen to me?" We kissed for the first time, and it was simple and lovely.

He was very serious and this scared me a lot. He was a young White male from a very prestigious family, and I was a Black, servant girl, and this was the 1950s. He must have never thought about what would happen to us, but I really liked Joe. He was real nice for a White boy and he never made me feel different. My mother, on the other hand was very upset whenever she saw us together. She would scream, "Lula Mae, gyal yo betta get yerself in hay an put dese dishes away."

There was always something to do; shelling peas, hanging clothes, fetching wood, baking and cooking. There was also dusting, sweeping and polishing floors and silver in the big house. There never was a dull moment. The brightest moment of my life was when Joe brought me all his books that he didn't use anymore and I read them from cover to cover. If I did not understand something in the books I would mark it and when Joe came home he'd spend time explaining it all to me. He was very patient. Whenever Joe was at home he would steal me away and we would go to the back of the huts and sit on the log and we would talk for a while until someone missed him or me and started yelling, "Joe, or Lula Mae Where are you?"

Joe told me that he loved me very much and could not see himself living without me beside him. I became deadly afraid and wondered what would happen to me if anyone found out how we felt. I loved Joe too, but I could not release my full feelings because of our situation. We spent as much time together, hugging and kissing and planning our future. I figured it was all a dream, but Joe sounded so convincing. He told me "I will find a way for us to be together, I will!"

After Joe finished school and came back home for good. We started talking more and more and we became so serious I was having headaches. He was very special to me and told me I was the only one in the world for him. He wanted no one else but me. I did not know what to do. I tried to question my ma, but she said, "Dem white folks always want to have dey needs met by us colored folks. Gyal, leh me tell yuh dere is nuthin we cyan do. We jest have to let dem have dere way with us."

I never told her everything because I was afraid of what she might do. I was 18 years old and loved being with Joe.

"Great news!" Joe said one day, "I have figured out how we can get married and live together. We would have to run away to Alabama to an old doctor friend of mine."

"Could you really trust him?" Lula Mae asked tentatively. When she saw the look on his face she quickly added, "Nothing would be greater than being with you. I hope you believe that." That statement seemed to melt Joe's glum mood and he smiled.

"I love you Lula Mae and don't you ever forget that; I will do nothing to hurt you."

He proceeded to tell her about his doctor friend. He had met Dr. David Fitzgerald when he went to school and they got to talking and became good friends. He was old and lived alone in a big house and he had few servants. He told Joe that when he was younger, he had fallen in love with a Black girl but couldn't marry her because she was a servant in his mother's house and it was improper for a White man to love and marry a Black woman. He said, "She had the most beautiful eyes, they penetrated your soul. She had smooth black skin and she walked like a panther. When I thought of Nadine I couldn't eat, sleep or think straight." That was how Joe started telling Dr. Dave about Lula Mae.

He said, "My mother almost had a heart attack when she realized that I was in love with Nadine and would not let me see her. My mother was so smart; she led me to believe that she was sending Nadine away to become an accomplished Black woman, worthy of my affections. I trusted my mother and thought she had my best love interest at heart, but no, it was just a trick to send Nadine away and I never saw her again. She was crying very hard the last time I saw her. I was able to kiss her not knowing it was a kiss goodbye."

"Did you try looking for her?" asked Joe.

"It was no good for me in those days. I was young and everyone thought I had lost my mind. They could do whatever they wanted with me then. I had no say in the matter. Even if I did no one listened. I realize now that I should have fought them all. My parents, my church, my friends whoever was involved then. Now it's too late to even think about it. I beg her forgiveness for not fighting for her every day. Instead I went away and became a doctor. Since my parents' death, I inherited everything as an only child, plus I made lots of money, but I am not very happy. Riches never made anyone happy. I wish I had Nadine here with me to spend and enjoy all that I have worked for." He laughed when he said that. "I repeat," he said "Money is no substitute for a pretty, loving woman, and you can trust me on that."

Doc and Joe often sat for hours talking about his long lost love. He was always so sad. One day Joe asked him, "Did you ever find anyone else?"

"I never looked," he said. "I've had some meaningless relationships but nothing like her. She was real special. I cannot explain to you what it was like. She was the most beautiful darkie I ever did lay my eyes on. She had a regal look about her." He took her picture in his hand and looked at her as tears welled up in his eyes.

He spent the rest of his life regretting that he never searched for Nadine or fought his parents to find out where they had sent her, so he spent the rest of his life helping people. He was a very good doctor and was always in demand, he went over and beyond what he was supposed to do. He had a small practice, and also worked at the hospital. On Fridays, he would go to the other side of town in the very poor neighborhood and worked free of charge. Therefore, he had a large following; he made calls night or day, it didn't matter to him what hour it was, as long as he was available he worked.

The staff at the hospital loved him because they could always depend on him to do more than his share of work, and they showed him how much they appreciated him. Many patients owed Doc. because if they hadn't the money to pay, he still tended to them. Everyone who knew Doc. would do anything for him. He was revered in this small community; and rich and poor alike loved him. That was the reputation he had.

Joe sat remembering Doc and how he came to help him with Lula Mae. Joe told Lula Mae, "I'm not going to let you go. I love you and want to spend the rest of my life with you. I'll make arrangements for us to leave this place. I will be back from school soon and I'll have everything set up."

Lula Mae wondered if he was sane. He really must be crazy, and he wanted to have her hanged in the process. She kept her thoughts to herself and just smiled as she listened to him telling her of all the plans he had for them.

"I really mean it, Lula Mae, I love you and we will be together, I promise you." Although she knew he was crazy, he seemed so sincere that she did not know what to think or do. Although this sounded so crazy to her, it did awaken deeper emotions for her.

"I believe you, Joe, anything you say," was her answer after he kept asking her if she believed him, but deep down inside she could not believe him. He noticed that her eyes looked worried.

Joe graduated from college and came home. Lula Mae was happy to see him. Mrs. Kettering loved Joe and had lots of plans for him. He told her he wanted to relax for a while before making any big decisions about his future. She was okay with that. She had a couple of parties at the house and introduced Joe to the most eligible Southern Belles in Georgia. Girls, who were pampered, educated and rich, and as far as Joe was concerned none of them was his type.

They were so shallow compared to his Lula Mae.

While one of these parties was going on at the big house, Lula Mae went home and tried to study herself in the mirror. "What was it about her that Joe liked? Was it her hair? No! It was short and the hot comb kept it straight. She tried to comb it in very attractive ways but that still couldn't be it. She looked herself over, and over again, her eyes? Her pouty lips? Her slim figure? Her shapely legs? What was it that a handsome, rich, Caucasian young man like Joe could see in her? It left her baffled, but nonetheless, happy and contented.

CHAPTER 3

After a few months, he told Lula Mae that they would have to leave Georgia and head for the backwoods of Alabama. He told her about Doc, and how he was going to help them. They planned their escape just at dusk on Thursday evening. Joe stole the car to take them to the train station. As they left the Kettering's yard, Lula glanced back with a sad look in her eyes, "I'm going to miss everybody here," she said misty eyed.

Joe patted her leg, as he drove out of the yard, "I'm sorry," Joe said apologetically. "I will too, my dear, but this is the only way I know of."

"I left a note for my mother so that she wouldn't worry."

"She can't read," Joe reminded Lula Mae.

"Oh, she'll find someone to read it to her."

Lula Mae was trembling as if she were cold, but she wasn't; however, she could not stop shaking. She wanted to tell Joe to take her back home, but at the same time she wanted to be with Joe. She was terribly confused.

There was no point in starting an argument at this late time in the game. What was done, was done and she had consented willingly to the escape, and so she must suffer the consequences of leaving the family behind.

He left the car at the train station, as is often done, because he knew someone would take it back to the house. He took the train, and then used the bus to go to Alabama. At the bus stop in Alabama, Doc had an old Negro meet them at night and brought them to the house. Doc had arranged everything for them.

Joe and Lula Mae got married at Doc's house with a minister from a church that Doc attended. It was simple and beautiful. There was Doc looking all proud, Ms. Martha, head housekeeper, and her husband, Mr. Mike and two other servants.

Joe and Lula Mae stayed in Doc's house which was huge.

That night was just a blessed event for Lula Mae and Joe. Lula tried to remember all that she had read in books concerning the wedding night. She dressed in her loveliest lingerie that she bought when she went down town with Ms. Martha. She dressed and perfumed herself as best as she could. She was very nervous; and it seemed that Joe was nervous himself. He drew her to the bed, and started kissing her passionately. Lula found herself responding with ease, yet with wanton passion. Joe undressed her slowly and started kissing every inch of her body; then when the time was right he entered her and they made sweet love, passionate love.

After they were there for a month, he moved them down with the other Negroes, because that is what Joe and Lula Mae wanted. Joe worked in town at the hospital, in the Accounting Department. Joe got a job there as the assistant comptroller and he also helped out Doc at his own private office. Lula Mae worked with Ms. Martha and the other ladies and they were all kind to her, praying for her, "This gal don gon and get her a white boy loving her." They loved Joe and he loved them in return. Everyone got on very well in this community.

Lula Mae had the time of her life when she could openly pursue her love of reading. She was given books by Doc. and Joe took her to the library so she could see a variety of books. She loved it so much that most of her free time was spent going through magazines, reading and learning all she could about the outside world. Whenever Mr. Mike and Ms. Martha were going downtown to buy supplies, Lula would accompany them and she got whatever she needed. She also would pick up some magazines to see what was going on in the world and at the same time see the fashion news.

Everything was so undercover as far as their lives were concerned. However, Joe was the most romantic person in the whole world. He was even better than the people in the books she read about. Joe would not let her feet touch the door when they were entering their doorway. He would always pick her up and carry her over the threshold. She would be so tickled, but she told him I'm no longer a bride, you only do that when you get married.

12

He smiled, "every time I bring you into this house in my arms I marry you over and over again, and you know why, he winked sheepishly – we are going to have a wonderful honeymoon. That's the part I like."

One night while they were making love, Joe said as he ran his fingers over her smooth skin.

He said ruefully, "I love the blackness of your skin, your darkness exudes a sexual brilliance that takes my breath away." He would also say, "You remind me of a panther, getting ready to strike her prey, and that prey is me," he laughed and slowly glided his way up on top of her. He would always say she reminded him of some animal or thing.

Once he said "like a black rose still waiting to be created," or "a daisy, simple and beautiful." He would kiss her lightly and then say, "I'll love you forever that means until the end." With his loving words in her ear that is how Lula Mae fell asleep every time they made love. He never failed to tell her how much she meant to him.

She said to him one time, "When will I remind you of me?" He quickly replied, "You are the core of all my creations. You see, the panther could not get her agility unless she started out as you, the rose could not bloom until you fashioned her and the daisy come about because it had to find someone who is worthy to pick her up and lovingly place her in a vase on the table."

She asked him, "Is that why you brought me some daisies tonight?" and they both laughed.

They spent a lot of time together when Joe got home from work. He made good money and loved the people and the work. When he got home, he and Lula Mae would sit for hours talking about what their lives was going to be like from then on. They seldom went out, so they stayed at home and enjoyed themselves and each other's company very well. They turned on music and danced and pretended that they were at a ball. They moved the furniture away and had fun. Sometimes they would play cards or a couple of board games. They always were together and enjoyed being with each other. They held hands, and talked about everything and sometimes they would just sit outside and enjoy the sunset. They loved to hug and kiss. It seemed like hugging was a medicine for them. It made them feel secure and needed at the same time. Joe would carry her over the threshold and they would lie in bed talking and exploring their bodies before making sweet, special love to each other. The love they had for each other was the greatest thing in the whole wide world.

Six months into the marriage Lula Mae felt sick almost to death. She could hardly stand on her own two feet. She felt nauseous every morning and threw up everything she ate. Old mother Martha took one look at her and said, "Yes, baby youse with chile."

"Oh Mis Martha, I feel so sick. I feel so weak and miserable."

"It's awright chile, yuh'll git over it, an we all did" and she threw her head back and laughed at me. It was an uncomfortable feeling having a baby. I blew up very quickly. When I was five months pregnant, and Doc was examining me, he frowned; he also did it again when he examined me one month later. I knew he was keeping something from me and I told Joe. Joe talked to him about my suspicions and he decided to talk to us.

Doc arranged for me to go to the hospital and see a doctor, instead of the midwife I was seeing at home. After talking with the doctor at the hospital, Doc sat us down and told us what was confirmed by the doctor at the hospital. I was pregnant, but he heard multiple heartbeats and there could be two or three babies. "Sometimes, a baby would hide behind the other, but I do know there is more than one baby in there."

I almost fell over. He said I had to be careful. "You need to stay off your feet as much as possible, and give your back a rest." He had arranged to use a room at the hospital and had doctors who would be able to help us if we needed help. Anyway, I was to try to utilize the women in the house to help me with whatever I needed and not overdo my housework. "Rest whenever possible," they all urged.

I had three months to go but it could be sooner and there may be the possibility of a C-section. I was scared.

When I was about seven and a half months – I had to stay off my feet and Doc came to check up on me every day before going to the big house. He told me he had arranged to use the hospital in case there were complications. I was scared and he looked at me and patted my shoulder, "Don't worry, everything will be alright." I brought many babies into the world, and I'll take good care of you." He would also hold secret conversations with Miss Martha and once I saw her shaking her head as if she was very troubled. I asked her one day after he left what they were always talking about and she said, "nuthin much."

It started late one night when I thought I had to use the bathroom and when I got up lots of water ran down my legs. I was stunned – I did not know what to do. I screamed and Joe came running. He looked at the puddle of water and said, "Lu, Your water broke." I did not really know what he was talking about. However, he ran to get Miss Martha after helping me to the bed. Miss Martha sent him to get Doc and told him to get Ms. Ivey and Ms. Deanna too. I wondered what she was doing inviting everyone to see me birth this baby.

It was a long delivery. Doc said that he thought that he had everything under control. With the help of Ms. Martha and the other ladies he thought he could manage. He did not want to use the hospital unless there was an emergency situation. If he used the hospital records had to be kept and he had no control of their record keeping. Everybody was buzzing around carrying cloths, boiling water and poor Doc - he looked beat. He kept telling me to push when he thought the time was right. It was a hectic night. I was spent the next day. We went clear into the night, and when everything was done there were three little girls in this home. They were different but beautiful. They looked like little chimpanzees. They were so cute. Doc talked to Joe and said we were blessed to have him on our side. He was glad there were no major complications and that he was also glad they did not have to use the hospital. "Having a baby was a natural thing; it wasn't a disease," he explained to Joe. Everything could be handled at home.

The babies were premature by weight and they were wrapped up tightly and their heads tied. They had to have special handling because they were so tiny. It was also a good thing that he was a doctor. He was a tremendous help to us. We could not have had our lives if it were not for Doc looking out for Joe, me and now the girls. Lula tried not to show too much excitement whenever she looked at her three little miracles that God had given her.

Lula was up and doing for herself within a month, and would have gotten up earlier but the ladies would not allow her.

"You had a terrible ordeal in giving birth and you have to let your body rest, we will take care of you and the babies," they scolded. Miss Martha tied my tummy so that it would not bulge, and she showed me how to hold and bathe the girls, squeeze out my milk and put in bottles for them. This was also supplemented by a special formula as the girls got older and seemed to get hungry more often. I had all the instruction I needed to look after my girls, and yet Joe and I were not left alone to do what we could until it was night and time for them to go home. Doc insisted that they help me.

He said, "Although you may feel ok, you need a lot of rest, because you need to heal on the inside to recover properly."

In three months time with lots of care and special attention, the girls began to look like little babies should. I decided I was going to name the girls after the people I read about in my books. Mary Jane could easily pass for a white baby, Betty Lou was a real mulatto and Wendy Mae had darker hue than the others, but they were all beautiful. As they grew up I saw a little of what they would look like. We noticed that there was a distinct reddish mark on all the girls' legs and on Betty Lou were two marks. Miss Martha said, "Lawd dem dun got the biggest birthmark ever."

I said, "It's not that big but it's on the same part of their thighs." After a few months, after bathing them and wrapping them up, I lined them up together. At that moment I saw what the birthmark was. It was as if two hearts were carved into their legs but in such a way that it had to line up with the others. Betty Lou had the mark on both legs and when she was in the middle of her two sisters there were two distinct hearts on both sides of her.

"How amazing," I said and called Miss. Martha to see. "Three girls together form two beautiful hearts- three into two. That is so remarkable-three into two," I repeated.

I was so excited about the birthmarks that I showed Joe as soon as he came home from work, and didn't even have a chance to sit down. We were all amazed at these magnificent hearts. Joe said they had them because they were loved. I was so happy with my little girls. One day, out of curiosity I asked Miss Martha why they were so different.

She said, "Gyal, a Black woman cyan mek any kine of pickney, it all according to de fader; yuh dun gon mek a white gyal, referring to Mary Jane, a colored gyal, referring to Betty Lou, and a black gyal, pointing last to Wendy Mae." she laughed out loudly at me. "Yuh be supprise de kine of chillum Black and White partners mek; dey be Black to almost White; sum ah dem real funnie looking too," as she laughed and sat down hard on a chair. I could not help but laugh and started to think of all the mulatto kids we had on the farm and how they looked and I sat down and laughed with her.

When they were one year old, I began to see their individual characteristics; I was happy but at the same time I was scared for Mary Jane. She had beautiful reddish brown hair, few freckles about her face. She was clearly a white child; Betty Lou had a very clear olive complexion and thick curly hair. She was the most beautiful child I had ever seen. Wendy Mae, my special baby was brown skinned, with long curly dark brown hair, but she had a lot of my features on her. She was the cutest child and very loving, tender and compassionate of the three. What kind of life could I give my girls as a Black mother? I couldn't hide them away for ever. Would they be able to keep our secret? Would it be right for them to do that? What about schools? Husbands? What have I done? I became depressed and did not like the life I was living anymore. I began to wonder about Joe now. Was he sorry he married me? Would he want to leave and take the white baby with him and leave me with the others?

He informed me, "Nothing of the sort, Why would I do that? However, we might have a problem with the girls' upbringing so we'll take the time to figure out what is best for us and the girls. Since they are our girls they will be okay," he said laughing. "Don't worry," he said. But Lula really was worried.

When we ran away from Georgia we left a lot of burnt bridges.

I could not go back, nor could Joe. His mother was furious with him and had cut him off. He was no longer her son. She did not want people to know that her son had run off with a Black servant girl. Most of them knew from the gossiping servants anyway. It was hard for her to deal with her only son and heir running off with one of them Niggers. He was educated and could have any young white girl around here. She was very angry and did everything in her power to try to find out where he went but no one was talking. She would find him however, when she was ready. No son of hers was going to stay with a Nigger, not if she could help it. She was often offering money to servants who could bring her any kind of news about the two of them but so far no one knew a thing. She had her daughter, Lucy at least, and she would have to do for now.

* * * * *

Lucy and her husband Roy lived with Mrs. Kettering. Lucy was her father's princess and her mother hated her for taking away her husband's attention. However, Lucy was her flesh and blood and at least she was married to a white man and had two beautiful children, Roy Jr. and Linda. Mrs. Kettering was not close to the children or to Lucy and her husband. Lucy seemed to laugh at her when she would talk about missing Joe.

"Joe is living his life, give him a break. I wish I had the courage to do what he did," she said and laughed out loudly. Her mother could not stand that type of talk, as she was reminded of the time she had found Lucy with one of the Black boys in the barn when she was 16, and tore her behind and sent the boy off the plantation.

CHAPTER 4

Life was hectic taking care of three little girls who were just as frisky as could be. Doc loved them and he felt as if he were their grandfather. He would play with them in the house and they would jump on his back for piggyback rides. "Me, me, me now," shouted Mary Jane who would always be talking; it seemed that she would never shut up. Doc loved to play with his girls, who called him Pop-Pop. Pop-Pop would do piggyback rides until he was tired and then they would all fall down laughing. He was so very happy with his children as he called them. Mary Jane wanted a puppy and Pop-Pop got her one and they named the puppy, Sparky.

Sparky was a little Daschund who followed the children wherever they went. Mary Jane would sit and talk to Sparky and he just sat there and listened to her. She patted his back as she talked and he just wagged his tail every now and again, but he spent much of his time licking her hands, and her feet as if he were tasting her. She would smile and tickle him under his belly and he would turn over and allow her to play with him this way. They spent a lot of time together. Sparky was very good with the other two girls, and they loved him.

Doc felt a special affection for the girls because he was so close to Joe and Lula; plus the fact that he birthed them. It was clear that Mary Jane was his favorite although he denied it. It seemed that Betty Lou was just like me. We were both independent people; we did not depend on anyone for anything. Betty Lou was also the fighter; she didn't like to share her toys, and was always taking her things back from her sisters. She would also pull on Wendy's hair and make her cry; then she would run away. Wendy Mae was quiet and sucked on her thumb as if it were candy. Lula loved her girls and she had plenty of help from the other women on the plantation. However, there was always fear lurking at the back of her mind. Sometimes she'll look at Joe and it seemed as if he were in a pensive mood. She'll ask him what he was thinking and he's say nothing, but she knew that he was also worried about the girls' upbringing. He told her he had to save all the money he could get because they all had to go to college at the same time and it was going to be very costly.

"They can't go to the same school," I said, "it will be too much for them."

"It will be alright, you would be surprised how many bi-racial children are in college and doing fine," he replied.

"Yes, but none of them are triplets and trying to hide from their grandmother," I said.

"I miss my mother, Lula sobbed, "I don't know if she's dead or alive and my little sister, Janie. Oh, Joe, what have we done?"

Joe took her in his arms and comforted her. "Don't let it worry you, Lula Mae, I swear I will make it alright for our girls. They would want for nothing; they will be happy and well cared for, I promise you. Haven't I always kept my promise?" he asked her, as she looked at him disconcertingly, and shuddered at her thoughts.

The girls were two years old on July 15th and had a birthday party over at Doc's house. It was a lot of fun. They looked so pretty in their little pink and white dresses, with white ribbons in their hair and cute white sandals. Everyone in that neighborhood came to the party which was held in the yard. Pop-Pop went all out for their party; he wanted to do everything he could. There was lots of food; the children played games and everyone had a lot of fun. Everyone enjoyed themselves. Doc had special pictures made of his three little darlings. It was the most beautiful picture, then there was one with Joe, Lula and the three girls; then there was one with Doc and his family. Doc gave Lula some pictures in a small album, and he kept the three that he liked and framed them. They were always sitting on his mantelpiece.

Two days later, the girls were playing and Mary Jane fell down and busted her lip. She was crying so hard and her sisters were just looking at her and if they too were hurting. Lula picked her up and carried her off to clean her up and the other two came trailing behind her. They were all crying – it was so funny that Lula began to laugh. They stopped and started to look at her – stunned. She kissed Mary Jane's lip and said, "Mummy kiss your boo-boo," Betty Lou said, "I wanna kiss her boo-boo," and Wendy Mae said, "I want to kiss it too," and we all laughed and rolled on the floor. Mary Jane kept saying, ""Kiss boo-boo, kiss boo-boo mummy," and she'll run off laughing. This was the start of a loving relationship between Mary Jane and Lula. It seemed from then on that Mary Jane would look for any kind of scratch, old or new and run to Lula saying "Mummy, kiss boo, kiss boo-boo. Whenever Lula kissed her boo-boo she would say, "Love you mummy," and would throw her arms around Lula, and she would ask, "How much do you love me?"

Mary Jane would open her arms wide and say, "This much," copying this antic from Joe, who always showed them how much he loved them. It seemed that she would follow Lula around just looking for an opportunity to tell her how much she loved her.

Lula decided to teach Mary Jane the song, "Little Bo Peep has lost her sheep." Mary Jane was a very inquisitive person so she would search until she found the three toys we pretended to be sheep and bring them home. She had a fit if she could not find them all. Betty Lou and Wendy Mae got jealous and wanted their own songs, so she taught Betty Lou, "Jack and Jill went up the Hill," and she would grab her bucket and try to go up the hill with Wendy but eventually always ended up with Mary Jane because Wendy Mae would prefer to sit and suck on her thumb. Mary and Betty said "she's no fun." Lula gave Wendy Mae the song, Mary Had a Little Lamb," because as she sucked on her thumb, in the other hand she had a teddy bear which it seemed she never let loose. They were all happy now – they all had their own songs.

There was not a day that went by that Mary Jane did not come to be kissed, sing her song, and to tell Lula how much she loved her. One day as she was playing in the yard, Lula looked up from the book that she was reading to see her fall down and scrape her knee. She did not cry, but looked carefully at the scrape, took her hand and wiped it off, and then she hopped to where Lula was. As soon as she made contact with my eyes, she started crying, "Mummy I got a hurt." Lula smiled to myself as it did not seem to hurt when I wasn't looking, but as soon as she saw me she started crying. It was so funny; I could not help laughing at her. I picked her up, cleaned the scrape and kissed her hurt, I said, "it's just a boo-boo, let mummy kiss your boo-boo, then you can run along and play; but before you go, tell me, how much you love me?" I could always count on "this much" love from Mary Jane.

I loved my girls very much and they all returned this love in their own way. Mary Jane, however, was such a loving child, and because she liked her "boo-boos" to be kissed I nicknamed her Boo-Boo.

The children were taking on different personalities and were different in many other ways. Wendy Mae was Joe's favorite although he denied it vehemently. She was tender, loving, always would run to see if her sisters were alright when she heard them crying. She would sit near them and start smiling and trying to make them laugh instead of cry. She would bring her favorite toy to share, and would always pat them on the back to make them stop crying. Whenever Joe was at home she would make sure she was sitting on his lap or riding piggy back or holding onto his knees and he'll have to drag her along and it was fun for her. He would make loud noises on her bare tummy and she would laugh hysterically. The others would join in the fun sometimes, but Wendy Mae just had to have her time with her "daddy." He played, "This Little Piggy Went to Market," using her toes and she would say "again" when he had finished with the other girls. She could not get enough of him. She would come in the mornings on a weekend and as Joe's toes hung from under the covers she would grab each toe and play, "This Little Piggy" and he would imitate her and laugh hysterically. It was their game, and they played it often. She seized every opportunity to play with his toes while he was in bed. Sometimes if he saw her entering the bedroom he would put his feet under the covers and she would have to lift the covers up to find his toes. It was real funny for her.

Betty Lou was the fighter. She did not like to share and didn't care if you cried. As a matter of fact – it never bothered her to see

22

the others crying. She carried on with whatever she was doing. She was independent and from an early age tried very hard to do everything for herself. It was amazing to watch her try to dress herself, brush her hair and even clean up after herself. She was turning into Miss Independence all by herself.

Mary Jane on the other hand was a team player. If asked to do some chore or other, she would do it willingly, but she never voluntarily did it. She was fair, compassionate, and loving towards her younger sisters. She would always look out for them. She played the role of big sister very well. She was also Lula's shadow she seemed to follow her around wherever she went. She would walk beside Lula and pretend she was doing whatever Lula was. She would get a rag and dust if Lula was dusting, she would pretend to sweep when she swept and she'll talk to her all the while. She asked a lot of questions and Lula liked the way she always wanted to know what was what.

"Where is the dust going?" she'll ask or, "I have a white rose and you have a pink one, which one you like better?" Lula answered all her questions lovingly. She was a very bright girl, and she understood everything she was told. She was also extremely loving and caring. She would hold Lula's hand and sometimes would kiss her hand and say, "I love you mummy." At that time Lula would take her in her arms and whisper against her soft hair, "I love you too, Boo-Boo."

Lula thought about her children; Mary Jane was also a tattle tale, "Betty Lou broke the pencil, and she wrote on the wall." Betty Lou was one who did not like to be bothered so she'll swipe her with the back of her hand and she'll come running to Lula, screaming, "She hit me, she hit me," and she'll hide behind her skirt as Betty Lou tried desperately to knock her out. Lula would become the referee between them, and calm Betty Lou enough for her to leave Mary Jane alone. Mary Jane thought twice before dealing with Betty Lou. She played more with Wendy Mae who did not pay her too much attention, but would suck on her thumb and hold her teddy bear in the other hand.

CHAPTER 5

B ack at the old Kettering home in Georgia, Mrs. Kettering was beside herself. Someone had finally given her some news about Joe and his colored wife. She couldn't believe her ears. She still had a lot of clout, and could get away with a lot. After all, her dead husband was the mayor of this small town and everyone loved him and respected her. They would do anything to preserve his good name. She found out the town where he was staying and was waiting on other information. She wanted to know if he was still with that Negro girl. Her pressure went up every time she taught of her son living in the same house with a Negro. What was wrong with him? Why would he disgrace himself like that?

Her information told her that Joe had been spotted in Alabama. However, they could not pin point exactly where he lived. She upped the stakes. She wanted immediate satisfaction. After all, this was her only son.

When news came that he was married to Lula Mae and that they had children. She was livid. He would not leave that gal, and he had to come to his senses, one way or the other. She asked the contact, "How can we get rid of his wife?"

"What are you asking, ma'am?"

"You know damn well what I'm asking and while you're at it get rid of the children too."

"My conscience would not allow me to do that, ma'am, but I can find someone who would. It would take some persuasion, if you know what I mean."

"Just get it done and let me know when you're finished. I don't care what you do or how you do it just don't harm my son."

Mr. Demas went about seeking out the people he knew who would carry out the job in an efficient way. He went in search of

Curly. Curly was a thug who would do any thing for a dollar. He had no heart, and would kill his own mother if she had something he wanted. Curly owed Mr. Demas for helping him out when he came out of jail. Plus Mr. Demas would help him from time to time. Whenever Mr. Demas needed any dirty work done he sent for Curly. This time he told Curly "I need you to burn down an old hut for me during the wee hours of the morning. The job is in Alabama, and I want you there as soon as possible to familiarize yourself with the surroundings. Do the job quickly and leave. It's $5,000 for you." Curly was the type of person who did not ask too many questions and Mr. Demas liked that. He did not want to explain to Curly that he was going to kill a nigger and her three children. After all, Curly was a nigger too.

While they were finalizing the arrangements, the phone rang. Mr. Demas asked Curly to wait in the other room. Curly did so, however, he heard Mr. Demas say, "I just got the guy who is going to get rid of your daughter in law and the children for you. I will talk to you when the job is done."

He hung up the phone and came into the next room. Curly had moved from near the door to the far side of the room and picked up a magazine as if he were reading. Mr. Demas told him, "I'll give you $2,000 now and $3,000 when the job is done. I'll give you $500.00 extra for expenses. See me when you get back."

"O.K." said Curly, I'll be back soon for the rest of my money."

When Curly got to Alabama he staked out the place and familiarized himself with the people who lived there. After a week, he met Mr. Mike on purpose downtown and tried to strike up a friendship with him. He was kind to him and he found out that he came to the store every other day to shop.

"I like getting away from home and seeing all that is going on in town," said Mr. Mike.

"I know what you mean," said Curly, then he held his chest and laughed out loud, "especially if you have an old woman there to torment you."

"Nah," said Mr. Mike, "I got me a good woman, she's different."

They had a drink and the next time Mr. Mike saw Curly he

had his ankle strapped up well. Mr. Mike invited him to come home with him so that his wife, Ms. Martha could look after his ankle for him. He accepted the invitation, but he told Ms. Martha, "Don't trouble yourself; I just need to rest awhile before moving on."

"Where are you headed?" asked Mr. Mike.

"I'm from Georgia and I'm just passing through." He stayed a day with them sleeping outside in the hammock.

The next day he saw the house, he also saw Lula Mae and her three children and he thought they were the nicest people around. Lula Mae said "hello" to him and the little girls waved. When he realized what he had to do it made him sick to his heart. He was angry with Mr. Demas. He didn't mind doing anything to a man, but a woman and children. That was not his style. He was angry and began to mutter under his breath – 'that damn white trash think he gon have me killing women and children. What could she have done to him?' Mr. Demas was a loan shark and he could not figure out why this humble woman would borrow anything from Mr. Demas. He was angry and when he was angry no telling what he would do. He had to carry out the assignment or else Mr. Demas was capable of having him killed, because he knew too much, and worse of all he'll hire someone else to do the job.

On Friday morning, Mary Jane became sick with a high fever and Lula Mae took her up to the big house for doc to look at her. He loved all the children but Mary Jane touched his heart so much he couldn't help but love her. So when she took in sick and Lula Mae took her to the big house as they called it. Dr. Dave told her, "Let her spend the night so that I could keep an eye on the fever."

"You sure, doc?" Lula Mae asked smiling she knew doc took every chance he could to have the children stay with him especially on weekends.

He said, "You and Joe are wonderful parents, and need to spend more time together, plus the little ones make me feel young again. Ms. Ellie and Ms Jane are also here to keep an eye on her. You go on now and get some rest. You can do that now that Joe is away."

"O.K. Doc," but Lula was worried about Mary Jane, she al-

26

ways seemed to get high fevers, and she could not put her finger on why she got the fever.

Reluctantly, Lula Mae left Mary Jane with Doc and returned to the cottage. Joe was away for the first time and she was a little overwhelmed with the three girls. They were such a handful even with Joe's help. He spoiled them so much and they knew they could wrap him around their fingers so they did it. Lula Mae returned home then she went to Ms. Martha's house where the two girls were staying. She sat down to talk to Ms. Martha for a while. Ms. Martha was very glad to see her and treated her like a daughter. Lula Mae and the two girls stayed with Ms. Martha until it got dark; they had dinner with her and her grandchildren. It was a very relaxing evening. Lula Mae gathered her little ones who were very tired and went home. She put them to bed and turned in herself. She was fast asleep by the time her head hit the pillow.

Curly was so angry he could not keep this secret to himself. The nerve of Mr. Demas! Yet he knew he had to do the job, there was no way out. Either he did it or someone else would and he had to think about his own life, Mr. Demas would like to use him as an example of people who did not do his bidding. Curly decided to confide in Mr. Mike. He explained that he had a job to do and if he didn't do it someone else would. He told him that it had to be done soon and there was no stopping it. He was leaving as soon as the job was done and he had to decide when was the best time for him to do his job. However, he wanted to warn the people. Mr. Mike listened to him for a while and then asked him outright what the job was.

"I gotta wipe out a family. The orders come from way up."

Mr. Mike begged him to tell him who the family was and he said, "The gal in the white hut and her children."

Mr. Mike began to panic because he did not know what to do; he had to tell Doc and Doc would not be home until later, and Doc would know what to do.

"Is there anyway you could not do it?" asked Mr. Mike

"No! No! I think it is a family affair; I listened at the door of Mr. Demas office and heard him talking to someone who wanted this family killed. I know it was a woman because when Mr. Demas came into the room he said, "the bitch!""

CHAPTER 6

As she lay in bed asleep with her two children in the next room, Lula Mae had no idea that her life was going to take a drastic turn for the worse. It seemed that Mr. Mike went up to the big house to wait for Doc to come home. It was pretty dark and Doc had not returned home yet. In the meantime, Curly got his gasoline and started dousing around the house. He felt okay because he had sent out a warning. That was all he could do under the circumstances. Mr. Demas needed him back home as soon as possible. He had found the people and all he had to do was get rid of them and make it look like an accident. It was about 10:30 and the place was as quiet as a graveyard after 8 o'clock. He took his matches out and lighted one. As the match hit the gasoline and the fire picked up, Curly made his way out of the yard and headed home.

Lula Mae was dreaming away. She had recently read about England and she was traveling and visiting all the places she read about. She loved the English countryside, and then she was on a double Decker bus, then the subway, among other travelers just enjoying and taking in everywhere. It seemed as if she was jolted from her seat on the bus. She was startled and looked behind her to see what made her move. At the same time her eyes flew open and she realized that she was dreaming. She smiled to herself and turned over when all of a sudden she smelled smoke and heard crackling. She got up hurriedly to look through the window to see what was going on. Suddenly smoke was coming into her room. She panicked and opened the door and in came the smoke, she coughed and drew back for an instant. It seemed that the whole front room was in flames. She had to get to the girls' room on the other side of the hall. She fell to her knees and crawled, she felt the fire on her arms burning her. She got to the girls room and grabbed them each one in her arms and tried to go back out but it was too dark with smoke and she could not see nor get to the door. The fire was all over the floor, the flames were dancing around, and becoming fiercer - her feet were on fire; she could not walk but she had to save her girls; she had to get to a window.

She ran back inside the room, closed the door and opened the window. How was she to get the children out the window? They were awake now and screaming. She yelled for help and saw a lone figure running towards the house. She picked up Wendy Mae and was about to throw her on the ground outside when someone appeared and was screaming for her to throw her out and then for her to jump; she threw her into their arms hoping they would catch her. Then she tried to do the same for Betty Lou but she was so frightened that she bolted and Lula had to go after her. This was no time for her to leave this room, and so Lula used all of her strength and agility to go after Betty Lou. She grabbed her and ran back to the window. Her feet were on fire, as well as the bottom of her nightgown. She was about to faint, as the fire dug into her bones, she was done for, but she had to get Betty Lou out now. She looked and saw someone there who kept saying, "Throw her out, we'll catch her." Lula did not know if she was dreaming or if someone really said it, but she did so anyway. She had to save her self too, and get out now. The flames had engulfed her again and her feet and clothes were on fire. She was burning alive, "Oh God! Help me!" She threw her self halfway through the window and all of a sudden she could not move, she was in so much pain as the fire consumed her feet. She had to get out but it was too hard. Someone screamed, "Jump, Lula, come on! Come on! Don't stop now! We'll catch you. The girls were screaming, and she realized that Miss Martha and someone else was out there waiting for her to jump; she must have done what they said, because she did not know how she made it out. Someone was rolling her on the ground and with each roll she felt as if she was on a bed of sharp needles. She screamed silently, and blacked out.

The next thing she knew was that she was in Miss Martha's house and Doc was standing over her. He gave her a shot and told her to sit up right away. He looked worried. He was speaking very fast and she could not understand what he was saying. Maybe, she was still dreaming but she was in excruciating pain. He was showing her an envelope and said, "Lula Mae, listen to me and listen carefully. You have to leave here tonight and take one of the girls with you. You cannot stay here anymore. I have arranged for Mr. Mike to take you North to a friend of mine. She owes me a big favor and she will take you in and take care of you until you are able to look after yourself."

"Joe," I whispered.

"You cannot let Joe know you are alive," Doc was saying to me. "It appears that his mother was the one who hired someone to kill you. Now I don't think we can tell Joe that. He will never want to leave you and the girls and the next time you and the girls will not be so lucky. I have some money in this envelope for you. Ms. Martha will take Betty Lou and let her niece in Tennessee raise her. You take Wendy Mae with you."

"What about Mary Jane?" she asked.

"She is safe with me; I will figure something out. Lula Mae it is important that you understand what I am saying. You have to leave right now. I have given you a shot to ease the pain. Here are some pain killers and when you reach where you are going Gracie is a nurse. She knows about your burns she will arrange for you to see a doctor immediately, and she has someone who will take care of you and Wendy Mae."

He was pacing like as frantic father, and then he said, "I will arrange everything with a friend of mine at the newspapers and everything will be alright. You have to forget Joe and the other two girls for now. You have to get healthy and we'll see what happens from there on. Joe is expected back next week. I will talk to him in the morning. He must believe that you and the girls died in the fire. Do you understand? If not, Joe will search the whole world for you and the girls until he finds you and then he'll unknowingly put your lives in danger. Also, Curly's life will be in danger for telling us about this job. I thank God he had the decency to tell us before it went too far. Do you understand what I am saying?" She nodded while the tears rolled down her cheeks. "Why can't I take Betty

Lou with me?" she whispered.

"Because it's easier with one child than two, seeing that you are very sick. My friend does not have any children, so now she'll have you who will have to be taken care of, as well as Wendy Mae; don't let's add any more children for now. Give her a chance to get use to you first. You have 3rd degree burns on your legs; you have to take care of yourself."

"But I'll manage she cried, "Please don't let me lose Betty Lou, please."

"As Much as I would like to help you, I think it would be better for now. Let us see how you recuperate and then I'll let you know. Remember I love you too Lula Mae. You have to go now."

They brought Betty Lou and she held her in her arms although she ached and then let her go. Betty Lou was confused and was crying, kicking wildly and trying to reach her mother. Doc and Mr. Mike helped her to the car as she could not walk. Ms. Martha brought Wendy Mae to her. Ten minutes later she and Wendy Mae were headed north. Lula Mae cried all the way and nothing could dry those tears as they penetrated her heart. She didn't have time to think of the arduous journey ahead.

Lula Mae's heart was very heavy. She wanted all her girls with her, but Doc said they would be killed. Mrs. Kettering was an evil woman and she would not stop until they were all dead. Doc was right. I have to get well in order to take care of my children. I will have my babies back. I will! If it takes the rest of my life, I will have my babies back. Lula Mae was barely conscious as she sat in the car, she moaned and tried to focus but couldn't; eventually, she fell into a deep sleep.

Doc went home and was arranging for his friend to take Mary Jane and arrange an adoption for her. He was going to keep tabs on her and make sure that she was alright. After all, she was his little girl. He just wished he could keep her for himself. There was no way Joe could keep Mary Jane. His mother would not accept a black grandchild, even though Mary Jane looked Caucasian.

CHAPTER 7

The next morning Doc called in his favors with Jess of the newspapers. He had a little caption stating that there was a fire in Dr. David Fitzpatrick's property. Unfortunately, the family who was staying there was killed in the fire, burned beyond recognition. Dr. Fitzpatrick is very upset over the death of his beloved friends. The family will be buried on Saturday.

The mortician knew what to do. Plus Doc was giving him big money for his services. He had a coffin ready for Lula Mae and the girls.

When Joe arrived home on Saturday, he was in time for the funeral services. It took place three hours after he came home. It was small and personal. Just the people in the neighboring area, mostly Negroes who knew Lula Mae and her children were there.

Joe was beside himself. He looked terribly. He cried unashamedly and Doc had to give him a shot to calm him down after the services. He did not want a shot. He wanted to die with his family. "Oh, God how can you do this to me? They were good kids and Lula Mae was a wonderful wife and mother. I do not understand, Help me God!"

Joe was inconsolable, and he had to spend a week in bed as per Doc. He could not get over this tragedy. He felt it was his fault for leaving his family. "Only if I was here I could have saved them. I knew I could, nothing would have stopped me from saving my loved ones.

Joe stayed with Doc for another week to get himself together. Then he could not stay there any longer. The memories were too painful for him. He could not bare it any longer. There was nothing for him to salvage, no pictures, no favorite toy, nothing, everything was wiped out. Oh, he could not stand it any longer. Just when everything seemed at a loss, his mother showed up in her royal regalia. She came into Doc's house and was so sorry to see her son in the state that he was in. He asked her how she knew where to find him, and she said, "a mother knows when her child needs her."

He was so distraught and at the same time happy to see someone who cared for him that he just let her take over. She told him he could come back and recuperate. Later on he could decide what he wanted to do with his life. So eventually, he said his goodbyes to Doc and the people who took care of his family and who were the only family he had known for the past four years. He left.

Doc was sad to see him go, but he knew her type she would not leave him alone until she got her way. So the best thing for Joe to do right now was to leave. He did not want Mrs. Kettering and her spies lurking around his place. You never know who could be bought for a price. He was happy to see them go and knew he would not see Joe again. It pained him because he had begun to look on him as the son he never had, and his grandchildren. Just thinking about them brought tears to his eyes. Oh! What he would do to have things back the way they were. But now they were not meant to be.

That weekend when everything was quiet, Doc sat down and got out his book where he had had copies of the marriage, the children's birth certificates, and supposedly death certificates. He wrote everything down making sure he had names of the children and the people to whom they were sent. He knew where Lula Mae was because his dear friend, Gracie was taking excellent care of her and Wendy Mae. She was taking Lula Mae to a small hospital where she was a nurse and she was also being cared for at home by Gracie.

CHAPTER 8

L ula had first degree burns all over her lower body. At one point, the doctors were not sure they would have been able to save her legs.

She was operated on and grafted so many times that she lost count. She was undergoing extensive therapy. She hurt a lot but nothing could ease the pain insider her heart that she was feeling for her husband and two girls.

Gracie reported everything to Doc, and he kept in touch with her regarding Lula Mae and Wendy Mae. They were his family and he intended to do his best to take good care of them. This was a nightmare they were all going through and he hoped that he would wake up and find that everything was back to normal in the morning. However, it was not to be; because when he awoke in the morning, everything was still a nightmare as far as he was concerned.

When Lula Mae and Wendy came to Gracie's home it was nightfall. It seemed that they were driving for the longest while. She ached a lot, but she was so drugged that she did not know what was going on. After she was settled in Gracie's home, she looked at Gracie for the first time. She saw a small, Caucasian woman, around 40 years old, with wispy blonde hair, small frame and a pixie like face. She had light blue eyes, and stood 5ft 2 in her stockinged feet. She had a warm smile as she came closer to Lula Mae and said, "Don't worry! I'll take good of you and your little one. Now try and get some sleep, it will do you good."

Lula took her advice and went fast asleep; it was all she could do as she was so drugged up.

Doc wrote Gracie and told her Lula Mae and Wendy Mae had to change their names and that she was to get papers for them. He made calls, and sent her the money to take care of this. When Gracie got the necessary papers and showed them to Lula Mae she cried. She was so unhappy and she felt like a prisoner. Inside she was crying, but she did not know this woman well enough to cry in front of her. "What have I done to deserve this?" she asked Gracie.

"It's not your fault that some people are ignorant and are racists, just be thankful that your lives were spared."

She even had to change her name; it seemed that everything strange was happening so fast that she did not have time to think.

Gracie started calling her Sadie right away, but she would not respond. Lula Mae was now known as Sadie Anderson and Wendy Mae as Bessie Anderson. Gracie told her she was in hiding and it would be better for her in the long run. She knew Gracie was right but she did not like it one bit. She sure didn't feel like her old self. Here she was in a wheelchair because it hurt her so much to walk. She was going to the hospital once a week to change the dressing on her feet. It was such a painful situation that she usually blocked it out while they were doing it. The doctors were amazed at how quickly she healed, but they did not know Sadie; she was determined to walk again, and soon. It took her a good six months of her own willingness to help herself that got her out of that wheelchair, even though it was for just short periods of time.

Sadie remembered the first winter she spent with Gracie. She got up early in the morning and limped to the window. It was all cloudy and she had to take her hand and rub away the misty, cloudiness that prevented her from seeing outside. Once she could see outside, it was the most breathtaking scene she had ever witnessed. It had snowed all night and the snow covered everything in her sight, the houses, the trees, the street, sidewalk, the whole ground was covered with snow. It was like a picture post card. Sadie whispered, "Wow! What a beautiful scene." She looked up and saw that light snow was still coming down from the sky; it was a steady, light fall but every snowflake stuck to another and it was wonderful.

She wanted to rush in and wake up Bessie but she decided against it. As she continued to look at the snow, she saw snow just falling off the roof tops of the neighbor's house and making a big pile on the ground; It formed little peaks and it stayed that way for a long time, then suddenly, some of it fell further to the ground.

Sadie went to the front of the house and looked out; she saw parked cars covered in snow. They looked like little mounds. A couple of cars passed in front of the house and the tires left marks in the snow and muddied its beauty. However, it still did not lose its magnificence. Then she saw a lone figure walking. It seemed like a man, all bundled up, in coat, scarf, gloves, and as he breathed wisps of smoke came out of his nostrils. Sadie smiled to herself.

The snow was piled high in certain places but it looked very picturesque. Sadie loved it. She stood there staring at the snow for a long time, until she felt a little tingle in her ankle. She had to sit down and rest awhile.

CHAPTER 9

Sadie was a resilient person, she fought back and so her healing was much faster than they expected. She had to have three operations and some grafting, but other than that she was okay. The feet were burnt so badly that it left her with a permanent limp. At her last visit to the hospital, Sadie found out that she was pregnant. She was not too happy to hear that, but Gracie was very happy for her. Like Doc, Gracie never got married and had no children. She looked a lot younger than her years. She lived alone and welcomed the company. She fussed over Bessie and Sadie so much you would believe they were long lost relatives. As time went by, Sadie saw a very helpful and compassionate woman who went out of her way to help them. Sadie liked her and was very grateful. "I don't know how I could repay you for what you are doing for us but I'll make it up to you as soon as I get a job."

Gracie burst out laughing, "You owe me a million dollars already, how long do you think it would take you to pay me back." Sadie looked frightened.

"Relax, and get well, Dave has sent more than enough to take care of you guys, and I notice how clean you have kept your room, although it must be very difficult for you, that is enough for now." She smiled and patted Sadie on the back.

"You are the sister I always wanted," she said. Sadie looked at her own hands then looked at Gracie thoughtfully. Gracie saw what she did and burst out laughing, "I mean the Black sister I always wanted." They both laughed.

Sadie looked around her room as she sat in her wheelchair. It was a pretty large room. It was Gracie guest room. It was painted in a very light green color; there was a queen size bed, a dresser with mirror and a chest of drawers; there was also one night stand with a beautiful tiffany lamp on it. The bed linens were white background with tiny flowers for decorations, the curtains matched the bedspread. It was a lovely, spacious room and filled with light. Sadie loved it. There were books for Sadie to read and she did some reading but her mind was not completely free so she did not enjoy it as much.

Gracie showed Sadie how to change her dressing, take her temperature and many other simple procedures that she needed to take care of for herself. Gracie had a well stocked library and although most of the books were on medical issues, Sadie still found many that she was interested in. Sadie was an avid reader and was excited when she read books on racism. This subject fascinated her. She felt she was in deep shit. Here she was, an ignorant, Negro woman who married an educated White man and had four children by him. Oh, yes, there were mixed marriages and mixed children but they suffered from society. She started to look at Gracie differently and wondered what was going through her mind every time Gracie said something to her. She was on the alert, and since Mrs. Kettering tried to kill her, it just made matters worse. Yet, there was Doc. And he was the kindest person Sadie knew. There was no pretense in him. He was genuine, or was he? Lord, this was confusing, but from now on she would not let her guard down around White people. As Sadie pondered on these things, she watched her daughter who sat reading a book. Bessie was a lover of books like her mother and so they both read a lot. Auntie Gracie took Bessie to join the library where she had a variety of books to choose from.

When it was time for Sadie to give birth, Gracie was there beside her in the hospital as little Joseph Ryan Andersen was born. He was a beautiful baby and had the loveliest eyes. They seem to follow her around the room and they smiled as if to say "I know what you went through, and I'll make it up to you." She loved him with fierceness from the start.

CHAPTER 10

When Bessie turned four, Gracie decided to take her to a school where she could learn to socialize. Sadie looked at her and wondered what the other two girls were doing at that moment. Gracie loved to take care of Bessie, and sometimes Sadie began to find herself resenting the help Gracie was giving. However, she always had "Seff" as he was called. He was a beautiful one year old, but he looked everything of Joe. He was light skinned, with green eyes and a curly, auburn top for girls to envy. He was her pride and joy and she loved him with all her heart.

Bessie and Seff got along extremely well. It was as if they knew they had to stick together. They hugged each other, kissed a lot and Bessie would play "This Little Piggy whenever she saw his toes uncovered. He would play he was asleep until she finished. She had to play "This little Piggy whenever she saw toes sticking out" Everyone knew to cover their toes because Bessie could not resist playing with toes. She would giggle hysterically when the person jumped out at her. She never stopped playing the game even when she was a teenager.

Gracie was a special person and she helped Sadie very much. Bessie loved to sing and Gracie noticed that she had a very beautiful voice. So, Gracie arranged singing lessons for Bessie. She also arranged for someone to come in and teach her to play the piano. Bessie enjoyed it. What bothered Sadie most was whenever Bessie needed anything she always asked Auntie Grace first. Then Gracie would say, "If it's alright with your mother."

Sadie felt as if she were losing her children; sometimes she would say "no" just to show her authority. Then she realized that if it wasn't for Gracie, she and her children would not be surviving the way they were. The living was more than good. She did not want for anything; Gracie really treated her like a family member and not as an outsider; they talked a lot; she taught Sadie more about finances, and how to pick clothes that flatter her body, and she was great with the children who adored Auntie Grace; and what Sadie realized- Gracie did not have to do it. I feel as if I should hate her just for being White and rich; but then again, I would be doing to her what was done to me. Forgive me God. From then on, Sadie decided to work with Gracie and not against her; after all, she had Sadie's best interest at heart.

Sadie's feet were badly burnt and even with all the operations she underwent, she still had a limp. She started going for short walks after Seff started school. Later on, she ventured out further and further exploring the neighborhood. Gracie was at work, and the children were at school. The housekeeper, Ms. Helen never wanted her around, so she decided to take her walks when Ms. Helen came.

One day as she was sitting on a bench resting she thought of Mrs. Kettering and what she had done to them and the hatred boiled up in her so much. She thought of hiring someone to kill the old bitch. Let her see how it feels to have to run, and beg for your life for no other reason than someone didn't like you. It was horrible. She began to cry and as the hot tears fell she thought of Joe. She did not think of him so often now. Yet she missed him. She wanted to dismiss him from her memory, but she wanted her two daughters and did not know where to find them. White folks had ruined her life, but it was her fault. Where did she get off marrying one of them? Joe loved her deeply, and she loved him too. She couldn't blame him. He showed her all the love in the world. She smiled as she thought of all the antics he did to make her happy. Seff reminded her so much of his father, it was uncanny that the two of them were so much alike in character, and they don't know of each other. One thing was for sure, they both loved her deeply.

Seff called her "Duchess" and sometimes, "My Queen" as he bowed before her. He always made her feel like royalty. She loved that young man and thought there wasn't another young man like him in the world. He made her ecstatic. Mrs. Kettering took Joe from her but Joe left his younger self for her to love always. This was just like Joe. She smiled as she thought of Joe and the times they had together. He made love to her by touching her body and making her feel wholesome and beautiful. He never just had sex with her; he always made love to her whole body, as well as her mind. It was wonderful, just wonderful. Even if he didn't know they had a son, he was still looking out for her. She could never love any other man the way she loved Joe. Nonetheless, Joe was a part of her past and she did not want to talk about any of the past with her children. Let them have a good life and not have to look over their shoulders all the time. They shall be happy and contented children.

Sadie sat for a while each day thinking over good and bad thoughts. When she reached this part of her walk, she'll sit and rest and ponder on what to do, to get her girls back. On this bench she would sit and plan. She made plans to kill Mrs. Kettering –not do it herself but trying to get someone to do the job for her. Revenge tasted sweet in her mouth. She couldn't wait to get started. But how do you start? I can't just go up to anyone and ask them if they will be willing to kill someone for me. Oh, how I hated that woman – I could see myself holding her scrawny neck and wringing it until she turned blue and was begging for mercy. Even then I would not let her go; I would just laugh in her face. It was not even easy to find someone to kill the bitch. Sadie laughed to herself when she thought of the word, "bitch." She felt liberated – she had never called anyone names before, much less a White woman, who was her mother-in-law, or boss lady to her mother; but now she could have called Mrs. Kettering every foul name she could think of. She wanted the bitch dead, just because she tried to kill her and her children. Sadie was not going to let that bitch get away with it.

She started to think of ways of disguising herself and going back to Georgia to do the job herself. She began to bring a little notebook and pencil with her whenever she walked and would spend time writing down her thoughts. These were morbid thoughts, thoughts of murder, hatred and deep anger. There were detailed plans to draw Mrs. K away from the house and the help she'll get if she stayed in the house; plans to make Mrs. Kettering suffer and even to kill her in a most horrible way. She always felt good after writing about her murder plans.

She decided that it was too good to kill her, no; she was going to suffer first. She decided she was going to tie her up, set fire to her feet, then her hands and let her face burn a little. Let her know what it was like to burn in that fire. When she begins to beg for mercy, she would just laugh in her face. She would throw water on the fire and let her ache for a while, and then light her up again, this time beginning from the hands. She would let that burn until she could smell the flesh burning, and then for sure she will walk with a limp like Sadie.

She was smiling now, she liked the way she imagined it. Mrs. Kettering would be begging for her life, and she had the power to say "no." Sadie would replay these scenes many different ways but always was ending up with Mrs. Kettering, the bitch, begging for mercy.

The more she thought about it, the angrier she got. Once there was a nice old man sweeping the streets and as he passed by and talked to her she said candidly, "I need you to kill someone for me."

"Did I hear you right?" he asked.

"Yes, you did!" she replied

"Well, lil girl, let me tell you this, when someone done you wrong, all you gotta do is forgive them. The good Lord told us to forgive seventy times seven-that's a whole lot of forgiving. But you know, when you don't forgive you never have peace, and you cannot survive in this world hating other humans. You want to have peace deep in your heart and freedom. If you let the devil encourage you to hate, and not forgive, you begin to destroy yourself and you don't even know it; you get sick and even die. God loves us and we must love one another and not hate; we have to look for the good in everyone, Christ is in everyone you know. So my little girl, don't let anyone drive you to hate so much that you want to kill them, okay?"

Sadie smiled, and said thank you," but inside she was thinking, 'who the hell asked for a sermon; all I wanted was for you to say, "I'll kill the bitch for you."

42

As he was walking away, Sadie asked, "What is your name?"

"They call me Mr. Frank."

"Well, Mr. Frank thanks for the advice."

"Anytime, my dear," he replied as he walked slowly away, whistling.

CHAPTER 11

One day as Sadie sat writing her usual hate plots, it began to drizzle. She paid no attention to the rain at first because Sadie always loved the rain. However, she decided to go look for some shelter because she knew she could not make it home without being soaked to the skin. The rain had started to come in torrents. She really needed shelter.

As she started to walk in a different direction from home, Sadie was surprised to see some little stores as she turned into a little cobble stoned pathway. Among the stores there was a sign that read; "Second Hand Books", she was curious. She hurried into the bookstore and a middle aged white woman greeted her.

"Hi, how are you today?" asked the woman

"Fine, thank you," replied Sadie sheepishly

"Is there any book in particular you're looking for?"

"No, Sadie replied, I would just like to browse; I'm sheltering from the rain, if you don't mind."

"No problem, take your time, my name is Zoë, here's something to help you dry off," and she handed Sadie some paper towels.

"Thank you," said Sadie as she passed the towels over her hair, face and hands.

"Today is one of my slow days, so if you have any questions I'm right here trying to figure out which bills to pay" and she laughed. Her laugh was so infectious that Sadie joined in, soon they were both laughing.

Sadie thought, 'sometimes Caucasian people can appear to be very friendly, but deep down inside they are like devils. As soon as she thought this, Doc and Gracie's images appeared before her and she said out loud, "Well not them, they're good people."

Now Sadie had somewhere to go when she went walking. She would sit at her favorite spot, think some, write some, and then head for the bookstore. There she would go through the books, buy a few and chat with Zoë for an hour or so before heading home in time to see the children off the school bus.

Sadie and Zoë became friends and had a lot in common. She began to show Sadie little things about the bookstore, also talked to her about the new books she read.

One day she asked Sadie, "Would you like to work for me part time?" Sadie beamed. "A job! A real job!" She had never had a job. Gracie had told her she didn't have to worry about money because Doc set up money in the bank to come to her every month to take care of them and it was more than enough. Sadie was grateful to Doc but she was not interested in the money and so she never asked any questions about it. Now was a chance to earn her own money. She was delighted and could not contain her joy. "Do you really mean it?' " I mean, really mean I could work for you?" "No kidding, for real?" asked Sadie.

"Slow down, slow down, I really mean it because I have to close up the shop whenever I have appointments, or errands to run. I could manage a part time clerk, but the pay is small."

"I'll take it. I'll take it" and she almost wanted to hug Zoë but refrained herself. Zoë noticed her making an attempt to try to hug her then pulling back. Zoë went to her and embraced her and that was the beginning of a beautiful friendship.

- Sadie told Gracie about the job and Gracie did not seem too pleased. She told Sadie that she did not need the money. Gracie did not like the way Sadie talked about Zoë. She felt a pang of jealousy as Sadie talked about Zoë. "Zoë showed me this, and that and how to keep the books; how to pack the shelves, and I'm learning so much, and it's what I've always wanted to do; to be around lots, and lots of books. You know how I like to read. I know I will enjoy it, and Zoë will teach me all I need to know. I'm so happy," Sadie kept on and on. The kids were looking at her, and they both laughed with her.

Then they got up and hugged her, "I'm happy for you, my Duchess," Seff said, and Bessie just held her tightly. Her hug said it all; she didn't have to say a thing; it was like that between them. They just had to look at each other and it seemed as if they read each other's minds. She loved her children and they were happy for her.

Gracie seemed a little reluctant in expressing her joy for her. She did not know why, but she was going to get to the bottom of it. However, she was not going to let anyone and anything stop her from doing what she felt so right about. Here was another White woman trying to stop her from doing what she wanted and she felt an anger that she did not know she was capable of. I could wring her scrawny neck. As soon as she said it, she was saddened by the fact that she was going to dislike Gracie.

Gracie had done so much for her. How could I be so ungrateful? If it wasn't for Gracie, she and Bessie and Seff would not have a place to stay. This was a very nice neighborhood, good schools, and everything was beautiful. This was all due to Gracie; after all, she did not have to take them in, Doc or no Doc. Sadie felt like an ungrateful wretch, and smiled to herself. She didn't feel too badly about her feelings. What the heck, White folks always felt as if they had to run Black folks' lives. Gracie was no different. They showed you some kindness and then they want to take over your whole life. Tears welled up in her eyes and Sadie found herself crying uncontrollably. It seemed that all the anger and frustration was being washed away and she just let it go. Afterwards, she felt wonderful.

That night after the children went to bed, she approached Gracie and asked "What's on you mind, Gracie? You seemed stunned and upset when I told you about the job."

"Oh, nothing, really, I just thought that if you wanted to do something that probably you would take some classes at the university, I know some of the professors there and they would be happy to help you."

Sadie replied, "I think I could get all I need out of books, plus I was never comfortable around a whole lot of people and I don't want to start now."

"But, you don't need the money I have money saved up for you and I would like to take you to the bank and have you open your own accounts."

"Well! Well! Thought Sadie, now you realize that I am capable of handling some money." Sadie thought of the clothes Gracie bought for herself and the children. They were really nice clothing; clothes that she by herself would not have been able to afford; and, even so, she was timid about going into stores and shopping without Gracie. Most of the clothes Sadie had before were made by someone she knew in Georgia. She could see the difference from those clothes and the store bought ones that she and Grace brought home. Gracie showed her what to look for and showed her what type of clothes flattered her shape; what colors looked best on her; she also taught her about the textures of the clothing. As usual, Sadie was a fast learner. Soon, she was picking out all her clothes when she and Gracie went to the store. She loved her clothes; they made her feel like the people in the books she read about. She felt elegant in these clothes, and they made her feel good about herself.

Gracie continued, "The children are getting older and you need to make your own financial decisions. I understand it is time for you to run your life now that you are so much better, but a job? I never thought about that."

Sadie looked at her "What you mean?" snapped Sadie, "You never thought about me and a job, nor don't you think I'm capable of doing it?"

Sadie did not wait for an answer but continued, "Zoë showed me most of what I have to do and I understand fully well. I even gave her some ideas about displaying the books and she loved it. So I know it will work out."

"The mighty Zoë! All I ever hear from you is Zoë this, Zoë that, I'm sick and tired of hearing about Zoë," Gracie hurled at Sadie and walked out of the room.

Sadie softened as she looked at Gracie and she realized what Gracie was going through. She recognized it in a flash. Gracie was jealous! She needed Sadie and the children to depend on her. They were the family she never had and she saw them slipping away from her grip, and she did not like it one bit. Sadie felt sad for her but she was determined to get that job, and no one was going to stop her, especially a White woman.

That night before Sadie went to bed she looked at herself in the mirror, and liked what she saw. She was tall, very dark, and beautiful in her own right. She spoke well, dressed nicely, thanks to Gracie, and lived in a very nice neighborhood. She would earn some money and get an apartment for herself and her children as Gracie had done enough for them. These are some of the things she and Gracie will have to discuss. It was a scary thought, but it had to be addressed. After all, she did not want to be beholden to Gracie for the rest of their lives. She slipped in between the soft sheets and went fast asleep.

CHAPTER 12

Gracie wasted no time in teaching Sadie about finances. She was eager to learn and caught on quickly. It brought to her remembrance all the math Joe had taught her.

"Doc sends this amount every month for you and the children," Gracie told her. "I will show you how to balance a checkbook; I will take you to the bank and have you and Bessie's name on every account. I have already bought some stock for you- so I will show you how to read and follow the stock market."

"Do you think I need to know all of that?" asked Sadie, seemingly afraid. She was comfortable with Joe teaching her anything, but someone else? That was unheard of, at least for now.

"Yes, you need to know all that and more," replied Gracie. She looked at Sadie's face and saw the fear in her eyes.

"Don't be afraid. I will teach you all that I know and Bessie is old enough to be taught too. We'll have classes every month end when the statements come in.

Sadie was a fast learner, and so by the end of three months she had it all down pat. Gracie told her, "I'm so proud of you and Bessie – so from now on you two will sit and figure out what to do with your money and spend it anyway you want, just don't go overboard with shopping," and she smiled as they all hugged one ano-ther.

Sadie was happy to learn something new. She also noticed that Gracie had used very little of the money Doc had sent for them. She was scared now that she realized that Doc, and Gracie were taking care of her and her children. How was she ever going to manage without them? Gracie sensed her thoughts and said,

"You do not have to worry about a thing, my house is large enough for all of us and more, furthermore, I love the company.

You would not imagine what it was like coming home to an empty home. I love having you and the children here, and would not want it any other way, so relax yourself and enjoy the ride."

"I do not know how I will repay you for all that you are doing for us, but I appreciate it," said Sadie as she sobbed quietly. Grace came over to Sadie and took her in her arms, and said softly, "I know you do, Sadie, and someday you will be able to pass on the same kindness to someone who needs your help."

"I don't think anyone would need my help," she said. As Gracie walked slowly away, Sadie again withdrew any negative thoughts she had conjured up about her. She was just the nicest person she would ever know besides Doc.

CHAPTER 13

Sadie took the job with Zoë, working three days a week and loved every moment of it. She felt important. This was the first job she had ever had with pay, and she was going to enjoy herself. This job put her in the frame of mind to remember Joe. He knew how much she loved to read and did all he could to provide her with books, and magazines to read. Now she had them at her fingertips and she remembered Joe saying, "Books can take you wherever you want to go." Sadie became a bookaholic. She was an avid reader and was surprised at how many things she could learn from books. Joe had taught her well and she was grateful to him; now she was also grateful to Gracie for teaching her finances. She was able to bring home many books and read them. This way she was able to tell customers what books they would like, when they explained the type of reader they were. Sadie spent a lot of time reading and was amazed at the wealth of knowledge she acquired. Sadie would get lost in romance novels, cry at the dramas, laugh at comedies and just have a ball all by herself.

The children were avid readers too. Gracie made sure they had the latest children's books to read and they too would go to bed after reading a good book. Sadie was happy. She loved her job at the bookstore, she loved being with the children and Gracie, however, and she always thought of her other children. Sadie wanted to know what was going on with them. Were they happy where they were? Did their new parents love them and treated them well? These were questions that Sadie posed to herself each night and asked God to make sure that they were all right. She asked God to let her see her children again. It was a mother's plea right from the heart. She knew deep in her soul that God would one day answer her prayer.

The next morning as soon as the children left for school, Sadie went into the kitchen to have her breakfast and look through the newspapers. Ms. Helen was working in the adjoining room and she was singing as usual.

Gracie's housekeeper, Ms. Helen was a very kind, jovial woman. She wore a smile on her face and always greeted Sadie with "Gawd is good!" Sadie did not want to offend her, but she felt that God had dealt her a bad hand.

Today, Sadie asked, "How good is He?"

Ms. Helen looked at her and smiled, "As good as ya want Him to be, chile." Sadie looked at her then kept on reading.

Sadie noticed that whenever Ms. Helen took a break she would take out a Bible and would read it. She seemed so happy – like nothing in the world could affect her. When she was working she sang about Jesus and carried on in such a way you would think she was in church. She was kind and nothing Sadie said seemed to affect her. Sadie felt compelled to be nice to her. When Sadie told her, "Sometimes you really annoy me with all your crazy singing, don't you ever get tired?"

Ms. Helen just laughed and said, "Daling, if I dunt praise the lawd, the rocks gon cry out. I dun wan no rocks to cry for me. Gawd give me voice and I aim to use it. If I can't use me voice, I use my hands, or my feet, or shake my body," and with that she went into a dance. Sadie looked at her pitifully, and smiled, "poor woman" she thought – she has got to be crazy. Suddenly, she smiled at me pointedly and continued to sing and praise her God.

One day she said to Sadie "you need to get out de house and come to church and hear sum good preachin; maybe, you mite like it." Sadie did not like this conversation, because she knew once Ms. Helen got started about "Gawd" there was no stopping her. If she had to stay past her time for cleaning, she would. So Sadie quickly said, "I'll take you up on it soon. Sadie knew Ms. Helen would never give up, so Sadie agreed to visit her church just to shut her up.

And so it was, one Sunday morning, Sadie decided to take her children to church' Gracie had to work that weekend, and she was going to keep her word to Ms. Helen. She took the bus and she and the children had a nice ride to the church. She really enjoyed the service and decided she would come back. This is something else she could add to her life. She felt good about herself. She was doing things for herself and did not have to depend on Gracie to take her and her children to the church. As a matter of fact, she did not let Gracie know she was going to church.

That night at the dinner table, Sadie was telling Gracie about the church service she attended. "I dressed the children and we went to Ms. Helen's church. It was a beautiful service. I never thought I would enjoy it. I was expecting something quite different and so I was going with the pretense of getting Ms. Helen off my back." They all laughed. The singing was good, the people were friendly and I thoroughly enjoyed the sermon. The pastor taught about forgiveness. It rose up a lot of questions to problems I had not dealt with and made me think long and hard about my life."

"Oh! Questioned Gracie, "what problems?"

Sadie looked at her long and hard, "What problems? You don't have two beautiful daughters stolen away from you. You don't know the pain I feel for my children; what will become of our lives from now on," but instead she said out loud, "Oh! Nothing much."

When Ms. Helen came the next day, she asked me if I would like to read her Bible. – "Do you understand this Bible, Ms. Helen?" I asked her;

"I read, but could not understand the deeper meaning.

"Chile, I read what I could and ask de good Lawd to explain it to me. I read it over and over again until I gets it. It's no right way or wrong way to get it. But yuh keep comin to de church, and in the meantime I'll ask Pastor to have someone cum over and teach yuh de Word."

I said, "No thank you," but she insisted. Two weeks later Sadie got a call from the Pastor and he told her he was sending over Mr. Paul Thomas to speak with her.

Mr. Paul Thomas was a very handsome Black man, about 6 ft. tall, medium built, beautiful brown eyes that twinkled when he smiled and even white teeth. He had dark curly hair, with a neat part on the side. He was so striking that he almost took her breath away. His handshake was firm and his voice was melodious. She liked this man. Then it struck her – she did not have any dealings with men other than Doc and Joe.

It also struck her that she did not think of Joe a lot now. At first, she was in so much pain and had to be isolated and kept very clean because they had to peel the dead skin and treat her. All she could do was sleep after a session. Her body was growing with the child inside her and then she had Bessie to deal with. At times, she realized that Doc was right, and that she could not have dealt with the other two girls, a baby and a burned up body. She thought about the girls a lot. Every time Bessie did something remarkable she wondered if the other girls were doing the same things. Did they have a good day in Kindergarten like Bessie; were they riding the bus or did they have to walk to school, or was someone taking them in a car. She did not know whether they were split up or together. At these times, Sadie would sit and cry to God for His help.

It was nerve racking for her. She hated Mrs. Kettering more and more when she thought on these things. Her daughters would be twelve years old now and it pained her heart to think of them. She often wondered what they looked like at the present time.

On the days that she did not work with Zoe, Sadie would walk to her favorite bench and sit, and write her thoughts in her little book. Today, as she sat quietly, she heard someone whistling and looked up to see, Mr. Frank. As he came closer to Sadie he said,

"How are you, pretty lady?"

"I am fine, thank you, what about you, Mr. Frank? How is life treating you?"

"Just great, my child, just great; I am alive and well and breathing God's fresh air; I'm keeping God's earth clean, it's the least I can do for my Master."

"Oh, Lord," whispered Sadie as she smiled at him, I think I'm in for a sermon.

"Are you married?" asked Sadie.

He hesitated before answering. "No, baby, my woman done gone on to be with the Lord, it will be seven years next month, "he replied sadly.

"I'm sorry to hear that, Mr. Frank," Sadie smiled wickedly, "But I know a very special lady and you seem very suited for her. Do you have a girl friend?"

An expression of amazement flitted across his face, "Young lady! No! I don't, and haven't been looking either," he said with a wide grimace.

He turned around and came closer to Sadie, but stopped a few yards away as if she were going to bite him. He smiled gently.

"Come and sit with me for a while," invited Sadie patting the bench near her.

"Oh! All right, just for a minute," as he sat down heavily and smiled.

"That look in your pretty eyes tells me you're plotting something, aren't you?" he asked. Encouraged now, she smiled sweetly and said.

"Yes."

Mr. Frank did not appear to be upset.

"I want to invite you to church on Sunday, I want my children to meet a man who was kind enough to set me straight, also I have a very good friend named Helen Jones, and I would really like you to meet her. I feel it in my bones that the two of you will become great friends."

"Mmm. Very interesting, my dear. I don't like leaving my church, but I'll do it for you, my pretty one," he said, as he reached up and pushed back a wisp of hair that had fallen in her eyes.

"Thank you, Mr. Frank, I know you'll enjoy the service and my children and Ms. Helen will enjoy meeting you."

Sadie gave him the name and address of the church on a slip of paper from her book.

She could not write for the rest of the day. Mr. Frank has spoiled it for her, and he wasn't even Caucasian.

CHAPTER 14

Betty Lou was scared of daddy. He liked to put her on his lap to sit down and his hands always went into her panties. He would be making crazy noises as his fingers fondled her private area; however, when mommy came into the room he would stop. He told her how pretty she was. She loved her daddy but hated when he put his hand up her panties. She was now ten years old and she was maturing nicely. Mummy kept her eye on her, especially when daddy was around. She would make sure that daddy did not call her to sit with him. There were times when he drank that he and mummy would argue and she knew it was about her. She felt lonely. She was the only girl with an older brother, yet she could not get close to her mother. She never hugged her or told her how pretty she was, that's why she liked daddy. He would bring her little gifts and candy. He would take her for walks by the barn and do nice stuff with her.

However, when she was twelve, she had filled out nicely and always took pride in dressing and combing her long wavy hair. When she looked in the mirror she saw a very beautiful girl – no doubt about it' but she did not resemble mummy or daddy. Once she asked her mother who she looked like and her mother snapped at her so sternly that she never asked again. Later that night, her father said, "You look like yourself, you're just beautiful," and they both laughed.

Daddy was a very sweet, loving and generous man, but when he drank he changed into another person that Betty Lou did not like. He would say, "Lizzie come here and when she came he would say bring me another beer, then he would slur, "Gawd almighty how fine you look and lick his lips." Many times daddy would come up behind her to hug her then he would cup her breasts and say," Gawd, you're beautiful." One time mummy came in and saw him. Mummy screamed at Lizzie as they called her now and then slapped her so hard it left a mark on her cheek. She got after daddy too and let him have it.

Whenever mummy had to work late daddy would drink and then one night he came in the bed with me. It was the most horrible night of my life. I could not imagine that my daddy would want to hurt me so much. He would put his hands down my pants to my private area and massage me; he would also suck on breasts and bite my nipples. He told me he would tell mummy that it was my fault, and he pointed his finger at me while he said threateningly, "you know how crazy she gets when she sees you with me. Why, she might even kill you."

I cried myself to sleep and could not stand daddy anymore. I hated him. Lizzie endured his advances for two years and then decided to tell mummy. She was seventeen and she was not going to live her life like this. Not ever. The next time daddy came in, she ran out the room screaming because she could not stand to be touched anymore. Mummy was just coming in and saw her half naked running and screaming at her father. "He wouldn't leave me alone, and you won't do anything about it. I hate you both; I'm your own daughter and that is what you would do to me, she cried. He yelled "You are not my child- you're nothing but a half nigger, your own parents didn't want you. The only reason you're here is because we need the money the Doc sends to take care of you. So I don't feel badly because you ain't no kin."

Shocked at what he said, Lizzie gathered her clothes to cover her nakedness while she looked at her mother. "Mummy is that true?"

Her mother bent her head down and said softly, "yes, he's right," then she turned to him and said, "But it gives you no right to violate a little girl. She can get us all in trouble. What the hell were you thinking? You always think with your penis and not your brains, you bastard."

He started to beg her as she started to walk away. She grabbed the bottle of liquor on the table and swung it at him, he ducked and it splattered against the wall, and he left the house running and swearing.

Lizzie was confounded, what did he say I was not their child and who was Doc? There were so many questions in her mind that she was confused. She tried to talk to her mother but she didn't feel like talking now. Lizzie waited until the morning and asked her mother to please tell her the truth. She had always wondered why she did not look like them. Eventually, her mother told her, "All I know is that your father is white and your mother black – there was some disaster and you were shipped to me by my aunt. I was sworn to secrecy to protect your life. But now, Mr. Bigmouth had to let you know all about it.

She paused, then sat down heavily and sighed. Finally, she said, "It seemed someone was trying to kill your family and that's why you were sent to me. I do not know the whole story, and nobody talks about it. But now, you can't stay here anymore. I'm sorry" and she began to cry. Lizzie was forced to pack a bag with a few of her belongings and her mother gave her $500.00 and said I just got the money from Doc, plus some of the savings I had. Take it and go quickly before your father comes back. He went over to his sister's to spend some time. I'm sorry Lizzie, I'll keep praying for you."

"Where should I go, mummy?" she asked. "I don't know where to go or how to travel by myself. Please don't send me away," she cried. "I'll be good, oh Lord, don't send me away."

"You can't stay here, chile; it's better for you to go. I cannot protect you from your father any longer. He always had an eye for a pretty woman. You have grown into a beautiful woman, and it is hard for him to resist you. He has no conscience and before you become more scarred, you need to go. Get on the bus and go to another state and start over. You're old enough to do that. That's all the money I have now, just make it last until you get a job and a room in someone's house; and may God be with you." This was the first time her mother hugged her and they said goodbye.

She couldn't believe it. She was being put out on the streets. Where would she go? Who will take care of her? At least mummy and daddy took care of her. But wait they said they did it for the money. Where was her mother? She must have been some black servant girl who got caught up with the master and her mistress caught them and she ran like hell. She smiled to herself as she taught of this scenario. Then she got back to reality. Who was Doc? Mummy said she did not know anything and that she would not be questioned. It was too complicated. All she could tell Lizzie is that she used to live in the state of Georgia. Here she was seventeen years old and on the streets of Tennessee. At least, mummy gave her some money. She decided to jump on a bus and head for Georgia.

CHAPTER 15

After Mary Jane was settled with her new parents, Doc did some investigating on his own and was surprised and shocked to learn that she was placed with parents who were KKK members. They loved their little girl very much but never knew that she was a Negro. This could be devastating. What was he to do now? Could he go up to them and say "hey, your child is a nigger!" No, he had to leave it alone. It seemed that Mr. Ascott took his membership in the KKK very seriously. He was one of the leaders, a Grand Dragon. However, he was a devoted husband and loving father to his little princess. It seemed that Mr. Ascott could not father a child; his wife wanted one so badly that he would have done anything to get a baby for her. They were on a waiting list for a baby over three years, so when his good friend Harry told him of a doctor who specialized in adoptions and had a young child about two years old ready to go. He seized the opportunity to get this young child for his wife.

She was very pretty; maybe her real parents were rich. She had flawless complexion, reddish light brown hair, and blue-green, brownish eyes. She was just gorgeous.

One night while they were looking at T.V. a beautiful black woman came on and Maggie pointed and said, "Mommy, mommy, and started laughing and clapping her hands and she looked at her knees and said "boo-boo, Mommy kiss boo-boo." She was so happy that her parents were happy with her.

"Maybe this little girl had a mammy," Edgar told his wife, laughing.

They named their little girl Margaret Anne Ascott. Maggie as they nicknamed her was growing up very nicely and at five years old she had gotten used to them. She loved her daddy – he doted on her and bought her every new toy on the market. Mummy loved to dress her up and show her off to her friends. She was very, very happy. Yet, there were times as if something was missing somewhere but she did not know where or what.

By the time she was sixteen she knew what she wanted to do in life. She wanted to be an investigative reporter. She liked to find out things and did not mind how long it took her to get to the truth. She was also an avid photographer. Daddy bought her a most expensive camera for her 12th birthday. Now it came in handy for the work she did. She would take a picture of everything possible. It was an expensive hobby but she enjoyed it.

Maggie lived in a happy home. The only thing that upset daddy was talking about Negroes. Daddy hated Negroes and she hated what her daddy hated, and loved what her daddy loved. It was as simple as that. If it was bad then daddy should know because he was a good man and loved and protected her so much. She wanted to grow up and marry a man just like her daddy. Mummy was wonderful too, but in a different way. Daddy had a way of making her feel special, as if there was no other girl in the world like her and she enjoyed it.

He spoiled her rotten and she loved it. It was such a great feeling to know you were loved, protected and wanted. It gave her confidence and high self esteem to deal with the pressures she had in school. Daddy would sit and talk to her as if she were an adult. Sometimes he would ask her opinion. She'll look over at her mother and she would just smile and say, "Go on, let us hear what you have to say about this or that". Her mother loved her father and she also loved Maggie. They were a great, middle class family. Maggie could not ask for more.

The family went to church every Sunday and Maggie met a young man who sang in the choir with her. His name was John Holiday. John and Maggie started dating when she turned 18. She liked John a lot and most of all Daddy liked him too. He was tall, dark and very handsome. John liked Maggie a lot but sometimes his behavior was not what she liked. He would do things that she did not feel comfortable with, and he did not care whether she liked it or not. Those are the times when she knew that they would not be good together. He did not respect her feelings, like daddy did. This attitude of John bothered her a lot, but she kept it to herself.

Maggie decided to go to a local college and study criminal justice. She was blessed to get a part-time job in a small, local newspaper while she was in college.

James Henson was a fine young man who inherited the newspaper from a distant cousin. He started reporting everything that happened in the town. He was from New York and did not hold to all the going ons in Little Town Georgia. He would laugh out loud at some of the antics of the natives. He did not like the Klan. He was not biased or prejudiced, as a matter of fact, he reported about the Negroes as well as the whites. His newspapers began to have better sales. He called a spade a spade. The Negroes loved him because they thought he was a fair person. Maggie liked working for him. The pay was small but the exposure and the experience she was gaining was great. The only thing that kept them arguing was that he really thought Negroes were people, who were worth loving, and that it was all right to treat them like Caucasian folks. But then again, he grew up in the North, and she could tell that he did not care much for her father.

Her daddy hated Negroes and would do anything to get them out of town living in a small island – just coming off when they needed to do some work for their masters. She had no dealings with them because daddy saw to it that she never got mixed up with the likes of them. They were separated from white folks in many ways and so she did not have to deal with them. However, on her job it was different. Sometimes she had to go into a community, or home to find out what she wanted to know for her newspaper. She began to meet Negroes and some of them seemed like Caucasians. When she would tell her father that she had gone to see some Negroes about a matter, he would yell, "Hell, those people are nobodies, they don't count – you shouldn't be wasting your time on them. Tell about the greatness of your race. We are superior; we are God's people. We are blessed and they are cursed. The good Lord cursed them and made them our servants, right there in the Bible. Yes, princess, they are worse than filth. They steal, murder people, get drunk and they don't like to work; so keep far away from them Niggers. They are nothing, and don't you forget it." Maggie loved her father and intended to do as he suggested.

"That maybe true but James is my boss and he thinks differently and wants me to be objective in my reporting. He says that's the only way to be. Be true to your calling and report the facts, not your opinion," she would reply. However, whenever daddy got the chance he told her over and over again that Negroes were filth and the scum of the earth.

After graduating from college, Maggie got the position as James' assistant and she loved every minute of it. They both worked hard and they did most to their own leg work because they loved getting the facts for themselves. He's taught her that the interview is only 20% of the work, but 80% is the preparation, and that included many scenarios. It was hard work but she loved every minute of it.

CHAPTER 16

M
r. Thomas came as often as he could in the evening. Sadie learned a lot – she could not wait to read her own Bible which Mr. Thomas bought her. She made notes and she learned verses and learned how to meditate and trust in God and she felt like Ms. Helen and she could now understand the goodness of the lawd- as she told Ms. Helen, and they both laughed and hugged each other.

Mr. Thomas led her to the Lord and she learned what it was to have a personal relationship with Jesus. She realized that He was her Savior, that she was a sinner and was headed for hell. She accepted the Lord as her Master and Savior and she cried that night. She realized that she was plotting Mrs. Kettering's death in the most horrible way. She got on her knees and asked God to forgive her that night and she tore up the little book where she made all her notations about this horrendous crime she was to have committed. She asked God to forgive her for the murder she had committed in her heart. She was so happy she found the Lord. Bessie, Seff and Gracie were also led to the Lord.

Gracie was present over the two years Mr. Thomas came and she would sit and listen to him explain the Bible to them. He came because Sadie had difficulty traveling in the evening and she wanted to be at home with the children. Gracie loved the Lord and was consoled and comforted by His Word.

After one meeting, Gracie told Sadie, "I see you have a great admirer and she laughed." "What are you talking about?" Sadie asked innocently.

"Ah, come on, can't you see the man loves the dirt you walk on?"

Sadie replied, "Are you crazy? He is here to teach me the Bible and only the Bible, Thank you."

"Yeah! Right! Said Gracie, "you had better watch out – is he married?"

"He's a widower with two children."

"Ah-ha, you've been checking up on him," Gracie said.

"No way! He mentioned it because he was talking about Bessie and Joseph. He said they were lovely children and he admired how close they were and how loving to each other, that's all."

Gracie smiled and walked away singing, "Love is a Many Splendored Thing."

Six months later, after Bible study, Paul said, "Sadie, I'll like to take you to dinner on Saturday, are you free?" Sadie stretched herself backwards and looked at him with her head way back as if surveying him.

"You mean as in a date?" and she smiled.

"Yes, what's wrong with that? Will you come?"

"Yes, but I know I'll get a lot of teasing from the children and Gracie and as to Ms. Helen she'll be shouting, 'Praise de Lawd.' They all think I don't have a life, because I do not go out much."

"I agree with them," and he laughed as he took her hands in his, then raised them to his lips. He kissed her hands softly and said, "It will be my pleasure to take you to dinner."

That was the beginning of a beautiful friendship. They took walks after church, there were picnics with his children and hers and even Gracie accompanied them sometimes. They went to fairs, theme parks and places that she would not have dreamed of. Paul was always attentive, caring, and tender and Sadie realized that she was in love with this big, gentle man. This man who showed his love for her in every way without overpowering her; without forcing his intentions on her, yet, she could see the love in his eyes every time he looked at her. Sadie returned the feelings but tried not to give into them as she knew she was still married and nothing could come of this relationship. She confided in Gracie and told her of her love for Paul, and Gracie said, "You should tell him, and then try to get a lawyer and get a divorce. I'll find out details for you. You deserve some happiness; you can't live the rest of your life in limbo. Something's gotta give."

After being with each other for over three years, Paul declared his love for Sadie and told her he wanted to marry her and spend the rest of his life with her. They spent special time together, and it was always delightful with Paul. She begged him to wait until she could sort things out in her life, but she was not prepared to tell him everything yet. Some how or the other the time was not right.

One evening as they were coming home from services together they stopped over at Paul's house. It was the summer time and his children were at their grandparents' home. They got comfortable and sat talking. Paul took Sadie in his arms and started kissing her so passionately that there was no turning back for them. Their pent up emotions just burst forth and the next thing was Paul was undressing Sadie as he picked her up and took her into the bedroom. As he laid her on the bed, he began to whisper sweet nothings. "You remind me of a beautiful black orchid, and I feel like a bee who wants to pollinate you." Sadie couldn't help but laugh out loudly; she was laughing so hard that she started to cry.

Paul was taken aback, "What did I say? It's just that you brought out something in me; something I did not know I had. What did I say to offend you?"

"Nothing," she laughed, "It's not you, it's just...." And she laughed softly, "I'm sorry" she whispered. I just want to know if every man who makes love to his woman tells her all this crap, she thought. Paul made passionate love to her and they both knew deep down inside that this was wrong, but somehow it felt so right. They lay spent in each other's arms and Paul asked Sadie to marry him again. We can't live like this you know; I want you every moment of the day. I can't stop thinking about you. You are beautiful and I want you here in my arms. God knows I tried to wait, but you're tempting me every time I see you" and he started to laugh. "My Sunday school class members should see me now," and they both laughed. She felt quite happy being with Paul. She also felt safe and very much loved. It was a good feeling and one that she did not want to lose.

CHAPTER 17

Bessie graduated from High School, went to college for two years and got an Associates Degree and then decided to call it quits. She wanted to be a teacher but she was madly in love with David Scott. Bessie and David met in school, and struck up a friendship with each other that rivaled all friendships. Anyone who looked at them could tell that they were madly in love.

David was the tall, dark, and handsome type. He was in good physical shape since he worked out a lot. He always wore a smile and had one dimple that made his eyes light up. He was a light skinned Negro to Bessie's darker complexion. He and Bessie were ideally suited for each other. They were both unspoiled, innocent people and loved each other dearly.

David wanted to marry Bessie as soon as she graduated from the two year college. Sadie reminded her that she always wanted to be a teacher, and she told Sadie she would take it up later. "Right now I just want to be with David."

They would get married and live in the Barracks wherever he was stationed. He was a soldier, and she intended to follow him wherever he went. Bessie was so much in love with David that Sadie could not withhold her permission. She remembered how it was for her and Joe and wondered where he was right now. She wanted him to share this moment with Bessie. Bessie was always his favorite although he never admitted it. She smiled to herself and remembering how she would play this Little Piggy with his toes. She knew it wouldn't happen, at least not now.

Bessie made a beautiful bride. She had on lace over satin dress with tight fitting lace sleeves. Her veil had sparkles of diamantes in it, and she had a small train that was beautifully beaded. She had three bridesmaids, and a flower girl. It was a small, intimate ceremony and Seff was the father giver.

When the question was asked, "who gives this woman to be married?" Seff replied, "I do! And I don't want her back!" The whole church laughed. Everyone knew how much these two loved each other.

Auntie Gracie (as she was called by the children) was radiant at the wedding. She arranged everything and there was a small gathering at the house after the wedding. This was special for Gracie. She was like a mother to Bessie and Seff. She went through a lot with these two. However, two months ago, she was diagnosed with cancer. She was suffering a lot and the doctors gave her no more than six months to live. She went all out for this wedding and no one could stop her fussing over Bessie and David.

Bessie and David honeymooned in Florida, in Disneyland. Then David was going to be stationed in Georgia. Sadie was apprehensive, but she figured it had been 20 years ago.

Three months after the wedding, eight months after her diagnosis Gracie died in her sleep. We were all devastated. I was so glad to have Pastor James Goodwin and Paul Thomas to encourage me with the Word, reminding me that Gracie was a believer and her soul was at rest with Jesus. I need not worry. I missed her warm smile, and quick retorts to whatever we were arguing about. Sadie asked the Pastor to be allowed to say a few words about Gracie.

Gracie's home going was a wonderful experience for Sadie. The service was very well attended. Many of the doctors, nurses and staff of the hospital where Gracie worked filled the little church. It was interesting, this little black oriented church filled with equal number of Negroes and Caucasians. Gracie would have had it no other way. Pastor Goodwin called Sadie to say a few words.

Sadie walked slowly to the rostrum and stood tall; she looked out into the congregation and began to speak:

"My task today is very easy and pleasurable. I am here to tell you a little about my friend and sister, Grace Anne Madison. Gracie was a woman of integrity, she was fair, honest and compassionate; she didn't have a mean bone in her body. Gracie exemplified goodness; she became a Christian and her life said, 'If I could help somebody as I pass along, my living would not be in vain.

I'm here to tell you, her living was not in vain. My children and I are eternally grateful to Gracie for taking us in when our own relatives treated us with disdain and scorn; she took us into her home and acknowledged us as intellectual and responsible persons of equal status. We thankfully acknowledge the priceless benefits we received from her. She had this remarkable willingness to do what's good and right.

She loved to laugh and have fun; she had this infectious laughter that you had to laugh even if you didn't want to, and so the children will always have her laughter indelibly engraved in their hearts. Gracie loved as God loved, she was no respecter of persons, you could be Black, White, Brown, or Gray it did not matter to her. She loved you for who you were. And so today, I did not come to mourn her passing but to rejoice that her soul was redeemed by the Lamb of God and that she is trying to spread all over Heaven that tumultuous joy she gave to us. God bless you Gracie, I loved you, my sister.

Sadie made her way back to her seat, and as she sat down, Bessie reached over and hugged her mother. Tears were streaming down their cheeks.

The sermon by Rev. Goodwin was consoling and at the same time motivating others to live for Christ as Gracie had done. Bessie sang Gracie's favorite songs, "What a Friend We Have in Jesus" and "It is Well with My Soul." There was not a dry eye in the church. Seff and Bessie sang a duet, "His Eye Is on the Sparrow."

Gracie had no immediate relatives, so in her will she left the home to Sadie and money for Bessie and Seff to finish off their studies. She also left money for Ms. Helen, the church, few friends, and her favorite charities.

Sadie was grateful for a place for herself and Seff to stay. She was worried that probably they would have to leave now that Gracie had gone, but Praise de Lawd, as Ms. Helen would say, He had taken care of her and Seff.

When Sadie started working with Zoë, Gracie had taken her to the bank and showed her how to use the bank and manage her finances. She would be eternally grateful to God for allowing Gracie to help her and her children the way she did. Sadie was a fast learner and she knew how to keep her own books. This experience helped her with the bookstore's accounts too.

Bessie stayed with her mother and Seff for a little while, after the week's honeymoon. David had gone ahead to make arrangements for his bride to follow him. They told Sadie where they were going to stay but she had never heard of the little town and paid no attention to anything else. Soon Bessie was packed and she was saying goodbye to her church family, Seff and Sadie. Seff hugged his big sister and they both cried. He said, "And if that big ape doesn't want you, I'll take you back."

Bessie punched him playfully, "He is not an ape, and he's my husband."

Sadie and Seff watched her get on the bus and she was gone. She realized that Seff, her baby would soon be off to college that he and Auntie Gracie had arranged. Seff wanted to study law and Auntie Gracie was all for it. She felt sad but remembered how blessed she was and thanked God for His blessings.

Bessie had arrived safely in Georgia, and after church on Sunday, Sadie cried herself to sleep that night. She was grateful for Seff and loved him very much but she did not know where her two girls were and now Bessie had been married and gone off to her husband. She felt alone and wondered what Joe was doing at this moment. Did he ever think of them? Was he married? How can he be when she was still alive? No need to think of him, she had Seff. As if he read her mind, a tap was heard on the door and Seff asked, "Duchess, are you alright? May I come in?"

"Sure, Seff"

Seff came and sat on the edge of the bed and took her hands in his. "Duchess, you do not have to be so brave, you need to break down and cry like I did awhile ago" and he laughed.

"Not on your life! I'm just joking. I am a man! Men do not cry! I was glad to see her go. Now I have you all to myself," and he started crying. Sadie raised herself up and took him in her arms.

"You have been such a wonderful person, I just thank God for you- I don't know what I would have done without you, Seff." You have shown Bessie and me nothing but love. You are a God send."

CHAPTER 18

It was two years since Bessie went to Georgia with David. She had called Sadie and told her the good news - she was pregnant. Sadie was ecstatic. She was happy for Bessie and David, and she was going to be a grandmother. How wonderful!

Bessie hung up the phone from talking to her mother and left the little café on the barracks where they were stationed. Outside, she ran into Daisy another young soldier's wife. "Oh, Bessie, I need to talk to you. I need your help badly."

"What's the matter?" asked Bessie

I need your help, it's my mother – she's been diagnosed with cancer and the doctor said she has only six weeks to live. I need to go see her for a week, but I need my job. My mistress said if I can get someone to fill in for me it will be alright. It's not a lot of work, just making beds, dusting, polishing and light work and the pay is good. It's only 5 hours per day and you'll get transportation pay as well. Please, please help me."

"I'm so sorry to hear about your mother. I just finished speaking to mine. I would be devastated if anything happened to my mother right now. I don't think I could take it and she became teary eyed. "O.K. I'll help you but I have to clear it with David first."

When Bessie told David he told her, "Sweetheart, you know you would not rest until you help the whole wide world, so go ahead, but don't work too hard; remember, you're carrying the heir to my kingdom in your womb." David came up behind her and was rubbing her flat stomach. "Imagine, he said, this beautiful body will be more beautiful as my seed springs forth," he spread his hands and twirled around, "I am so happy, happy, and happy."

David was going on a two week assignment so he would be

away and was glad Bessie had something to do; this way she would not have all the time to worry about him.

The next week Bessie set off for the house of Mrs. Mabel Kettering which was two towns over. It was a beautiful plantation, and the people there were friendly. They took to her right away and showed her what she had to do. The house was real big. She had never been in a house like this before. It seemed that too many people were not living there. Mrs. Kettering lived on the west side of the house and her son and his wife and two children on the east side. She and another girl, Mindy would do all the cleaning.

On Thursday morning, as Joe, his wife, Sarah and his two children were at breakfast he noticed Bessie and she had a striking resemblance to Lula and he kept looking at her. When his wife and children left the table, he asked, "What is your name, young lady?"

"Bessie, sir," she replied. She felt scared as she did not mingle with a lot of white people.

He said, "You remind me of someone I knew years ago, and she died in a fire, but I still think of her often." He seemed to be in a trance, and Bessie offered, "Sorry to hear that, Sir, real sorry," and she went about doing her work.

The next morning, Joe was not feeling well so he told Sarah that he was not going into the office today. He was going to relax and take the day off. Sarah was happy as he never took care of himself. She had some errands to do and she was going to be out of the house most of the day, so he will get some rest.

Bessie went along doing her work as she was scheduled. Today was her last day at this home. She enjoyed the work, and the people. Everyone was nice to her. She hummed as she dusted and cleaned the children's room. She finished early and decided to do Ms. Sarah's room. She entered, humming softly as she emptied trash. As she passed by the bed she saw toes hanging out of the rumpled sheet. Bessie could not resist the feeling that came over her and she went quickly over to the toes, took one in her hand, and started singing "This little Piggy." She was giggling so much that she did not see the startled look that came out from under the sheets. Joe was flabbergasted, it was Wendy Mae. He shot up out of the bed and when Bessie realized what had happened she tried to run, but he was out of bed and caught her. She began to cry and cower, "please sir, I didn't mean any harm. Oh! God! I'm sorry, I'm so sorry."

"No, No, I'm not going to hurt you. It is just that my little girl used to do that to me and now, you, who look so much like my Lula, you are doing the same thing. Why did you do it?"

"Oh! I don't know. I usually do it to my mother and brother, I'm so sorry, sir." She was crying hysterically now and he had to wait to calm her down. He was sure she was Wendy Mae. He had a gut feeling, and he was never wrong about such things. He had to find out more about her mother, but a brother? He got a glass of water and gave it to her and told her drink it. She took the glass but could only sip it slowly. He wanted her to hurry up and calm herself so that he could ask her some questions but he could see that she was afraid.

He took her hands in his and said, "Bessie, when I first saw you, you reminded me of my first wife. Her name was Lula Mae, she was a Negro. We had triplets – 3 most beautiful girls. When they were about 2 ½ years old, they all died in a fire in Alabama. That was about 18 + years ago. I had gone away for a week, and then I got a call from Doc who gave me the bad news about Lula and the girls. I was devastated. The love of my life had died and our children. Ten years ago I got married again and Sarah and I have two beautiful children. However, I miss my children and Lula; everyday I think about them. When we lived in Alabama, our youngest daughter, Wendy Mae loved to pinch toes and play, "This little Piggy" because I taught it to her, and every day, sometimes 3 or 4 times a day she would take my toes and play this game. So you can see, when you did that to me this morning, it brought back memories and then again you reminded me so much of Lula that it was too much for me. So, please relax; you just have to tell me about your family."

Bessie listened, she remembered Auntie Gracie talking about Doc but she never saw him or asked any questions about him. She told Mr. Kettering what her mother looked like, but said she had no sisters only a brother named Joseph Ryan Anderson. Joe was stunned; his name was Joseph Ryan Kettering. Bessie continued to tell him that she was married and was only filling in for the week for another soldier's wife. Bessie's husband was on assignment for another two weeks and she decided to help out a friend. She didn't know who her father was because Sadie never talked about him. He could have been White; she always wondered about her hair texture, and length; they were more in line with mixed breed girls, also Joseph was very light skinned, sandy colored curly hair and blue-green eyes. He was very handsome.

"My name is Joseph Ryan Kettering; there is something fishy going on. How old are you, Bessie?

"Twenty-one and my birthday is September 15th.

"That the birthday of our triplets," he volunteered.

"How old is Joseph?"

"Eighteen," she replied

"She must have gotten him after the fire."

"There is something else," she said, warning up to him, "My mother was badly burned in a fire and she had to have several skin graftings and a few operations. She also walks with a limp," Bessie explained.

"Bessie, I can feel the connection between us, you used to be my special girl, you followed me all around the house, while you sucked on your thumb, and you had a little yellow teddy bear that you carried around with you all the time. Do you remember any of this?"

She shook her head, "No, sir – Mr. Kettering, but I do have a favorite teddy bear."

"Bessie, you have to help me clear up this mystery. Would you be willing to help me?" She nodded, "yes," what else could she say?

"Okay, do not tell your mother anything just in case we are wrong but I doubt it. I will make arrangements for you to accompany me to meet Lula. When was the last time you went home?"

"Last year, sir and I just found out that I was pregnant so I would like to see mummy."

"Congratulations, my dear, I am so happy for you," Joe said.

"Okay, let your husband know, then call your mother and let her know you're flying in day after tomorrow to see her. I will be there to straighten this out. I will tell no one and I expect you to do the same. This is crazy. I have to know what is going on."

Mr. Kettering helped her to her feet and Bessie left the room. Her head was reeling; this rich, White man said he used to be married to her mother and that he is her father; worse of all he said she was one of triplets, and that she had two other sisters. He really must be crazy, a loony bin as Seff would say. Nonetheless, she had to go through this with him to show him that he was wrong; and at the same time there were some similarities in his story that she needed to clear up.

He told her to take the day off. He was going to take her home in his car. Bessie knew she should be uncomfortable but he seemed to fit in her life so easily like Auntie Gracie that she did not protest.

Two days later, Bessie and Mr. Kettering were on a plane headed for Connecticut.

CHAPTER 19

When the car pulled up at the house, Sadie was very excited. She told Seff who came home on the weekends that Bessie was coming and that he should be nice to her now that she was going to be a mother. Bessie came out of the car, and a man was paying the taxi driver; she did not pay much attention to him as her eyes were on her daughter who looked beautiful as she ran up the walkway. Sadie hugged her tightly and they both were laughing so hard it was funny. After hugging Bessie, Sadie noticed that the person had followed her to the door as he came forward she looked at him for the first time and her heart fell. Her heart stopped beating; all the blood rushed to her head, she got very, very dizzy; her body kept spinning around, around, around. She was able to make her eyes focus for a moment, yes, it was a ghost.

Sadie whispered "Joe" and she fainted. At that time Seff came out of the room, shouting, "Where is the mother of my nephew? Did you....Duchess, what happened" and he ran to see what was wrong with Sadie. He noticed Joe, and asked, "Who the hell are you; and what did you do to my mother?"

"It's okay, I can explain," said Joe apologetically.

"My name is Joseph Kettering," he answered as he cradled Sadie in his arms. He picked her up and carried her over to the sofa.

Bessie asked, "Is she all right?" Joe smiled and said, "She'll be all right. She just needs to get over the shock of seeing me again."

"What is going on, and who are you?" Seff asked again looking questioningly now at Bessie and then Joe.

"I am Sadie's husband and I think I am Bessie's as well as your father"

"What?" said Seff.

Sadie was stirring so Joe turned his attention to her. He said to Bessie and Seff. "Please let me have some time alone with her."

"Joe" she whispered, "How...."

"Hush, Lula just let me hold you, sweetheart; I must be dreaming. I couldn't believe it when Wendy Mae, I mean Bessie came to the house and guess what? I was at home sick and was under the sheets with my toes out; you know how I never liked to cover my feet. She saw my toes and started playing our game. I let her finish and then I got hold of her. She was frightened, and scared stiff. After calming her down, I got details from her and here I am.

Tell me Lula what happened? How could you do something like this to me? This is some cruel joke? I don't believe you of all people would do something like this to me. All the way in the plane coming over here, I told myself I was dreaming. This was not happening, at least, not to me." He got up now and started pacing while he talked, as only Joe could do.

"For eighteen years I thought you and the girls had died in a fire, now I come to find out that you are all alive and well, and no one bothered to inform me that I had a wife and children. I even had a son. What the hell was going through your mind, Lula?"

"Calm yourself down, you were always a little hot headed," she smiled.

"Hot headed! I am downright angry, you do not know what your 'so-called' deaths have done to me, I was in agony, in pain and suffering, knowing my wife and children were killed in a fire; how can you be so insensitive?" Joe asked.

"Oh. Joe you do not know how many nights I cried for you, to feel your arms around me telling me all those wonderful things you used to tell me, and how our lives have changed. I could not contact you because I was ordered by Doc not to do so. You see, Joe, and this is hard for me to tell you, but I have to let you know so that you may understand why I did what I did."

Here Sadie put her head in her hands and sobbed quietly. Joe came closer to her and took her in his arms. "Shhh, just relax, and take your time; there's no hurry."

After a few moments, Sadie raised her head and continued between sobs, "Your mother paid someone to murder me and my children. She found out where we lived, knew you were away and had a man named Curly set fire to our cottage. It was a good thing Curly saw us and decided that a nice family like ours should not die because of "racist white folk" as he put it; so he told Mr. Mike what he had to do but by the time Mr. Mike found Doc, Curly had already set the fire and I was trapped in bed with Wendy and Betty. I was able to save my babies, but I was badly burnt and had to leave right away and Doc told me only to take Wendy, as it would be easier for me." As she retold the events of that night the tears trickled down her cheeks; she just let them flow because they were washing away all the years of pent up hurt.

Encouraged, she continued, "Mary Jane had a fever and was in Doc's house when the fire started. Doc took care of the details and I was sent to live here with a friend of his. Her name was Gracie Madison. Gracie died two years ago and left me this house and some money. I worked in a book store part time, recently I bought it as the owner wanted to retire; and Seff and Bessie encouraged me to buy it. Doc warned me never to get in touch with you because you would travel the world to be with us and that your mother might try again and this time we would not be so lucky. I have no idea where the two girls are."

Relieved now, she turned to him, "What about you? Tell me what you have done over the years. I did not expect to see you ever again; but I'm so glad I did."

"I was horrified when I learned that you girls died in the fire. I attended your funeral and stayed with Doc for awhile until my mother showed up and wanted to take care of me. I was so out of it that I didn't think anything of it. Doc urged me to go, and I was in no mood to fight him, and being exhausted I let her take me home. He came to sit next to Sadie.

"I was a zombie for months, did nothing, just laid around the house. Eventually, I got up, and started working at a prestigious law firm. Seven years ago I married a wonderful girl named Sarah and we have two children. Stephan and Sandra, ages six and three. She's a wonderful wife." When he said the word, he realized what he had just said, "Oh! Lord! We are not legally married; I am a bigamist. What shall we do Lula? I love you and I also love Sarah." He got up again and held his head in his hands.

"This is so complicated. I am going to have to call Sarah and tell her, but not now. As for my mother, I think when I get back I shall wring her scrawny neck."

Sadie busted out laughing. Joe looked at her puzzled. "I have already done that a few years ago, I murdered her, I hanged her, I pulled her toenails out one by one, you name it, and she died many days very, very, slowly."

Bessie and Seff appeared in the room, "We heard laughter," said Seff, "Are you alright, Duchess?"

"Yes, I am, my Prince; come and meet your father. Joe is going to stay the weekend with us so that you guys can hear everything that happened and get to know him."

That night was torment for Sadie, "how dare he get married again; he did not even try to find us; did not give a damm, the bastard." She remembered how he had told her his love would last forever, well, was this forever? No, it was only ten years, ten freaking years. Her thoughts were running like a runaway train. She wanted him badly, but her heart was sore, he had failed her, and this was not supposed to come from him. He was the love of her life. She wanted him to make love to her like he did in the olden days and tell her how beautiful she was. What would God think of this? She was still married to him, so she would not be committing adultery. Well, God was almighty, He would understand. She needed to feel his arms around her right now. Oh! How she hated him. Another White person making her life a living hell, but this time it was Joe, the love of her life. He was living with his mother who tried to kill me and my children; while now he has a white wife and children and everything is honky dory. Oh! Those people! How I hate every last one of them. It was almost morning now because she and Joe had spent most of the night talking. Finally, she drifted off to a fitful sleep.

When she woke after a few hours of sleep, she had to remind herself that she did not dream everything; that Joe was in this house with the children and she was here. He had remarried and had a wife whom he loved and two children. She remembered her thoughts and felt sad. Sadie remembered the first sermon she heard on forgiveness and tried hard to remember how to; why should she, and when. Nothing was coming through but she remembered that when all else fails call on Jesus.

Sadie fell on her knees and sat quietly. She thought of Joe who had always been kind, loving, compassionate, and very romantic. He had been a wonderful father, and husband to her. Poor Joe, he was a victim of his circumstances. Oh! Lord Jesus, forgive me so that I can forgive him. He waited ten years thinking I was dead. He wasn't unfaithful. I believe that if he knew I was alive he never would have gotten married. Forgive me, I was the one who knew I wasn't free to love another man and I fell in love with Paul. What a mess! Lord, give me the strength to face this situation, Holy Spirit lead me, guide me, tell me what to say to ease Joe's heartache. He must be in torment – a Black wife who turns up after seventeen years, another wife and two children whom he loves dearly. Oh, Lord help him".

Sadie stayed on her knees and quietly communed with God until she received His strength.

At breakfast, Joe and the children were like old friends. He was fascinated with Seff, "you are a very handsome young man, and I like how, you call your mother, 'Duchess' I think it befits her."

Seff smiled and said, "Thank you, kind Sir"

"Why are you called Seff?" asked Joe.

Everyone laughed, and Seff said, "I could not say "Joseph" so I said "Seff" and the name stuck with me; I like it though."

Joe turned to Bessie, "I heard I am going to be a grandfather," she smiled.

"I would like to meet my son-in-law when he comes back."

After breakfast, Joe announced that he had to call Sarah and tell her what had happened as she did not know why he had left the way he did and it was only fair to prepare her now.

Sarah answered, "Hi, sweetheart, where are you?"

"Sarah, you would not believe what has happened," he paused, "I don't know how to explain this to you, but, I found Lula and one of the triplets, and also I have a son. Sarah they look fine and everyone is wonderful. I am so happy right now you wouldn't believe it. My wife is alive; my children are alive, oh! Thank God!"

Sarah was silent for a while, then she said, "Joe, Joe, I am happy you found your wife and children, but do you know what you are saying? Listen to yourself. Do you know what it means about our marriage? You said my wife is alive, does than mean I am not your wife? What are we going to do about that?"

Joe realized how insensitive he had been and to break this news to her over the phone, what the hell was he thinking. "We should not be talking about this on the phone so I'll explain everything when I come home. Just take care of yourself for me, I love you" he added and he hung up. He put his head in his hands, and said, "What a mess."

When he rejoined Lula and the children he was a little calmer. He had missed out on his first son's birth, and he wanted to know all about him. He went over to Seff and they started talking. Seff asked, "What should I call you?"

"You can call me Joe – since you are Seff you will be an extension of me." They both smiled. He asked Seff, "What are you studying?"

Seff replied, "I want to be a lawyer and a minister." Joe could understand the Lawyer part, but a minister; that was something else. "Why the ministry; Do you think you have been 'called', as they say?"

"Yes, I do, and I take it very seriously, but at the same time I would like to help poor Black people who cannot afford a rich lawyer," and they both laughed.

"I'm doing a lot of research now for a law firm here in Boston, and I enjoy it immensely," he continued.

"What about your love life; Do you have a girlfriend?"

"Yes, I do; her name is Cindy Butler. She is the cutest little lady next to Duchess. I think Duchess and Bessie like her, if not, she would not be my girlfriend. Cindy knows what I want and is willing to wait for me for at least two more years. I do have some money Auntie Grace left me so I can take my time and only concentrate on studying. Duchess instilled in Bessie and me a love for reading and so I do not mind hitting the books." He smiled as he turned to Bessie, "I guess the books hit you." She raised her hand to smack him and he held her hand, drew her into his arms and said softly, "No more fighting with me until we have my nephew safe and sound."

"Niece," she said.

"It had better be boy, I'm banking on it," Seff retorted.

Sadie sat smiling at her two children and Joe just sat there thinking to himself. What a remarkable fellow! He reminds me of myself at his age. The weekend soon ended and Joe promised to keep in touch and come back as soon as he can; bringing Sarah and the two children with him. Joe and Bessie left for the airport.

Although Sadie and Joe did a lot of talking all through the night, they both were hurting. He felt betrayed by Doc, his mother and Sadie. She felt betrayed by Joe. Her Joe; who had promised to love her forever, proved that there was no such thing as forever with him. It was quite an unforgettable weekend.

In the plane, Bessie and Joe engaged in small talk and Bessie felt quite comfortable with him, and told him so.

"That's because you were always my favorite as your mother stated. We had a special bond together. You followed me around like a lost puppy dog. You sucked on your thumb and always had a teddy bear in the other hand. Your sisters were always playing with each other or their toys, but you, you followed your daddy around, and I loved every moment of it. I'm so glad you're alive Wendy, I mean Bessie," and they both laughed.

Joe took Bessie home and promised to keep in touch with her. Bessie could not wait for David to come home next week to tell him all that happened.

Joe went home and he was livid. After talking to Sarah they decided that they have to move out of this home, something they should have done a long time ago, however, his mother had always said, the estate belongs to you anyhow, stay here take care of it, and it will be alright. I do not know everything and I prefer you being here. She had helped him so much after the death of his wife and children that he felt badly; wanting to move away and she always made him feel badly when he mentioned moving. Sarah and he spend all weekend talking about this and they both decided that they had to leave.

He told his mother he wanted to talk to her. She went in the study and sat down; she thought probably they were going to have another baby or something like that. He started out by saying, "I saw Lula Mae, and two of my children this weekend. What she told me made me see red. I cannot believe you would pay someone to kill my wife and children."

Mrs. Kettering was flabbergasted, "what are you talking about? You attended the funeral, and told me all about it. How could this be?"

"You tell me!" He screamed as he walked around in circles.

"Lula and my youngest triplet, Wendy Mae, are safe. Did you know that Lula was pregnant at the time of the fire, but did not find out until she was being treated for her burns? She had 3rd degree burns all over her body, had to have skin gratings, and a couple of operations, and then come to find out that she was pregnant with my son. How could you pay someone to kill them? Oh! Yes! The young man confessed to one of Lula's neighbors who told Doc; only it was too late by the time Doc found out, the house was already on fire."

Her face was stricken. She was thinking, you can't even pay people to do things properly; all that money for nothing. Better she had done it herself.

"Good Lord, Joe. I'm sorry; I was so ashamed when you ran off with that Nigger gal, but now that she is okay, I'm glad. You have Sarah and the children so you don't have to worry about her now. I'll send her some money; just let me know her address." She walked over to the desk, pulled out a drawer and her checkbook.

"Put that away! Do you think Lula wants to hear from you? She doesn't need your money, she wants her children." He was screaming at the top of his lungs; "her two older girls are still missing to her. She has no idea where they are now. She had to run for her life with Wendy and leave the other two to be split up with different people and now she has no idea where they are. I am going to spend the rest of my life trying to find our two girls. Sarah and I are moving out and there is nothing you can do to stop us now. Not after trying to kill your own flesh and blood. You swear that you love Sarah, now she is not even my legal wife because of your interference."

She stood up, looked him dead in the face and said, "They will never be my flesh and blood! Never! No bloody Niggers are going to be in this family. Not if I could help it!

Go after your Nigger woman and her children, see if I care. Poor Sarah, she and the children are the ones to suffer through this." She got up, felt a sharp pain in her chest and slowly, very slowly sat back down. Joe had already stormed out of the room.

CHAPTER 20

oc was nearly 86 and he still went to see a few patients. He was getting tired, and knew he had to take care of himself. Doctors were all the same; they made bad patients. He never took his own advice. He was getting very frail and he knew the end would be soon. He had to put things in order. He had to right the wrongs he had done. His thoughts were very erratic nowadays. Oh, God if only you could forgive me. I thought I was doing the right thing, but sometimes you are just trying to control peoples' lives. I loved those children as if they were my own. Joseph and Lula Mae were the children I never had. However, I really messed things up for them by trying to protect them. I destroyed their lives. Forgive me God. He thought about the things he found out about his favorite girl. She was placed with members of the Klan. Oh my God what a travesty! The Klan, of all people. It was like a death sentence without knowing it. He decided to sit and write them a letter explaining her heritage to them. She was old enough to hear the truth. He was also banking on her mother to help her as he learned that Mrs. Ascott did not go along with her husband's ideals and that she loved Margaret very much.

He got out paper and wrote everything he could and asked them for forgiveness for allowing them to adopt a Black child. It was not his intention, and the doctor who gave them the baby did not know they were "Partial" to Blacks. He tried to put it in a nice way. He explained that her father was a Caucasian man who married a Black woman and they had triplets, and that he was the attending physician. Margaret was the oldest of the three. They had distinguishing marks on their bodies which was very unique. Margaret and the younger sister, Wendy Mae had these marks on the left and right thigh respectively. The middle girl, Betty Lou had it on both thighs. When these three girls are together at the thighs, the birthmarks formed two distinct hearts. It was if God was setting them apart from everyone else. I hope you can continue to love Margaret as you do, and forgive an old foolish man for making a terrible mistake. Please remember that if I had known Dr. Avery was going to give Margaret to you, knowing your husband's ideology, I never in my wildest dreams would have let it happen. She remembers nothing of her biological parents and maybe she doesn't know that she is adopted. I suggest when you tell her that you explain these things to her. It will be hard on her but it would be best that she is told the truth about her heritage.

He knew his end was near. Gracie had gone on, and she left Lula Mae, Bessie and the boy the house and some money to run things. He had set it up for Gracie so he knew what was going on. He had the lawyer explain to Lula that money was at her disposal to pay bills and feed and clothe them as always. He felt obligated to help them. He was also glad to hear that Sadie, as Lula called herself now, was working, Seff was in college and Bessie was married. They were doing marvelously well. Tears came to his eyes as he thought of his family.

He was putting his things in order; ever so often he made necessary changes. He made his will, leaving a small amount for all the children. He left his house to Mary Jane and Betty Lou. He had already sat down and wrote letters to Mr. & Mrs. Ascott through his lawyers; telling them of Mary Jane's heritage. He decided that they should mail the letter after his death.

Doc was searching for Lizzie. He had a detective trying to find her and he finally heard what had happened to her. He had traced her to Georgia and was waiting word from the detective. It had been a year and no one seems to know where she had gone. He was determined to find her and take care of her. He had let her foster parents know he was very upset over what went on, and wished they had written to him, when it happened. They were trying to be smart and still try to collect the money even though she wasn't there. He let them have it. He stopped the money right away and that was the end of them. They did not know where Lizzie was and it seemed as if they didn't care. "Oh! My God! What that poor child must have gone through. I will find her if it is the last thing I do. I owe it to Joe and Lula," he said out loud.

Doc visited his lawyers to update his Will and file papers with them. Now he gave them a very large brown envelope that needed to be dealt with when he was gone. There were letters in that envelope concerning his family.

CHAPTER 21

L izzie got off the bus and looked around. This place seemed like deadsville. It seemed like a very small town. She walked from the bus station down the street and came to a cafeteria; where there was a "help wanted" sign. She went in and asked for the job. The woman looked at her and her bag and asked, "Are you from around here?"

"No she replied. I just came off the bus and I need a job and a place to stay."

"Well! Well! Whad duy yuh no."

"I need someone like yesterday- the job doesn't pay much and it's a lot of work. Do you still want it?"

"Yes, I need a job and I also need a place to stay," replied Lizzie in her Southern drawl. She wished she didn't sound so country.

"There's a room over Ms. Nellie's; I'll tell you where it is and just tell her Ms. Margie sent you."

Lizzie picked up her raggedy bag and headed for Ms. Nellie's home.

Ms. Nellie was a tall, Black woman with a round face, and dark piercing eyes. Her head was tied with a scarf and part of it hung down the side of her face. She smiled as she welcomed Lizzie and Lizzie saw the most beautiful smile in her life. Her eyes closed up and her cheeks puffed up and she had nice, even dentures. Lizzie smiled back.

"Come in chile, you must be tired."

"Thank you," said Lizzie. "Ms. Margie sent me; she said you had a room to rent."

"Yes, my daughter got married and went with her soldier hus- band up north, and I am here by myself, so I would like the com- pany."

Lizzie worked in the cafeteria washing dishes, cleaning and sometimes they even showed her how to fix some simple foods. She was learning a lot, but at night she was dog tired. Ms. Nellie would always be up to help her in anyway she needed. She also wanted to talk to Lizzie and sometimes Lizzie was so tired she'll fall fast asleep while Ms. Nellie was talking to her.

After seven months, Ms. Nellie died suddenly. It was a heart attack. Her daughter sold the house and the people who bought it wanted Lizzie out. She missed Ms. Nellie and now she had to find another place to stay. She found lodging with a friend who came into the cafeteria frequently. Maisie came into the cafeteria and you can see she was an uppity Negro. Ms. Bernie would make snide remarks behind her back.

Lizzie asked her one day why she did not like Maisie and she said. "If you like selling your body you could look like her," she turned up her nose and walked away.

Lizzie rented a room in the same house with Maisie's mother. Maisie began to talk to her. "You're such a beautiful young woman; I know you can make a lot of money if you knew the right people."

"I could?" asked Lizzie.

"Yes, just let me know when you're ready and I'll introduce you to my friends."

Lizzie remembered what Ms. Bernie had said about Maisie, and she was skeptical. The fancy clothes, jewelry and money Maisie had fascinated her. Here she was breaking her back, working in a stinking cafeteria making no particular money, and she could not even save a cent to get her out of this situation. It was dead-end street if she ever saw one.

She began to talk to Maisie some more and Maisie told her she could be making up to $300.00 per week. She was making less than $100.00 per week, even when she got tips. She had to pay rent, and pay for other necessities. It was hard for her to put away any particular money. Maisie made it sound glamorous. Lizzie would stay with a Ms. Greta Henson. Ms. Greta ran the business and all Lizzie had to do was be company for some of the gentlemen who visited the home. It sounded easy, and Lizzie was excited. Now she would be able to save some money and then try to find her mother who might be working like a slave in somebody's kitchen. Lizzie could not wait to get started.

Maisie took Lizzie to Ms. Greta and she loved Lizzie right away. Lizzie was even more fortunate because Ms. Greta told her she had a room for her and that she did not have to travel back and forth; she would live on the premises.

When Ms. Greta explained to Lizzie what she had to do – "just be nice to the gentlemen I send in to you, and everything will be alright."

Ms. Greta spoke to Maisie and told her to slowly enlighten Lizzie as to what would go on, and then take her shopping for some decent clothes.

"Spend as much as possible, I have a feeling that this one will bring me some real money. She's got the figure, the looks and youth; so train her well, my dear."

Lizzie got her first customer two weeks later.

A very mild mannered white, man who came in and did not do much talking but asked Lizzie to undress slowly and dance for him. She thought this was going to be it, but when she undressed to her underwear, he said,

"Take the bra off very slowly;" she did, and then he said "peel your panties off and kick them up in the air." This was getting weird; after she was naked he wanted her to straddle him and call him daddy. She remembered her father right away and tried to run from the room but her clothes were all over the place. She tried to pick up something but he grabbed her by the hand and flung her on the bed, "I like the feisty ones; ooh I do." He threw her on the bed and got on top of her.

"Get off of me, you creep" she screamed. He looked astonished, because she was frightened.

"Didn't they tell you what was going to happen?" he asked her as he strapped her down and covered her mouth.

She shook her head and said, "Not really, Ms. Greta said I had to be nice to the customers."

She remembered what Maisie had tried to show her and how she told her to pretend she was somewhere else when "it" happened, but she never really said what. Now she understood.

"Be real, honey you are in a whore house – that makes you a whore."

"I ain't no whore; get off of meh."

"Not until I get what I paid for"

"yuh ain't pay meh nuttin. Yuh creep."

Lizzie tried to get up but he would not let her. He jumped on top of her, pried open her legs and had his way with her. She screamed and he enjoyed her screaming, grunting and saying "come on, baby, say it for me," Lizzie did not know if she would live or die. She was hurting and wanted to die.

She was still crying hysterically when he left, and Ms.Greta came to her and soothed her, "Don't cry honey, its better as time goes by."

"Gets better?" she thought. "What was she talking about? I wasn't going to do this again. No! No! No amount of money was worth this pain, this humiliation. First, it was daddy, now was it to be every man she met? No! She could not do it!

As if she read her thoughts, Ms. Greta said, "Honey, this is business. Just think of something pleasant, and let them have their way. The money is good, and now what do you have to lose?"

She laughed as she said this. "I'll tell you what I'm going to do for you. I'll let you relax for a few days, but after that, you have to get back to work or leave; it's as simple as that."

Ms. Greta was thinking that with Lizzie she had to make back the money she had already put out, so she smiled sweetly and patted the young girl's shoulder.

The girl was young and fresh; and she was absolutely exquisite. She had never seen such beauty other on a porcelain doll. Lizzie had it and many of the men were tired of these old beaten down women. They wanted something new. She was already seeing the dollar signs.

Many of the older women came to console Lizzie and Maisie her friend who brought her to the house began to tell her of her first experiences and how she cried and wanted to disappear and go anywhere but in this house. However, she got over it quickly when she got her first money and she could buy what she wanted. She looked at it like this. Here, she had a roof over her head, good food; saw a doctor regularly and it wasn't so bad. She had regular customers, and she knew how to handle each one of them. She knew what each wanted and how they wanted it and she did it-simple as that. She talked to Lizzie every day and told her that it could only get better. Lizzie relaxed a little and tried to put her mind at ease. She was already alone, and had no where to go, no one to turn to, no money other than the $100 she had left. She told her self that she would save up her money and then split. Ms. Greta took out a portion of the money for room and board and she still would have a generous amount at the end of the week.

CHAPTER 22

hree weeks after that incident, Ms. Greta was away and her assistant, Ms. Susie was in charge. One of Janie's regular customers, Mr. Richardson came in unexpectedly and Janie was away, he was drunk out of his mind, and demanded that someone be sent to his room. Ms. Susie was beside herself. This had never happened before while she was in charge. She tried to find another girl and no one wanted to take him on.

"Hell no! Cassie told her; tell him to come back when Janie's here. He knows the rules."

But Mr. Richardson wanted to have some fun and he was not leaving. Susie thought of Lizzie and decided to send Lizzie in to him.

When Susie came to Lizzie, she was sitting on the chaise peeling an apple and eating it. Lizzie said, "I just want to finish my apple."

Susie said, "Take it in with you." Lizzie took the apple and the knife and went in to see Mr. Richardson.

Mr. Richardson was a tall, burly built, Caucasian man. He had thinning hair, dark blue eyes, and probably was handsome in his younger years. He seemed like 50-60 years old. She thought 'what was this old man doing in a place like this?' However, she smiled and said, "How are you doing?"

"Fine," he grunted. He was obviously very drunk, and his hands seemed to tremble.

He seemed a man of small talk, oh boy what was I getting myself into this time, Lizzie thought.

He yelled, "Get undressed" and turned to a bag he brought with him. He took out, a scarf, handcuffs, a small stick and some sort of cream. Lizzie was wondering what all the equipment was for. Was he getting ready to go to work afterwards, and wanted to make sure he had everything with him. What was the reason? She was soon to find out.

Mr. Richardson told her to lie on the bed and stretch her feet apart so he could shackle them to the bedposts. She protested and she begged him not to let her do this. She started to panic as she did the last time and as much as she tried she felt the blood rising up in her. Instead he slapped her and pushed her down on the bed; he had the shackles on the left leg and somehow snapped it to the bedpost; she struggled and started kicking with her right foot so that he could not get a grip on it; that's when he began beating her about the face, one slap after the other. He took his fingernails and drew blood on her back and legs. "You damm whore, just shut up; you Black bitch," he screamed.

She heard herself screaming and was hoping someone would come in and save her but nobody came. He grabbed the scarf and put it around her neck and began to pull. He jumped on top of her within a minute was inside of her; and he started yanking the scarf while riding her. She was being torn from top to bottom, she screamed for help but no one came to help her. She realized that the soft music was being played in all the rooms and maybe no one wanted to interfere. They thought she was enjoying herself. Oh, my God. He was tightening the scarf – she was going to die. She started to feel for something to hit this monster, she felt nothing, she stretched her fingers as far as she could and they touched something. She wrapped her fingers around the knife she used to pear the apple.

She grabbed the knife and swung it into his neck, into his shoulder, into his back, into his side, over and over again while she screamed, "Get off me! Get off me!" She began to soak and realized that it was his blood that was spilling on her. He slumped over and she pushed him off and he fell to the ground. She got up, but her left foot was in the stirrups and she could not break free. Suddenly, Ms. Susie was in the room, she screamed, "Oh my God! Oh my God!" She took off the shackles from Lizzie, and Lizzie ran naked outside screaming for help. Everyone else came running now; she was hysterical and could not breathe. She fainted and fell

95

to the ground.

When she came around, Ms. Greta, Ms. Susie and the girls were all standing in the room. Ms. Greta was saying, "What the hell happened? Do you know that you just killed Mr. Richardson. A murder in my place! How dare you! I don't need this type of shit, I don't want any publicity. I should have gotten rid of you the first time you acted up. And you! Susie, you should have known better than to put an old pervert like Dennis with this young child. What the hell was going through your mind? Why didn't you send him away? Both of you know the rules, if Janie isn't here no one else can take the shit he does. He knew he wasn't supposed to be here. He must have been drunk as a skunk and now look what the hell's happened? I have to call Sergeant Sonny Matthews and see what he can do for us. I don't need this shit, I really don't need it."

Det. Matthews, a tall, heavy built Black man, came and he, Ms. Greta and Ms. Susie went into her office to talk. Next thing I know the ambulance, police cars and swarms of people were all over the house. It was crazy. Police came and they were taking Mr. Richardson's body away in a body bag. Lizzie wad crying again. What was going on? She had killed Mr. Richardson, she was going to jail. Oh. Lord, what have I done? What have I done? She cried.

Det. Matthews came in to her and asked her, "Do you remember what really happened?"

Lizzie started to explain, "He tried to kill me; and I grabbed the knife to stop him because he was not listening to me; I could not speak while he choked me. I was scared," she cried. Lizzie continued, "He was telling me to "Scream baby scream!, but he was choking me and I could not breathe, much less scream. I just wanted to stop him from hurting me, that's all."

At last the questioning seemed to be over, and she tried to calm herself, while the officer went over to talk to Ms. Greta.

She was crying so hard and sobbing, that she was not making sense. Det. Matthews said to Ms. Greta, "It's bad. Richardson was too well known to put this under the rug. There will be a trial and the whole nine yards. If there is anything I can do to help, I will but murder is out of my hands." He turned to Ms. Greta and asked, "What the hell was wrong with him? He's a sicko; you know that;

why would you send such a young girl into him? She's beaten to a pulp, and all the marks on her neck, scratches on her legs. It looked as if he used a rake. Good God! What do people go through for some money! I would advise you if you have a camera, you need to take a few pictures before they take her away, and don't let her talk to anyone, until you can get your lawyer present."

Ms. Greta got out her instant camera. She used this camera to take pictures of the men who frequented her place. They never knew she had their pictures; this was her security. Now, she took pictures of Lizzie, pictures of the bed and the room; then she put the camera and the pictures away. It was time like these she was glad that she invested the money to buy this expensive camera.

CHAPTER 23

The private detective, Derek Hicks, had slacked off because he had other pressing jobs, but he did not want to disappoint Doc. Doc had taken care of his mother when she was ill and she did not have the means to pay him, yet he showed up every week to treat her and even give her medicine that she needed. She looked forward to seeing Doc. And that pleased her only child. He vowed he would repay Doc if it was the last thing he did. Doc insisted on paying him, and he paid him handsomely for the work he did, expense account and all. Doc's estate deposited his paycheck every month religiously.

He had a great description of the girl and after two and a half years seemed to be making some progress. He found where she worked in the cafeteria, found the home she lived in and then she vanished. He knew she would be somewhere around and decided to stick around a little longer. While looking at the television in one of the flea bitten hotels he stayed in, he saw a news flash.

The announcer was saying, "Twenty year old prostitute indicted in murder of prominent businessman." A picture of the business man was flashed on the screen- a jovial looking man, in an Italian suit, then the face of the young prostitute. Derek dropped the donut he was about to eat and yelled, "It's her," he got up out of the chair, went closer to the TV, and then started for the door, but where was he going? He sat down back and wondered, "Is that the girl?" he had to find out more before telling Doc.

She was a very beautiful girl. She had high cheek bones, beautiful, heavy, very silky light brown hair; light brown eyes that sparkle; and an oval face. She was drop dead gorgeous. She stood around 5ft.5in in her stockined feet. She seemed to have some bruising on her face. She was in handcuffs and taken into prison by two female cops. How could he find out about her? The cops would not allow anyone to come near her. This was a murder case, and she was looking at the electric chair. A Black prostitute killing a white, prominent, business man- Oh! Oh! She was going to be locked away for good. He was sure she was the kid he was looking for – she matched the description the foster parents gave him as well as the cafeteria owners.

* * * * *

Mr. Hicks spent that week trying to make sure that Lizzie was the girl he was looking for, and that there was absolutely no mistake. He got as much as the facts as he could get and then decided to wire Doc to let him know that he had found his girl.

Doc was flabbergasted. He had to take a seat; this was not happening. Not his little girl. He couldn't take this; he knew he was dying and this would bring it on more. He had to do something and do it quickly. He thought of calling Joe and confessing everything to him, afterwards, he thought against it. Mrs. K might just be mean enough to pay the whole jury to kill the poor child. No, he had to get a good lawyer, if not, she was doomed. There was no justice for a Negro killing a White person much less a prostitute and a pillar of the community. He got busy thinking of a good lawyer. He called in his chips to Artie Kingsley, a criminal lawyer. After explaining what was happening, Artie said, "I would love to get on this case for you, Doc. But, right now I'm on a very important case, so I'll get back to you with the name of the best lawyer I can find to help you."

Mr. Kingsley hung up the phone, and pondered about whom he could get to do this job for Doc. He was a good old friend, but defending this Black prostitute was not his idea of a prominent case, and he was into cases that could make him somebody. However, he told Doc that his law firm would be willing to do whatever possible to help him, and he meant it. Doc sensed his hesitation to take the case, so Doc was already thinking about whom he could use, but he decided to wait on Artie because he would know of a better lawyer then he could think of.

Artie called Doc and told him, "I have spoken to the young lawyer, named Ernie Spaulding and he is going to take on the case."

Doc said, "I wanted you to work with him because you are more seasoned, and experienced in these types of cases." Doc knew that Artie was a senior partner in the firm of O'Reilly, Kingsley, and Duggan. This was a very prestigious firm in Atlanta. Doc told him he would take him up on his offer to help in any way possible.

"If at any time Ernie needed help from my law firm, I would drop whatever I am doing and help him."

"Thanks," said Doc. "It doesn't matter what it costs. If he needs you, be there," and Doc hung the phone up.

Doc then called the young man, Ernie Spalding, a reputable, criminal lawyer who lived in Atlanta. Doc spoke with Spalding and arranged for his services. He was going to defend Lizzie. He had one thing more to do and that was to inform Sadie that Lizzie was in jail and needed her. He felt she needed her mother most of all. Should he write Joe and tell him? No! Maybe his mother might intercept the letter and then where would Lizzie be?" She didn't need that type of attitude now; she needed love.

Ernie Spalding was a good guy and he did a lot of pro-bono work. People needed representation but they didn't have the money to pay. Artie was a good friend of his and he would throw him a couple of jobs that their big firm would not touch because it wasn't big enough. Artie figured he's kill two birds with one stone. Doc was great and he owed him but he was not going to spend his time representing some nigger gal. Not even for Doc. Ernie had the time and he was pretty good. He never lost a case, and bless him, he didn't mind representing Negroes. He was the man Doc needed. After calling Ernie he took Doc's name off his blotter and left the office.

Ernie had a few things to straighten out, then, he could find out all the details he needed for his case. He did not have a lot to work on so far, as the murder had only happened two months ago. He left home and headed for the small Georgia town south of Macon.

As far as the prosecution was concerned, this was an open and shut case. The girl admitted killing Mr. Richardson. No one seemed to care why she did it. He had his work cut out for him, and he knew it.

When he arrived in Applegate, Georgia, he was not surprised. Small town atmosphere, where everyone knew each other and exactly what was going on in the town. He headed for a boarding house. After settling down, he went to get something to eat. Anywhere in the south the food was always good. He returned to his room to have a good night's rest.

The next day, Ernie got a local newspaper and headed for the cafeteria to have some much needed coffee. The newspaper, called The Daily Record, was very thorough in reporting the news. The editor, James Hansen, was an amicable young man who appeared to welcome any news for his tiny news staff. He seemed fair at reporting the news the way it was. He was a little radical in his beliefs. He had a young woman reporter on staff that was in training with him and the rest of the staff was minimal. He reported news on Blacks as well as Caucasians and this caused some disturbance amongst the Caucasians. They felt he should not take the time to report anything on Blacks as they did not want to read about it. They let it go as they all said, "He's a Yankee."

Ernie met the young editor one night at the bar and they struck up a conversation. Ernie decided to let him know that he would be representing the young lady. James' eyebrows shot up, "You will be?" Greta surely must have more money than I imagined."

"I was not hired by Greta, and I'm not at liberty to tell you who hired me; I would like to ask you a favor. Would you happen to know a very good private detective that I could hire?"

"Sure, here is my card, call me in the morning and I'll have this information for you."

Ernie decided to go into the newspaper office to get the name of the detective. James met him, "Come on in and have a cup of coffee."

A young girl passed by and he called her in to introduce her to Ernie. "This is my assistant, Margaret Ascott. Maggie is assigned to do the story on Elizabeth Edwards. She's a very good investigative reporter and one that I am very proud of."

Maggie smiled as she extended her arm to Ernie, "Welcome!" she said and left them alone. James decided to give him the name of the detective he recently met, Derek Hicks.

CHAPTER 24

Ernie talked with Doc and got all the information he needed. He then sent Derek Hicks to visit Lizzie's old home and to find out all he could about her – "do not leave any stone unturned," he told him, and Derek did just that.

He did all Ernie's leg work for him and the two were both eager to win this case for this beautiful young woman who they knew would be put in jail and the key thrown away. Artie Kingsley had mentioned that if Ernie needed any help from his law firm he was not to hesitate to ask. Ernie intended to take him up on this offer. Let them see that the big wigs were getting involved with this case. He intended to use lots of publicity, newspapers, and such for Lizzie's sake. Otherwise, she would be pushed under a rock and forgotten.

Ernie saw his client and spoke with her many times. He tried to explain the process to her as simply as he could. All she wanted to know if she could say she's sorry and could she go home.

"I'm going to get a real job and don't mess with nobody."

She had no concept of the depth of her crime on the community and what was in store for her. She was clueless. She was lucky to have Doc as a friend. He was going to make Doc proud, Ernie thought.

CHAPTER 25

aggie was excited about this case. At least there was a Caucasian involved, even if he were dead. This young colored girl didn't have a chance. Mr. Richardson was a prominent man and one of daddy's acquaintances. Daddy thought that she just down right had murder in her heart and wanted to bring him down like an animal. He was angry that Mr. Richardson visited the whore house, but you know, "men will be men" and he laughed, "But look where it got him."

Mom and dad discussed the case at length each giving their own opinion but both agreeing that she had no right to kill him. Maggie listened to her parents and tried to be impartial. She had set up some interviews with neighbors of the Richardson's and one with Mrs. Richardson. She was also trying to get Ms.Greta to allow her to interview the girls to see what she could find out, but she was not budging.

"No way," she said, "I don't want my girls splashed all over the news paper; after all, they have not done anything wrong. I am not looking for any publicity. We need some peace; the TV people were out here and had the capture on the tube for everyone to see; now we want to be left alone."

Maggie was very persuasive and finally got an interview with Mrs. Richardson. She invited Maggie in and said, "You are so young, what are you doing out of school?" They both sat down and Maggie got out her tape recorder. She was so happy, daddy bought it for her. It enabled her to talk freely and concentrate on the person. She still made notes but it was minimal. She liked Mrs. Richardson and the two were soon talking like old friends.

After a while she said, "Turn that damn thing off."

Maggie did, and she continued in her Southern drawl, "You know, you think you know a person, and then you find out that you don't and you really don't care. I married Dennis when we were young and crazy. He was every woman's catch. He had a good education, good family back ground, handsome football player, you name it, and he had it."

"Did you date in high school?"

"Yes, on and off. When any other person got between us, we always ended up together again; there was no splitting us."

"Two years after we got married, we found out that Dennis could not have children. I was devastated. Dennis told me he was sorry almost every day. He was obsessed that he couldn't father a child. However, it didn't matter to me that much and so I told him I wanted to adopt and he was very upset about that. I think he was very disappointed that we were not going to have his children. It frustrated him a lot but he tried not to show it."

"Did you ever pursue the adoption process?"

Yes, and he led me to believe that it was okay, he would go along with the adoption for my sake. Then I began to pick up on little signs that it was not okay."

"What did you do, then?"

"Well, eventually he told me he did not want some other man's child in his house reminding him of his inadequacy."

She lighted another cigarette and then continued, "Sex with Dennis was always wild – and I enjoyed him a lot but after awhile, things got worse over the years so much so that I did not want anything to do with him. He turned me off sex.

He was brutal and angry in his lovemaking like he wanted to beat the devil out of me or something. I would be bruised and ached when he was finished with me, and so I stayed away from him. I knew he was visiting the whore house and was happy for him. Whenever he saw them he would leave me alone. So, I turned a deaf ear to his goings on. A woman has to protect herself, you know. He saw a Negro whore named Janie, and also one named Anne; so I was surprised that this young gal was doing him. She's no more than a child but no one will look at that. The only thing they will look at is that she's Black and she killed a good ole White boy."

She shook her head and drank some coffee while she inhaled

deeply on her cigarette. She looked deep into my eyes and said, "Poor child, I feel sorry for her. I believe what she said, He had a lot of anger when he wanted sex and he got off on some weird stuff. I couldn't take it and so I was happy when he saw Janie." She started to sob now – "but other to that he was a good provider and friend when he wasn't drunk.

Please do not print all that I told you. You seem like a nice young person. By the way, you look just like Lizzie with your hair in a pony tail. She really is a beautiful Darkie."

"Yes, she is" agreed Maggie, but secretly she was upset, how dare she say she looked anything like a Nigger. If daddy heard her he would tell her where the road to hell was, and direct her how to go there. The two women sat silently for a while as a radio played in the background softly. At an opportune time, Maggie thanked Mrs. Richardson for the interview and promised to stop by again to see her.

"Please say hello to your parents for me," said Mrs. Richardson.

Maggie realized that it was because of her father that she got the interview with Mrs. Richardson.

James said, "It doesn't matter how you get it, as long as you get it." He always made Maggie feel as if she did something very important. She admired this handsome, young man who wanted to do well by everyone. It didn't matter whether you were Caucasian or Negro. He was also level headed and did not get as excited as daddy. Daddy got heated over the least thing while James was cool, calm and collected. She loved daddy but she could easily fall in love with James. He was a man compared to John who seemed so immature. John was a lot like daddy. John hated Negroes and sometimes he would talk about what he would like to do to them. At first, it never bothered her because that was all she heard from her father, but now that she worked and talked a lot to James, he had a different perspective on life and on people and she was pulling more to his side. At times, it frightened her. She wanted to be fair to all people, but when ever she got into it with her dad – he always won. Negroes were the scum of the earth and will always be that to him. Mummy was different, but she never argued with daddy. All she would say was, "Now, now Edgar, calm yourself down, don't get so excited, remember your heart."

Maggie was able to see Anne who used to service Mr. Richardson. She told Maggie that she really could not talk to her because Ms. Greta would be very angry, and Ms. Greta had always been nice to her. Maggie told her that their talk would be confidential. She was skeptical but talked a little. She told of the beatings but he gave her extra money on the side, without Ms. Greta knowing, and she needed the money to take care of a sick mother. She only saw him when Janie was indisposed and healing from the beating he gave her before. Ms. Greta would not allow him to come to Janie more than once a month. Once she had broken bones where he had beaten her up so badly. Anne never suffered as much as Janie but it was enough to put her to bed for a few days. Maggie promised Anne that she would not let anyone know they spoke, and thanked her for her honesty.

The trial was supposed to start in a few months. It was going to be big for this small town. Maggie was excited that she was covering it for the newspaper. She investigated every little detail she heard.

Her mother once told her, "You never stopped digging until you come up with the answer." I remember when we told you Santa Claus brought you your bike and you wanted to know how he got it down the chimney. I found you the next day trying so hard to fit the bike in the fireplace and send it up the chimney. I had to tell you he brought it through the door and then he went up the chimney. Even then, you tried to peep up the chimney to find out how he climbed up and there were no stairs. Lord you were something to handle."

She came and sat in a chair and faced her beautiful daughter.

"Now, look at you, we could not fool you then and now no one will be able to make a fool of you. You are using that same inquisitive spirit to do your work. I am so proud of you, Maggie," as she got out of chair and came behind her daughter and hugged her tightly. She ran her hand through her hair and then kissed her on top of her head.

"I love you Maggie."

"I love you too, mommy," she said. She noticed that whenever she said that she felt very sad and she did not know why, she repeated it to herself, "I love you too mommy."

Maggie did not finish college. She went for two years after high school and then dropped out. She said she knew enough to write and she knew how to be nosy, she didn't need a college degree to do that. James had confidence in Maggie. He saw some of the work she had done and was very pleased. She took pictures to bring her words to light. It would serve its purpose for the paper. She had a lot of potential. He did not mind investing in her, but that bigoted father of her was a bad influence on her life. It was a pity that a beautiful, warm, loving, girl like Maggie could have a father like Edgar Ascott.

After being with Maggie for a few months, James realized that he was in love with her. However, she had a boyfriend, and he was not one to play second fiddle. He did not want to do anything to interfere with their working relationship. He would bear his pain in secret. He had gone home at Maggie's for dinner with her parents and her boyfriend. He liked Mrs. Ascott, but wanted to hold Edgar's nose and rub it in some filth. He really was obnoxious, and John seemed to play up to him, and encouraged him, especially when he kept belittling the Negro race.

Whenever James voiced his opinion, he yelled, "Ah, whadda you know? You're a Yankee. You're a young one; you'll soon see it my way. They need to be constantly put in their places, and kept in line."

He hit the table with such force as he and John laughed when he made his fingers into a gun and said, "phew." James had had enough and it was getting too complicated for him. He had to sit and watch Maggie and John together and then listen to her father berate every other race was too much. James got up, thanked them for a swell dinner and genuinely told Mrs. Ascott that he enjoyed the meal, said his goodbyes and left. Maggie walked him to his car and felt a strange urge to kiss him, and she pecked him on the cheek.

"Thanks for coming, I enjoyed your company."

"I enjoyed dinner," he replied, and he got into his car.

CHAPTER 26

Maggie went in to see the Detective who was in charge of the case. She was shown in to see Detective Matthews. He was a chubby, Black man in his early forties. He had piercing eyes that seemed to look straight through her. He smiled as he got up to shake her hand, "Sit down Ms. Ascott, please."

After she sat down, he enquired, "What can I do for you?"

She smiled back, "Thank you Detective Matthews. I wanted to know if you could tell me, since you are the arresting officer what you found out about Elizabeth Edwards.

"Nothing, other than what is said in the news; she claims she killed him in self defense. It's up to the jury to believe her."

"Do you believe her?" Maggie asked.

"Well now, he drawled, it's not up to me in these matters; I let others decide. I just try to bring all I can to the table, so they can sift through what is what."

He did not intend to tell Edgar Ascott's daughter anything. Her father was the meanest, son of a bitch, Negro hating, Klansman in all Georgia. She needed her information from someone else; he wasn't going to do her dirty work for her. Nevertheless, he was polite to her and answered her questions as best he could but did not offer any information.

Maggie sensed awkwardness with the detective. He seemed reluctant to answer her questions and just did it out of courtesy. When she got back to the office, she expressed this feeling to James and he looked at her and said, "You have to realize that lots of Blacks are not going to trust you." He paused for a moment, then continued, "How can I put it nicely? Your father's ideals may have rub off on you and they are not going to give you anything more."

"But that's not fair," she retorted

"Hey, that's life; get used to it."

Maggie tried a different approach. She went to see Ernie Spalding. He welcomed her into his office and she sat down to talk to him. Maggie was interested in Lizzie's background. Where was she born? Who were her parents? Any background information he could give her. He had no problems working with the newspaper and he realized he could use them. He answered all of Maggie's questions.

When Maggie got back at the newspaper office, Maggie said, "I'll like to take a trip to Tennessee."

"What's in Tennessee?" asked James

"Lizzie came from there. I would like to find out more about her background, and I also wonder if she has any family there. What do you think of the idea?"

"I think that's what a good investigative reporter would do, so go for it."

It was another problem convincing her father to let her leave town.

"Oh, I don't know about you going there. You never know who you'll come in contact with. Investigating niggers could be a terrible thing," he said "I..."

Maggie came up to him and hugged him, "Daddy, I'm a big girl now and I can take good care of myself. I will not take any risks, and furthermore it's my job. I just love getting to the bottom of things; so don't you worry about me. Just take your heart medicine and relax, ok?"

Maggie paused, and then she continued, "James thinks it's an excellent idea and he's even given me an expense account. I'm enjoying my work," she smiled as she walked away doing a jig.

"Be happy for me" she turned her head back to him.

"I am, you know that."

CHAPTER 27

Maggie arrived in Tennessee and decided to find a room to relax. She went out that night, surveyed the small town, and then when she went back to the hotel, she talked to the hotel clerk. The next morning, after getting the directions to the high school, Maggie was sitting in the principal's office of Glenmore High School. Mrs. Stedmore was very prim and proper. She sized up Maggie as she asked a lot of questions. "I just wanted to know if there were any special friends of Lizzie that I could interview." She explained that she was working on a case and needed information. She did not say what type of case she was working on. Mrs. Stedmore reluctantly gave her the names of two people, a young man named Teddy King and a young woman named Abby Croker. "I'm afraid they are no longer in school."

"Do you have an address, please?"

"We probably have an old address; I'll give you what I have and you can work from there."

She gave Maggie the addresses of both young people and wished her luck. Maggie thanked her and headed out.

Abby was working as a cook in a local cafeteria. She was scared when she saw the young White woman asking for her. Maggie had asked her boss if she could be spared for a few moments. She gave him her card, and he saw the name of the newspaper, 'The Daily Record,' and he said, "Okay, but remember we're coming on to the lunch period which is pretty hectic, so make it quick."

Abby smiled when Maggie mentioned Lizzie's name.

"How is Lizzie?" she smiled showing even white teeth.

"She's fine," Maggie smiled back. "Tell me about your relationship with Lizzie.

"We wuz bes friends; we talked a lot. She wuld come home wit me, an we wuld sit an talk."

"What type of things you talked about? Maggie asked

Abby bent her head, and solemnly said, "Stuff"

"What kind of stuff?" asked Maggie

"You know, we shared a lot. I had no mother; I lived with my stepmother, but we both had problems with our parents."

"What kind of problems?"

"Why you asking me so many questions about Lizzie? Where is she?"

Maggie decided to tell her.

"I am trying to help Lizzie; she is in jail for murder. She is claiming self-defense and I believe her that is why I want to know everything about her so that I can help her."

After allowing Abby to digest what she just told her about her friend, Maggie continued her interview.

"Now, what kind of problems she was having with her parents?"

Abby put her hand on her heart as if to feel if it was still beating, "Lizzie in jail? For murder? No! No! No! Not the Lizzie I know, why she wouldn't hurt a fly."

"This is the kind of thing I want to hear about Lizzie so I can form a picture of this young woman," Maggie said.

"All right, her mother didn't like her, and her father liked her too much," Abby started to ramble aimlessly, "if you know wat I mean. He was always trying to jump in her pants. She was very unhappy and she had to run away. I miss her a lot. I hope you can help her."

Abby started crying and moaning softly as she hugged herself. "Poor Lizzie," she whispered, they'll kill her in jail."

"Whoa, hold on, slow down, you're going too fast for me," as Maggie smiled, Abby continued.

"Lizzie and I both wanted to save ourselves for our husbands, she offered. She liked Teddy and he was madly in love with her. She put her hands to cover her mouth, 'poor Teddy,' what will he say when he hears about this. Lizzie and I talked about them two getting married and she giggled. Now Lizzie is in jail and I'm here working my fingers to the bone just to make a living. It's sad, so sad, and not fair."

They talked for a little while longer and it seemed to Maggie that there was no more pertinent information so she thanked Abby and left.

* * * * *

Maggie found Teddy in the mechanic shop working on a car. He wiped his hands on a towel and came to her. She did not offer her hands to this Black man. He was handsome for a Black man, and she realized that she had never been alone with a Black man before. She looked around her casually, and he noticed her fear and smiled, "It's o.k.maam; what do you want to see me bout?"

I'm working on a case involving a friend of yours and would like your opinion on her character, and what you remember about her." After allowing him to catch his breath, she offered, "the person in question is Elizabeth Edwards and your relationship with her."

He beamed, "Lizzie? Why I loved dat little rascal. She up and left town and didn't even tell me or Abby where she wuz going, just up and left like dat. I thought we wuz friends. Do you know where she is? Did she send you to look for me? Is she back in town?" He was smiling from ear to ear. He looked real handsome for a Black boy, Maggie thought.

Maggie held up her hand, "Wait, a minute, I want to know about your relationship with her and if you can tell me why she left town?"

"Oh, I really don't know much; I heard rumors, but I don't know. I think she ran away because of her father. He was always drunk, you know, and maybe he tried something with her, I don't know she never told me, but she loved her daddy. He liked to buy her beautiful stuff, and her mother was very jealous of their relationship. That's all I know. Is she alright?"

Maggie explained what had happened and Teddy bent his head and sighed, "My poor little rascal, some man dun gone and made her angry, my poor little rascal."

Maggie looked at him amazed at his saying. "Why do you call her little rascal?"

"We used to look at a program called the Little Rascals and she loved it. I told her she loved it because she wuz a rascal herself, and it made her smile, so I called her my little rascal. Dat was my pet name for her. My poor, poor, rascal, poor rascal," he repeated as he shook his head from side to side in disbelief. It seemed as if he was crying, so Maggie left him to his grief. After she left he wondered if he had told too much. I have to be careful next time he told himself.

It was early afternoon when Maggie came to the house of Mr. & Mrs. Edwards. Mrs. Edwards offered her a seat in a neat and very clean, small sitting room. Maggie glanced around the room. There was a vase of fresh flowers, a table on which there were pictures of the family. One picture was of Lizzie around the age of twelve. Maggie noticed a slight resemblance to herself in her facial structure. She could pass for my sister, she thought. It is so strange how God can make Blacks and Whites look a little bit alike sometimes. However, Lizzie was one damn good looking young lady. Nobody can dispute that.

Mrs. Edwards was also a very pretty Black woman. She smiled, wondering, wanting to know what this beautiful young woman wanted with her. Maybe, she was coming into some money. "What can I do for you, Miss?"

"Thank you, for seeing me, Mrs. Edwards, Maggie said as she sat down. "I just wanted to ask you a few questions about your daughter, Elizabeth."

Immediately, a scowl came on her face and she retorted, "I have no daughter." She was afraid that Doc had sent someone to investigate her husband's interference with Lizzie. I told that man he was going to cause us trouble.

"Lizzie was not my chile, she was born in Alabama; and my aunt asked me to do her a favor and keep Lizzie. We took her in and I was told to change her name. We named her Elizabeth, but I think her name was Betty Lou, I don't think I ever knew her last name. Doc handled all the paperwork for us, anyway. My aunt did not say for how long we were to keep Lizzie, so when Lizzie got grown she just left."

"Who were her real parents?" inquired Maggie.

"I don't know, but her father was White and her mother Black, and she had two other sisters. I think they were triplets. I only found this out lately from my aunt before she passed. She was a servant of Doc's."

"Who was Doc, do you know his full name?"

"I might still have an address on the envelope I got from him every month. She got up and then came back with a piece of paper on which was written Doc's name and address. "As I was saying, Mrs. Edwards continued, "Doc paid us handsomely to take care of Lizzie as her parents could not take care of her. It seems there was a fire and her mother was badly burned and could not take care of Lizzie, and that's all I know."

She spoke about Lizzie as if she was speaking about a piece of furniture. Poor little rascal, she thought and laughed. This woman did not like this child. Maggie decided to go for it, "what was Lizzie's relationship with your husband like?"

She flinched as if stuck with a pin and said, "They had a real good relationship. I mean they loved each other, like any young girl who loves her father."

"But, according to Lizzie's friends she ran away because of her father," reported Maggie.

Mrs. Edwards got up, looked Maggie deeply in the eyes and said, "This conversation just ended." Maggie realized that she had hit a raw nerve. She thanked Mrs. Edwards for her help and left.

She had to go to Alabama and find Doc. She needed to find out about this young lady's parents who would send her to such a cold, conniving woman. No wonder she had to run away. With a father who was molesting her and a mother who didn't give a damn, 'poor little rascal' she thought.

CHAPTER 28

She put in a call to James and told him what had happened so far. "Good work, and of course, you should go to Alabama. Don't worry about a thing here, I have it covered. This is your big break and don't you let anything come in your way. Plus you have a chance to travel all by yourself, but please promise me that you will be careful. I don't want to start missing my best assistant." She could tell he was smiling. She liked James a lot. Sometimes, she felt as if the two of them could be together because they had so much in common. When she compared him to John – wow! That was another thing. John seemed like a little boy compared to James. She found herself thinking more of James than of John. However, daddy liked John for her. John and daddy were so much alike it was if he were a younger version of daddy. She loved her daddy so much and did not want to do anything to upset him especially now that the doctor said his heart was weak and had started giving him some trouble.

* * * * *

Maggie jumped on the bus for Alabama. She was very tired when she reached Trey lawn, Alabama. She found a boarding house and got a room for a few days.

She went to the address she got from Mrs. Edwards. She was amazed to find a beautiful structure of a house, a mansion, she would say. It had fantastic architectural workings on the outside. There were huge pillars in front; a beautiful porch. There was a gazebo and the surrounding area near the gazebo was absolutely breath taking. There was a rippling brook which extended from a water fall; there were lots of trees, shrubbery, huge rocks in the water, and flowers. There was a walkway that led to the back of the house, but turning to the left you walked into a beautiful garden. There was a huge back porch at the back of the house with a seating area; a swing, and built in seating. It was fabulous. So this is where this Black girl accused of murder was born. I can't believe it. Black people did not live like this, and then she remembered about Doc.

Surely, Doc was white and he owned this place and Lizzie was the daughter of one of his servants. She looked at the house again, and a strange feeling of nostalgia came over her. It felt as if she had been here before. She thought to herself, "this place is warm and inviting.' She felt at home here, felt the peace and love in this place. She closed her eyes and smelled the air.

Turning her gaze away from the back of the house she saw from the main house were three cottages; even these were well fortified and one can see that the first one must have been rebuilt because it seemed bigger than the rest and it also looked as if the paint was newer. There was a little garden by the front porch and the house looked well kept, even now. However, you can see there was some decay settling in on the other two houses. Doc probably owned ten-fifteen acres of land right here. He must have been a very rich man. So this is where Lizzie had her beginnings. Quite impressive surroundings for a Black girl, Maggie thought enviously.

As she walked in the yard, there was that strange feeling again as if she had read about this place in book. It was as if she had been here before. She could not explain it, but she did not feel uncomfortable even when some young Black children saw her and came running towards her.

One little girl around six or seven ran up to her and smiled, "Hi, yuh looking fuh Doc?"

"Yes, is he at home?"

"Nah, he bin gone to de doctor fuh a long time, Ms. Ellie up de house"

"O.K. she said as she headed for the walkway to get to the front of the house. The little girl waved goodbye. Maggie looked after her. She was a pretty little Negro girl and very pleasant. She smiled to herself.

As she walked she looked to the right of her and further towards the back of the house she saw a woman hanging out clothes, and called to her, "Hello there, how are you? May I have a word with you?"

The woman took the clothes pins out of her mouth and put them in her apron pocket, "Yes, ma'am," she replied.

"I am looking for Dr. Fitzgerald; do you know where I could find him?"

"Yes, ma'am, he's in the nursing home," replied Ms. Ellie.

"Oh! I'm sorry to hear that, but is there somewhere we can sit and talk?"

"Yes ma'am," and she asked, "Do ya want to be inside or out?"

"Out, please," said Maggie.

The woman led her to the newest cottage and pointed to a chair on the front porch. "Please sit, ma'am, my name is Ellie, what can I do for you?"

"Ma'am; would you like some lemonade, ma'am?"

"Yes, please," replied Maggie

As they sat down an old dog came out wagging his tail. He headed straight for Maggie and started barking excitedly.

"Come Sparky," called Ms. Ellie; but Sparky got more excited and started licking Maggie's feet and jumping up on her. Maggie loved animals and began to pat Sparky and this made him more excited.

"Are you o.k. Sparky?" Maggie asked, "You seem a little agitated, tell me what's wrong?"

She bent over and was rubbing him, and the dog got excited, wagging his tail, with this tongue sticking out, trying to lick Maggie all over.

"I have not seen Sparky act like this in all these years; my, my, what a change!" Ms. Ellie said.

"Is he your dog?" Asked Maggie

"Yes, and no, he used to belong to Doc's grandchildren, especially Mary Jane. She was the one who wanted a dog and Doc got Sparky for her," explained Ms. Ellie.

With Sparky panting feverishly at her feet, Maggie introduced

118

herself. My name is Maggie Ascott and I am here to inquire about a girl who lived here when she was young. Her name then was Betty Lou; do you remember anything about her; or her family?

Miss Ellie nodded, and looked away sheepishly.

"Whatever you can tell me about this girl will be helpful."

Maggie could not help noticing how gentle and soft-spoken Ellie was, she seemed almost kind. Daddy would be surprised how some Niggers are just like White people. Ms. Ellie had a sweet disposition and a good attitude. Maggie liked her, in spite of her own ideals.

"Ellie, please tell me whatever you remember about Betty Lou if you knew her."

She noticed her tone had an edge to it as if she was ordering this Nigger to bow down in her presence, but Ms. Ellie was so polite and nice to her, she just let it slip. It seemed as if daddy had followed her, "Show them whose boss, baby, don't let them ever get the upper hand."

"Mos I could remember bout Betty Lou wuz she wuz a little gal about two years old, I was a little younger than her mother, Lula Mae. They lived in a cottage on this here land but it caught fire, and then Doc built another house for Ms. Martha and Mr. Mike on the spot. Ms. Martha and Mr. Mike died and gone on to glory. They was my aunt and uncle; my mama's sister. Doc took care of everyone here and now I have this house for me and my family. She pointed to the other cottage, further back. "My cousin, Aunt Martha's son Jesse and his family live there in the house where Lula Mae lived with her family; and the other cottage belongs to Ms. Ivey and her sister, Deanna. She looked at her garden and explained, "I love to work in the ground and I grows anything I put my hands on," and she laughed.

"When Betty Lou and her sisters lived here they spent a lot of time in Doc's house," she continued. "He was like their grandfather; they called him pop-pop."

She smiled and continued, "Everybody loved them, and Ms. Lula and Mr. Joe." She looked at Maggie who was making notes on a pad, "Is Betty Lou all right?" Ms. Ellie asked quietly.

"Yes" replied Maggie. She did not feel she had to give this Negro any explanations. After a while, and not too much relevant information Maggie said, "It is getting late and I have a few errands to run so she asked Ms. Ellie, "Do you mind if I come back again to see you? I might have some more questions."

"O.K" said Ellie.

As she was leaving the grounds, she saw a gardener working in the garden, near the gazebo. She headed towards him to watch. He looked up at her enquiringly, and she said, "Oh, don't mind me; I was just admiring the flowers."

"Oh! Yes, ma'am dey is just beautiful," he stated then he began to point out some of the flowers. Some flowers were enclosed by smooth; round rocks in a circular form, the flowers were arranged in such a beautiful way that you could not help admiring them.

Mother Nature smiled sweetly as she looked at this garden, Maggie thought.

"Dese are marigolds," the man said as he pointed to some bright gold flowers, then he went down the line and pointed out flower, after flower, and telling Maggie what they were. "Here we have a pole I put up here so that all these beautiful perennials surround it and it looks like a lamppost. It's really a nice touch to the garden, don't you think so?"

She was pleased that he had asked her opinion, as if she knew anything about gardening. She just smiled.

Here we have Spider Lilies, then some carnation like flowers, here again we have all types of lilies, purple, pink, white, yellow orange and lavender water lilies. Dey just love the water and cling to it for life," and he smiled. "We have here Hyacinths, and Lady Lotus, some beautiful purple flowers with yellow in the middle; he held on to one and said, "Here we have the pretty Sagittaria, these white flowers with the purple dot on each petal. Dey are so many beautiful flowers in dis here pond dat you feel in heaven when you sit and watch dem." He turned his gaze on her and asked, "Do you have a gardener, Ma'am?"

"Yes," she replied thinking of her mother out in the sun trying to keep the little flowers she had looking presentable. Here was a garden, with these round smooth rocks bordering the flowers at some areas, while in other areas there was a fragrant lilac hedge.

You can sit out here and paint, read, or just drink lemonade and feel as if you were in paradise. She realized that she had gotten an education and she did not know what the gardener was talking about, but she had heard the names of some of the flowers from her mother. He was still talking, "Flowers are one thing; but the trees at the back, and he pointed to some huge trees; I mean they were gigantic. "Dey are wonderful to me – dey give us all dat dey have- fruits, vegetables, and nuts, dey shade us, and de birds and small animals live in dem. Dey give us all dat we need like wood for fur- niture and oxygen. I love dis world out here," he laughed heartily; "I can get lost in it all day."

He laughed again as he gestured with his hands. This gardener seemed to know what he was talking about. She enjoyed listening to him.

"What is your name?" Maggie asked.

"Buster, Ma'am," and he bowed to her.

She smiled to herself. He seemed like a nice old man, just wanting someone to admire his handiwork. She said goodbye to him and left Doc's house.

CHAPTER 29

T hat night when Maggie called home she told her father, "Daddy, you would not believe where Lizzie was born. The house is a mansion. It could hold three houses the size of ours in it. The yard is beautiful too; there is a gazebo, and a beautiful flower garden. It is like a fairly tale, daddy, you just wouldn't believe it."

"Remember a white man owned it sweetheart, them niggers can't own anything like that. Hurry and come back home, I miss my little princess."

"I miss you too, daddy."

Her mother was happy to hear the good news and she missed Maggie a lot. They had never been apart. "Mommy, it's like I have been here before. The place seems so familiar, like I have been here in a dream. It seems like a piece of Heaven. Mommy you would like it here.

The gardener gave me an education about plants and flowers that was interesting. I mean, he really held my attention. He showed what plants needed the shade, the ones who loved the water, and the ones that thrived on sunlight. He seemed to have this all in his head, and worked diligently and tenderly with the flowers as if they were his little babies. It was fun watching him. I really enjoyed the garden, and now I have a better appreciation for plants and flowers after watching Buster, that's his name."

Maggie sighed then continued, "The flowers were telling their own story. Some were standing tall and erect, others were crouching low, crawling along the ground in beautiful shades of purple, pink and white. Some seemed shy, while others were bold and their brilliance came forth. Some were like little children running wild, only stopping when they met the walkway. It's a story any writer would love to tell, mom; it's as if there were telling a story of God's love for the earth."

Maggie continued excitedly, "I can see you now sitting on the porch or in the garden, and have those Niggers tending to you," and she laughed.

"But seriously, mom, I would love to see you in a place like this. I know that you would enjoy the rest of your life in this atmosphere."

Her mother smiled at the thought and said, "Now, Now, Maggie stop acting like your father; learn to accept people for who they are, and not what they look like. You must learn that especially in the type of business you're in. You have to realize that you're getting older now and I want you to live your own life, not hang on to your father's, or my ideals; remember they are not your own, thank God."

Maggie did not like the conversation at all. It seemed as if her mother was always disagreeing with her father, whenever she got the chance to do so, and she never did this before at least not in the open. Maggie was surprised. "O.K. Mommy, I love you, and miss you."

"Same here, sweetheart," replied her mother.

CHAPTER 30

For the past five days, Teddy could not concentrate on his work at the shop. He was thinking about his 'little rascal,' he wondered what was happening with her. The lady did not tell him too much other than Lizzie was arrested and in jail for murder. She had murdered a white man. He ached to see her again, and wanted to be there for her; he just had to arrange the time with his boss to go see his Lizzie. He had to make inquiries as discreetly as possible.

Teddy was so distressed that he was not paying much attention to the piece of metal he was soldering to put on to the car he was working on. He needed this piece of metal to fit in the right spot and so he was trying to make it fit. He turned on the welding machine and as he started to work he realized that he did not have his goggles on; he figured he would be alright this one time; it wasn't much, just a little piece of metal to work on. As the flames came out in a burst, Teddy slipped and fell and the machine fell out of his hand. The sudden burst of flame shattered a piece of glass nearby and sent slivers into Teddy. He fell to the ground and held his face as blood seemed to be pouring out of his eyes. Teddy screamed and fainted. His boss, Mr. Mimsy Andrews heard the scream and came running. He saw Teddy on the ground, quickly assessed what had happened and he put Teddy in his own car and took him to the nearest hospital.

Teddy's eyes were affected. He could not open his eyes, and he felt terrible. The doctors did all they could for him and he was left all bandaged; as the doctors had to surgically remove slivers of glass from his face. They did not tell him the prognosis of his eye condition, as they could not be sure right now. They had to wait to see after the bandages were off, and some healing had taken place, only time would tell.

While Teddy was in the hospital, all he could think of was his 'little rascal' in a jail cell, what would happen to her? Who was going to see her? Did she get a lawyer, and if so from where? Would they hang her? Oh, God No! Not my little rascal. He loved her so much, and was very hurt when she left without telling him that she was leaving and where she was going. However, that seemed irrelevant now. He was more concerned for her than for himself. He wished he had a lot of money now; instead of the couple hundred dollars he had saved. He really wanted to help her. help to help her. He had to contact a lawyer and he had to get out of this hospital soon.

* * * * *

Abby heard about his accident and came to visit him in the hospital. He was happy for the visit. He could talk to Abby, they were good friends. He told her of his plans and what he wanted to do to help his little rascal. She was impressed but said, "Do you think your little money could hire a lawyer to defend Lizzie, and where would we get a lawyer from to go to Georgia and help her?"

"I don't know yet, but I will sure find out," he replied.

Ordinarily, Teddy was a shy person, but somehow he got the courage to confide in one of the doctors who seemed very sympathetic towards him.

"How would I go about finding a lawyer to defend someone in jail in Georgia," he asked Dr. Hicks one day. Dr. Hicks asked Teddy a lot of questions and then he said he did not know of anyone right now but he sure would do his best to find out answers for Teddy and instruct him in what he should do. This is all Teddy wanted to hear, he had to get out of this hospital so that he could help his little rascal.

Teddy was wondering what it was like in jail for Lizzie; she had a mouth on her, but beneath the bark was a loving and caring person. Would they be able to see this side of her in jail? Or would they treat her like a criminal. His heart ached for Lizzie, she really did not deserve this, and she had no one to help her. He had to do something and do it fast.

Teddy was discharged after two months. He could see pretty clearly out of his left eye, however, his right eye had severe damage and he needed an operation that would allow him to have better vision. It would be costly and since his coverage would not pay for such an operation, it was out of the question for now. He wore a black patch over his right eye, and he thanked God that he could see out of the left eye.

He was at home with his mother fussing over him. He loved her very much; even his father was extra special good to him. They had always had a good rapport with one another in his family. They respected one another and since Teddy was their only son they both doted on him. His older sister was a good person, but she got married early and moved away with her soldier husband.

Mr. Andrews told him he could come in and run the office when he felt better, but he would not get the same pay as a mechanic and he agreed. Anything was better than staying home being an invalid.

When he went back to the hospital for his follow-up visit and saw Dr. Hicks, he was told by Dr. Hicks that he had talked to a lawyer in Georgia, and he found out about Lizzie's case and was told that she had a very good lawyer and a prestigious law firm representing her. Teddy was surprised, but happy. "Thank God," he said and thanked Dr. Hicks for his help. He did not know if these lawyers would talk to him so he asked Dr.Hicks, "May I ask you a big favor?"

"Sure, anything for you Teddy," he replied

"Is it possible for you to find out when her case is coming to trial so that I can make arrangements to be there, or better yet, is it possible for me to go and see her," asked Teddy.

"I'll see what he can do and I will let you know; come back and see me in three weeks by then I should have some answers for you." Dr. Hicks liked his young patient, and understood his need to see his old friend.

CHAPTER 31

Maggie called James and told him every-thing that happened so far. He said he had to be in Alabama and that he would look her up.

James arrived that weekend and they spent much of the afternoon going over all that had happened, all the interviews she did, when James said" Maggie, I'm proud of you, but save some of it for tomorrow and he began to laugh, Good gracious! You are so excited about this case. I just love to see you so exuberant; it rubs off on poor old me."

He held his chest and started to laugh so hard she joined in and said, "You're too silly. Let's go to dinner, my treat," and they left the hotel for dinner.

They had a wonderful dinner and a few drinks. They were both light headed as they walked back to the hotel. When James took her back to her room, she asked him if he wanted to come in since the night was still very young. He said, "Sure, why not," as he stretched out his hand in front of him indicating that she go ahead of him. He was slightly drunk and he knew it; but he felt good. He sat on the couch and patted the seat next to him for her. She came and sat next to him and she started laughing too. She realized that she too had a little too much to drink, but she felt relaxed. James and she talked for a while and she started to turn her neck from side to side.

"Tense," he asked,

"Just a little," she replied,

"Let me help." He turned her around and began to gently massage her neck and shoulders. She put her head back and closed her eyes as he continued to massage her upper body. Suddenly, she felt his breath on her face and he was whispering, "You're so beautiful, my precious one, so beautiful." She felt his lips on hers and she found herself reaching for him, pulling him closer to her and began kissing him passionately. It was such a frenzy that before she could think, he was undressing her. She found herself wantonly trying to undress him. He picked her up and carried her to the bed. Maggie was in a frenzy she did not know if she was dreaming or not, but right now she did not want to wake up. Her body was on fire; she was burning with desire and James was here to satisfy that longing. He kept whispering, "I love you, little Maggie; I really do."

She heard herself replying, "I love you too, James" and then they gave in to a night of excitement, making love repeatedly. She never felt such joy. She wanted him more and more. When they were both spent they fell off to sleep.

In the morning, James was the first to awake and when he realized what had happened he shook her gently to wake her up. She sat up and asked him "What's wrong?"

He answered cautiously, "I did not mean to take advantage of you, I'm..."

She put a finger to his lips, "Shhh, I know. I knew how you felt about me from the start, and I feel the same way, I love you James Henson. If I didn't this never would have happened."

He smiled, "Why you little seducer, you took advantage of my drunken condition." He took her in his arms and they made love again.

While they were having breakfast in the little diner, they discussed their future. She told him she would tell John, but it was her father that worried her the most. He had it in his mind that she and John were to be together and she did not like to go against her father. John's parents and hers were very close and spent a lot of time together. She felt it would not bother John too much, but she knew she didn't love him, at least not the way she loved James.

Maggie and James decided they were going to go to the nursing home to see Doc. Doc had been recently transferred to the nursing home for complete rest while the doctors on staff could keep an eye on him. Maggie and John made arrangements to go and see Doc. When they got there Doc was seated in a wheelchair.

This old, Caucasian was tall, but weather beaten. He face was wrinkled, and it seemed as if he had freckles as a child. Now the

128

freckles seem to spread all over his face. He had a little beak of a nose. His eyes were sunken in and he had a few hairs clinging to his bald pate. His hands were shaking as he held the newspaper in his hands. He put the paper away as they entered the room.

The nurse introduced them as newspaper people. He was surprised. Why would they need him? What did they want? He hoped nothing that he had done in the past had come back to haunt him. His body was sick and frail, but his mind was very alert. He looked at the young woman and she reminded him of Mary Jane when she was a child. He thought that this is what she would look like when she grew up. James held out his hand to him and started by asking, "How are you today, Dr. Fitzgerald?"

Doc replied slowly, "I'm fine, thank you," however, he was looking at Maggie and he asked her, "What did you say your name was?"

"Margaret Ascott," she replied.

"Ascott! Ascott!" He said as he held his heart and took a deep breath.

She was concerned and asked, "What is the matter?" Doc closed his eyes and leaned back in the chair. They were both surprised.

They heard his whisper, "Mary, my Mary, you came back, I knew you would come;" He sat forward now as if reaching for her, " Boo-Boo, its pop-pop, I'm your pop-pop."

He looked at her pleadingly; held out his hands to her as he whimpered, and she stood there looking at him with puzzled amazement. It was too much for Doc and the nurse who did not leave the room right away, asked them to leave as he was very sick. He cried as she left, "My Boo-Boo, my Boo-Boo, don't go Boo-Boo."

As they left the home, James said, "That was strange, it seemed as if he took you for someone else; maybe you reminded him of someone; poor old chap."

She was silent and thoughtful for a while, then she said, "Do you want to hear something funnier? I felt as if I knew him, like he brought back memories, but memories of what? Isn't that strange?"

"Very strange," he replied, puzzled by what had taken place.

Maggie was so uncomfortable that she started straightening her chain around her neck, brushing her clothes as if some kind of insect was crawling over her; then she would run her fingers through her hair. She decided then to take a comb out of her pocket book and pin her hair up.

She felt like crying but she did not know why she should feel like this. She held James' hand and they left the home.

CHAPTER 32

James and Maggie went back to see Ms. Ellie. She was in the big house this time. She invited them in and told them that she was keeping the house together for Doc as he wanted to spend his last days in his own house. Ms. Ellie told them that Doc's grandchildren spent lots of time in this house as pop-pop loved having them. When she mentioned the word, 'pop-pop' Maggie's heart skipped a beat. That was what Doc told her, "I'm pop-pop," he said, as if she should know who pop-pop was. She couldn't understand what was happening to her, but she felt as if she was in a circle and the circle was closing in on her. She couldn't put her finger on what was bothering her, but her mind was unsettled. She had to get to the bottom of this.

".. all over the house with each one of them on his back, giving them piggy back rides, and they would even spend some nights over here," Ms. Ellie brought her back to reality.

James said, "In other words, they spent as much time in this house than in their own home."

"Yes," Ms. Ellie said.

"Where is their home?" asked James.

"It was burnt down, but Doc rebuilt the house and that's the one I'm living in now."

"Do you mind if we take a look around this house," asked Maggie, "It's so beautiful."

"Sure, no one is here but me, and I'm sure Doc would not mind. Anything to help his grandchildren is okay with me," and she smiled as she got up and led the way.

The house was very spacious. It had a lot of light and seemed extra huge. There were about six bedrooms. Four were upstairs and two were on the main floor. The house had two stories. Only the bedrooms were carpeted as far as she could see. There were hard-wood floors in the surrounding rooms, and tiles in the bathrooms and kitchen. The house was real modern as far as Maggie could see. You could also live here and not see the other members of the family if you did not want to. As they left the house, Sparky, the dog, ran towards Maggie and kept barking and wagging his tail excitedly like he did before. She stooped down and patted him.

"Hi, little doggie," she said as she rubbed his back, " you remembered me from the last time I was here?" He jumped in her lap and started licking her face. She fell back and started laughing, and he was all over her. James stood by watching.

"If he weren't a dog, I really would be jealous, he's all over you. I would say he's in love."

CHAPTER 33

Doc sat in his chair reminiscing over the past. He remembered how he felt about these two girls, Mary Jane and Betty Lou. He remembered how for months, he had a detective trying to find Betty Lou and he finally heard what had happened to her. He had traced her to Georgia and was waiting word from the detective. It had been a year and no one seems to know where she had gone. He was determined to find her and take care of her. He had let her foster parents know he was very upset over what went on, and wished they had written to him, when it happened. They were trying to be smart and still try to collect the money even though she wasn't there.

He let them have it; "Why would you send a child out into the world with no particular money? Where was she to go? Do you know what could have happened to her? You should have written me, or gotten a phone call to me, or a wire to me, anything so that I would have been able to protect her. Now I have to spend money to unscrupulous people to find this young lady."

He stopped the money right away and that was the end of them. They did not know where Lizzie was and it seemed as if they didn't care. Oh! My God, what that poor child must have gone through. I will find her if it is the last thing I do; I owe it to Joe and Lula, and most of all I owe it to myself. I had promised Lulu on the night she left here that I would take care of her other children; and I will keep that promise.

Once he knew where Betty Lou could be found he started the process of helping her in any way possible. He thought of how he had decided to mail the letter to the Ascotts. He had put the letter in his briefcase so that he would not forget to mail it the next day. The next day, he felt sick and had to be taken to the hospital. After being in the hospital for a while he was taken to a nursing home. He was in the process of making arrangements to return home so that Ms. Ellie could employ a nurse to help take care of him. He just wanted to be home. When out of the blue, here comes Ms. Maggie Ascott and sent him into a tailspin that he knew he could not come out of.

CHAPTER 34

Sadie was at home when Joe called and told her he had news that Doc was sick and in the hospital. "I think he must be a 100 years old now," Joe laughed.

"Yes" Sadie said "he must be pretty old."

She began to think of the old man who had shown her so much love and no condemnation because of her black skin, but took her as the daughter he never had. She felt sad. He would always say, "You and Joe are the children I never had and you have given me such beautiful grandchildren." He really had a genuine love for her.

Sadie decided to go visit Doc. She was no longer afraid of anyone. She got the name of the hospital from Joe and told him what she intended to do.

"He really would like that, Lula, I mean Sadie. You know something, I can't get used to calling you Sadie."

"That's all right, you can call me anything."

"Thanks again, Lula for signing those papers so that I can straighten out my life. Now I am legally married to Sarah again. We hope to see you soon, as you promised," and he hung up.

Sadie arranged with Anne who helped her in the bookstore that she would take charge while she was away. Anne was a great help to Sadie. She loved to read, and had a knowledge that was exciting to Sadie. She was also well read. She would critique most of the books they bought. She gave Sadie tips of what to look for, and how to skim the pages. Sadie liked this petite, blonde young woman who was a young mother of two. Her children were in school and she just wanted something to keep her busy. She and Sadie had a lot in common so with this in mind, they became close friends and Sadie hired Anne to work part time in the bookstore.

Sadie had a harder time telling Paul that she wanted to leave for a while to take care of Doc. He loved Sadie and would miss her terribly, however he knew she had to do what she knew was best for her and Doc. According to Sadie, Doc was like a father to her and she felt it was her duty to help him as much as possible. Sadie felt badly that she was not able to help her own father. Doc accepted her and loved her like his own child, the least she could do was be there for him, whether he needed her or not.

Sadie made plans to go to Alabama to see Doc. When she arrived she made arrangements to stay in a rooming house near the hospital. After the setback with the reporters he was taken back to the hospital. Sadie went everyday to see Doc. He had suffered a stroke and was not able to speak. He also had cancer. The first time he saw her, he cried like a baby. She spent the whole day just holding him and comforting him. He looked at her and grunted as if he were trying to tell her something.

She just took his hand in hers, looked deep into his eyes and said, "I'm here to take care of you, just like you took care of me. I don't want you to worry about a thing." Sadie spoke with the doctors, nurses and wrote down all that they told her about Doc. She did not want to forget anything when she called Joe to tell him. What she didn't understand, Joe would find out and explain to her. She was comfortable with Joe explaining things to her that she didn't know.

She worked with the nurse everyday to learn to take care of Doc. She made notes of what she had to do; she made a list of the medications; what they were for; and when to use them, also what side affects to look for. Sadie stayed with him for one month, going home to see Paul on weekends. She arranged for Doc to go home after the doctor said he had little time left. She always remembered Doc saying he would like to die in his home surrounded by his family. She signed him out of the hospital and took him home.

It was difficult returning to the old place. Things were the same, yet different. The house where she lived with her husband and children had been rebuilt; although it had different occupants, it still brought back memories. Sadie did not spend a lot of time going over the grounds, Doc needed her help and this is what she was here for. The old folks she knew had long been gone and only little Ellie was there that she remembered. She was all grown up and beautiful. They talked a little, but then she went to tend to Doc.

After she got Doc settled in and made arrangements for a certified nurse to come in three days a week, she made arrangements for the type of food he needed; she got a wheel chair so that she can take him out into the gardens where she would read to him.

Sadie always walked with her Bible, and so she read passages of the Bible to him and told Him about Jesus, His death, resurrection and how He was our Savior. Sadie had a hymn book and she also sang some songs for him. Sadie had a beautiful, sultry voice and she belted out those hymns in such a way that she and Doc were just having fun praising the Lord in song. Doc knew some of the old hymns and so he hummed along. He would tighten his grip on her hand sometimes and grunt to tell her something. She could not understand what he was trying to tell her and so she just nodded her head and smiled. He seemed frustrated that he could not tell her what he wanted, and he would cry. Sadie spent this time reassuring him not to worry, but just relax and take it easy, everything was all right. Sadie would say to him, "Don't worry, God is in control of everything." She told him that Joe was coming to see him soon. He looked at her; she said with a smile, "Joe and I are in touch with each other."

Every day she would tell him a little about what had happened in her life after she left him. She told him about Gracie, Bessie, and Seff; how she found Joe again; his marriage to Sarah and the kids. He shook his head, and Sadie told him, "It's alright, I am in love with a wonderful man named Paul and we plan to get married in the near future. He managed a slight smile. He also held on to her hand and squeezed it hard.

Sadie continued, "I was very upset with you for a while. I wanted to take all my children with me when I left here. I knew I could manage with them but you did not trust me to handle myself and the children. I knew I could and I miss my girls, I still do. I have no idea where they are, do you?" Doc looked at her with a strange look in his eyes. She was not sure of what he was trying to say to her. Tears came trickling down his cheeks, and he looked so remorseful. She felt sad for this old man who had shown her nothing but love. I have forgiven you Doc – you don't have to worry."

He began to sob and Sadie felt so sorry that she had spoken to him about her hurts. She patted his head and soothed him and he was soon sleeping peacefully.

Everyday for the next two months, Sadie read the Bible to Doc. He seemed interested and smiled when she talked to him about Jesus. She told him how she had come to know Jesus and that she and her children, Bessie and Seff were believers and loved the Lord, Jesus Christ very much. Sadie was sure Doc was going to Heaven, she prayed for his salvation and he nodded and squeezed her hand when she asked him if he understood what she was saying. She was so pleased for him. She had read and discussed most of the New Testament to him. He looked forward to the times when she took him into the garden and read to him. She enjoyed it too. Doc loved to hear her read the Psalms. Once as she read a Psalm, he perked up and listened silently. She was holding his hand as she read and every time he heard something he loved and agreed with, he would squeeze her hand and smile. He did this all through Psalm 62, (KJV)

"Truly my soul waiteth upon God; from Him cometh my salvation. He only is my rock and my salvation; He is my defense; I shall not be greatly moved. How long will ye imagine mischief against a man? You shall be slain all of you; as a bowing wall shall you be, and as a tottering fence. They only consult to cast him down from his Excellency; they delight in lies; they bless with their mouth, but they curse inwardly. My soul, wait thou only upon God; for my expectation is from him. He only is my rock and my salvation; he is my defense; I shall not be moved."

Here he would squeeze her hand as if to say, "I agree."

Sadie continued, "In God is my salvation and my glory; the rock of my strength and my refuge is in God. Trust in him at all times, you people, pour out your heart before him. God is a refuge for us. Surely, men of low degree are vanity, and me of high degree are a lie; to be laid in the balance, they are altogether lighter than vanity. Trust not in oppression, bad become not vain in robbery; if riches increase, set not your heart upon them. God had spoken once; twice have I heard this; that power belongs unto God. Also unto thee, O lord belongeth mercy; for thou renderest to every man according to his work."

* * * * *

Sadie asked Seff to come to Alabama to meet Doc. He came and stayed with her and was with her until she was ready to leave. Seff and Doc bonded instantly. Seff would wheel him out into the garden every morning and read to him. He would also tell him stories about flowers, or anything that came to mind. Doc would smile and drool all over himself listening to Seff. Seff would wipe the drool and the two of them would go for a walk, while Seff sang to him. Doc would hum and smile, try to move his hand until he got tired. Seff would exercise his hands and feet by extending and retracting his legs and arms. It was also plain to see that Doc loved Seff. Sadie was glad he did come to help her.

When Doc went back to his room; Seff stayed with him; whenever he was in pain, Seff would give him his pain medicine and hold his hand while he rode out the pain. He would cry like a baby and Seff would massage his big body and talk soothingly to him. He responded like a baby. Sadie said to him one day, "I think you're not in pain as much as you want Seff to believe. You just want to be pampered" and he gave her a lopsided smile.

Remember Seff is a wonderful grandson and he knows what you are going through emotionally, physically or mentally. He knew all that you did for me and his sisters and he will never let you down. Doc was crying now. Sadie wiped away the tears and said, "You need to take your nap now, we'll be back later."

CHAPTER 35

J oe brought Bessie who was now seven months pregnant to see Doc. just before he died and he was so happy to see his son, daughter, and grandchildren together that he cried, drooled, smiled and squeezed their hands. He was beside himself; he just didn't know what to do. One Thursday afternoon three months to the day she brought him home from the hospital, Doc died peacefully in his bed with his children and grandchildren at his side.

Joe and Seff were helpful to Sadie and Ms. Ellie who cried many a day when she thought of Doc. Joe handled the funeral arrangements although Doc had arranged everything before hand. Sadie was in for a surprise when his will was read. Doc had left his estate to his two granddaughters, Mary Jane Kettering, and Betty Lou Kettering; he also left a small amount of money for Bessie, Sadie and Joe. He took care of the help and also left some money to his favorite charities.

Sadie held onto Joe and cried. She cried so much that she tried to justify why she was crying. She loved this old man who befriended her and took her as his daughter and never forgot to tell her in so many ways that he appreciated her. She didn't agree with him when he told her to leave the two girls behind, but now in hind sight, she realized that it might have been too much going into a new home to someone she didn't know with three children. Maybe the person would not have welcomed them; and she was so sick. She remembered those days of pain where she didn't even see Bessie. Doc was right, I was too sick to look after us all and then I was pregnant.

"Good Lawd," as Ms Helen would say, what was I thinking? However, I do thank God that he brought me through it all. Doc you were the greatest dad I ever had, and I loved you very much.

She felt good saying it loud, I loved you, Doc. Even though her heart was breaking and her arms were aching for her daughters, she was crying for Doc. "I loved you, I loved you! I did!"

Joe held her close, and allowed her to let loose all the pent up feelings she was holding up inside. As he held her, Sadie began to relax; she forgot everything that was happening to her now; it was a dream. Joe and she were back together; nothing had happened the children were grown and gone and here she was with the man she loved. She began to kiss Joe passionately and Joe although taken aback did not pull away. Sadie wanted to be loved and made love to; she did not want to be alone and sad. This was her husband, her Joe, who fought everyone for her. He loved her like no one else could.

Sadie quickly opened Joe's shirt and helped him undress, then she tore at her clothing. Joe was absolutely speechless but, nonetheless, he enjoyed the feeling and he knew what Sadie was feeling. They gave into their feelings and Joe, stopped her and quieted her, "My lovely buttercup," he began "I just want to drink in your beauty; let me look at you; your face, your neck; your breasts, your sweet tummy; your patch of sweetness; your thighs, knees and feet. He kissed each part of her as he spoke. "I love you Lula Johnson, I will always love you."

Joe entered her and she abandoned herself to this man whom she loved, trusted and adored. She enjoyed their lovemaking this time because she had initiated it. She was always a willing participant in their lovemaking before but somehow or other she didn't have to go after Joe; he was always there and willing to love her. Sadie cried softly afterwards; she was crying for Doc, for Joe and his family, for her children and for herself. What a mess! What a tremendous mess! Sadie lay in Joe's arms and they chatted until she knew Seff would come looking for her.

"Joe," she started, "this"... He put his finger to her lips and kissed them gently, "is closure" he finished.

"Yes," she said, "we started our married lives here, and here we just ended it."

'Thanks," she whispered and went to get dressed.

Joe later promised to get on the bandwagon to look for his

daughters. He promised her he would do everything in his power to find them.

Sadie went back home to Boston. She had missed Paul and although they spoke everyday, it just wasn't the same. Today she stood by the front door with her hand over her eyes shading them from the sun as she eagerly awaited his visit. Paul showed up and took her in his huge arms. She felt safe and at the same time she remembered being in Joe's arms. What a difference! She loved both these men, but in a different way.

Her love for Joe was a wild, exciting, crazy, mixed up, forbidden love. Paul's love was stable, sure, relaxing and strong. She had been blessed to have the two most wonderful men in the world to love her.

While she sat in the book store one day, she asked the Lord, what her purpose in life was. The Holy Spirit ministered to her soul and showed her. She had been born into poverty but had come into riches; she had come out of darkness into light. She had given her heart to God and was allowing the Spirit to lead her life. She thanked God for the revelation and for his blessings. She thought about her children and cried. You have two wonderful children and a beautiful granddaughter; count your blessings the Spirit said.

CHAPTER 36

Edgar Ascott had a bad heart. He had slowed down his activities a lot, and had retired from his job as a firefighter. He spent most of his time at home. His buddies would visit him and they would chat for a little and then he would get tired and they would leave. His exercise consisted of going from bedroom to den, where his wife waited on him hand and foot. He extended his exercise to sitting on the front porch after getting the mail. He had some money put away to take care of his family and he was very proud of that.

Maggie had returned home from her travels and she spent a lot of time helping her mom take care of daddy. She did not like to see daddy sick. She accompanied her father to the doctors and asked a lot of questions. Basically, he needed a lot of rest and to take things easy. So it wasn't an easy afternoon for him when he picked up the mail and was leisurely reading when he came across a letter from the law firm of (O'Reilly, Watson, & McLennan). He took the letter out and read the name at the bottom of the letter. It was signed David Fitzgerald. The name sounded familiar. Maybe, he wondered if the firm had made a mistake in addressing the letter to

Mr. & Mrs. Ascott instead of Margaret; Edgar put the envelope down, and started to read, halfway through the letter he began to perspire so profusely that he had to hold onto his heart. He could not breathe, he started to cough and gasp for air. No, No, this was not happening to him. Not his princess, Oh! God! No! Not his princess – she could not be, be, b-e-e-e Black. He tried to get up to call for his wife but no words came. He slipped to the ground as the pages fell out of his hand. When his wife found him he was unconscious. She gathered the mail and dumped it all in a sewing basket while she waited for the ambulance and Maggie.

Edgar was pronounced dead from a massive heart attack.

* * * * *

After the funeral, Maggie was a wreck. Her hero had gone; this man at whose feet she sat and listened to stories about life, about culture, about good and bad as he saw it. She enjoyed his talks immensely. Lately, she did not agree with everything he said but she chalked it up to growing up and having a mind of her own. She loved her father and he was a great influence in her life anyhow.

Maggie took a few weeks from work to help her mother who missed her husband of over 40 years. This was very hard for her. On one such day, Maggie and her mom were sitting at the table drinking sweet tea when mom said, "I will never forget his face when I saw him; it was if he had seen a ghost. Something frightened him badly."

"What was he doing, Mom?" Maggie asked

It was as if she was reliving that day. Maggie urged her to continue.

Encouraged, she continued. "He had just gotten the mail, I watched him go to the mailbox and he came back and sat down to read it. I usually checked on him every now and then to make sure I did not miss his calling me. He was reading the mail when I got out to him. As a matter of fact, he had a piece of paper in his hands, he kept saying, "No! No! No!" I grabbed him and put him to lie on the porch, called for the ambulance and you, and then I picked up all the mail and put it in the basket I was holding in my hand when I got outside."

She got up and picked up the basket and took out the mail. She started to read the opened mail and got the shock of her life. "Oh Jesus, she whispered, "this is what brought on his heart attack."

She was staring at Maggie now.

Maggie got afraid, "What's the matter, mom? What is it?"

Essie took her daughter by the hand and led her to a chair. She was weeping softly; Maggie was a little irritated as she did not know what was wrong. She just hated being in a position where she was helpless. "Mom what is it, please tell me?"

"I don't know where to start, Maggie, I don't," she began.

"Start from wherever you're comfortable and it will all fall into place, please mom." Essie's sobs came more forceful now, she couldn't talk. Maggie extracted the paper from her hand and she started to read. As she read, she turned a lighter shade of pale; this letter stated that she was adopted, and not only that it stated that she was bi-racial. "BI-RACIAL," she could not bring herself to say the word, "Black."

"Mom what is he talking about, am I adopted?" she demanded.

Essie could only nod her head. When she saw the look on Maggie's face she knew she had to get herself together to help her child, but somehow she felt helpless. She had let Edgar talk her out of telling Maggie that she was adopted when she was twelve, then eighteen. Now it was too much for her to deal with two devastating things at the same time.

Edgar felt he would lose his princess if she thought she did not belong to him. He was scared that she would want to search for her biological parents and he said he could not take that then. Now, she wished she had insisted. Maggie grabbed her car keys and ran from the house. Essie got up to go after her but she was already driving away.

Maggie was crying, the tears were just streaming down her face; no need to wipe them away, they were flowing too fast. Adopted and Black! Adopted and Black! Adopted and Black! Black! Black! Black! It must be a mistake. I was White. I could never be Black; daddy would not adopt a Black baby. He hated Blacks, he hated Blacks, and he could not love me if I were Black. Oh, God! The letter said he didn't know. Oh, God! Oh, God! Why me? I never did anything to anyone. Why am I Black? She found herself driving like crazy, she did not have a place in mind, and suddenly she ending up going to the job, maybe James was there. She had to see someone she could trust.

James saw her car and came to the door of the office to open up. He was surprised that she would be here at this time of day. As she exited the car, he noticed she was crying and looked very upset. He came to meet her and held her, "Good Lord, what's the matter?" he asked,

"My life is ruined! Ruined! I can't live in this town anymore. I'm done for! James tried to take her in his arms but she just pushed him away.

"Leave me alone, don't touch me! Wait until you hear what I am! I am a Nigger! A Nigger! A big, old, nasty Nigger; she kept hitting her chest, as she exclaimed, I killed my father! This man who loved me because he thought that I was White like he was; I killed him; he was reading the letter when he had the heart attack that killed him.

"What are you talking about, Maggie? You're not making sense, calm down and let me know what's happening." She gave him the letter she held in her hand. He read it, and then looked up slowly.

"You poor thing," he said, "But Maggie it is not your fault that your parents did not tell you they adopted you. It's not their fault that you are Black. There is nothing wrong with being adopted or being Black." Then everything sunk in; "Oh! Oh! Your father with his beliefs about Black people could not stand the fact that he had adopted a Black child. James thought to himself, the irony of all this; what news, "Master of the KKK adopts Black child. What a heading this would make. He knew this would upset Maggie and so he changed his thoughts. If only he could make her understand that being Black was not a disease or a crime, just a state of being. However, he knew her father had indoctrinated her so much it was seeping out her pores that Blacks were inferior; they were dogs; and not fit to live on the same planet as Whites. Worse of all he had done it to his only child, a child whom everyone knew he adored and he never knew she was a Black child. What a travesty! He thought.

CHAPTER 37

Maggie could not live with herself. She had killed her father. She took to her bed and had the most horrible nightmares. All her friends were standing in a circle and she was in the middle and they were all pointing at her and saying, "Nigger, Nigger, Nigger get out of here, Nigger. She would wake up screaming and her mom would come in and try to soothe her.

"Maggie, you have to stop this, you're only hurting yourself. Once and for all, you did not kill your father, his heart was bad. The doctors give him a few months to live. He was dying. You had nothing to do with it. I wish I could make you understand that it was not your fault."

Essie sobbed as she touched Maggie's head, "My baby, my baby, I love you, I always loved you."

Maggie was sobbing uncontrollably.

"You have to pull yourself together; I love you whether you are Black or White. It doesn't matter to me. You are my baby; I loved you from the moment I saw you, and so did Edgar. He would never hate you. I think if he had lived you would have made him see Blacks in a different light. Yes, he hated Blacks but that was just because he never give himself a chance to know them and his father was racist and brought up Edgar the same way. I went along with him because as you know he was basically a good and kind man. I loved him, Maggie but he was wrong to put these racist ideas into you, and now it has backfired; you hate yourself. When is it going to stop? Must I lose you too?"

"Oh! Mom I don't know, I can't face people now. I feel they are all feeling sorry for me. I don't know what to do."

"But no one knows about this. You make it seem like everyone in town knows about our business. Get a grip on yourself, and pull yourself out of the doldrums, please."

Essie went over to put her arms around her daughter, and said, "I'll tell you what, get up, get dressed and go to work. You were happy working on that murder case, get back to work and take one day at a time."

CHAPTER 38

Maggie was back at work and it felt good. Mom was right. She went through the motions at work and she avoided James as much as possible. They had no future together now. He would not want a Black woman for a wife; nor would John. She was destined to be a spinster. Somehow, parts of the letter kept nagging at her; triplets; birthmarks on thighs – one sister had it on both thighs and it formed two distinct hearts when they were together. That must be something to see; it was also very weird. She touched the birthmark on her right thigh. Three girls, two hearts, three into two, it was amazing that three girls together formed two perfect hearts. She smiled as she thought about it, 'three into two,' – what a mess!

Maggie pondered these things in her heart as she went to bed one night. She began to fantasize about what her siblings looked like; what her parents looked like, and wondered what they were all doing right now. Did they think about her? Why was she give up for adoption? Why weren't they looking for her? Would she want to go with them now? She could not imagine herself living with Black people. No! Not now! Not ever!

CHAPTER 39

Maggie spent most of her time at home; she and her mother were cleaning out her father's things to give to the Salvation Army when Maggie came across something that shocked her into reality. In the back of his closet was suitcase; when Maggie opened the suitcase, she found white clothing. She took it out to figure out what it was because she never saw her father in any white clothing other than tee shirts. When she held it up, she saw that it was one of the clothing that the KKK's wore. She was shocked and held her hand over her heart. Essie came in and saw what had happened.

Maggie was extremely distraught, Essie said, "I never meant for you to see that. However, you knew how he felt about Negroes."

"Yes, I did, but I thought it was all talk. I never knew he was really, really involved with the Klan."

"That was a long time ago. Maybe, he regretted the decisions he made in his youth and decided to quit. He hadn't been involved for years and years. Don't let it bother you now."

CHAPTER 40

Lizzie's case was scheduled to start in a few weeks. What Maggie learned was that Lizzie was well represented. She had a lawyer, and it seemed that there was a law firm, O'Reilly, Watson and McLennan, in Atlanta that was backing this lawyer. This was going to be an interesting case. Maggie was at the courthouse many days during the pre-trial. It was interesting and she did a wonderful job reporting the events. During one such session, pictures were shown of Lizzie practically naked, with bruises, blood dripping off of her. The sergeant was explaining the condition she was in after the murder. Ms. Greta snapped these pictures of her as she ran na-ked from the room. He pointed out every mark on her body and then he said, "Those two marks on her thighs are birthmarks." Maggie's ear picked up. "Birthmarks on thighs." She had to see the pictures. Could this be…. No it must be something else. She was very eager to see those birthmarks. The pictures were evidence, and she was not sure she could get to them, but she would sure as hell try. What was going on in her life? Who was this girl who reminded her of someone, and whom she had a burning desire to help free. She did not like Negroes and she did not care for them, so why was she so 'gung ho' to help this one? Maybe God wanted to help Negroes. However, she had to find out about those birthmarks; Lizzie was also adopted just like she was so it was imperative that she found out the truth.

CHAPTER 41

aggie got to Ernie Spalding and asked him to let her see the pictures. He wanted to know why she needed them so urgently. She assured him that it was for her own personal benefit, but that it was very important. He told her he would see what he could do. She enlisted James' help. She told him what she suspected and wanted to see the pictures. James arranged for her to see the pictures and when Maggie saw the pictures, she clutched her heart, and cried out, "Oh, God no."

James tried to hold her, but she ran from him, crying, "Leave me alone, I'm not only adopted, I'm Black and now I have a sister who is a murderess, Oh God what more?"

Maggie drove home, not knowing how she did it. Essie came to the door when she heard Maggie's car, as she wasn't expecting her home so early. Essie quickly dried her hands on her apron as she opened the door. Her heart sank when she saw the tears on her daughter's cheeks.

"What is the matter, Honey?" she asked as she hurried across the porch. Maggie ran into her mother's arms. Mother and daughter stood swaying from side to side, as Essie gently led her into the house and sat her down on the couch.

"Hush, let me know what happened?" she asked.

"Well, I found one of my sisters today, and you would not believe who it is, guess who? You would never guess, but I think that the Black murderess is my sister." She started crying so much that Essie did not understand one word she was trying to say to her. After a while, she told Essie what had transpired at the courthouse.

"Oh, you poor dear," was all that Essie could say. She did not know what to say to ease her daughter's pain. Maggie could not finish her assignment, so James took over Lizzie's case.

152

CHAPTER 42

Teddy had worked hard and long hours at the shop, in order to make up enough money for his trip to the prison to see Lizzie. Dr. Hicks said that the lawyer had arranged for Teddy to see her for an hour in two weeks. Teddy was excited and when he found Abby and told her the news she wanted to go too. She was crying so hard that Teddy said he would try to see what he could do, plus he needed the company because he did not know what he would do when he saw his little rascal in that jail cell. He asked his parents to lend him the extra money and they gladly obliged.

Two weeks later after Abby had gotten permission to leave her job; they both were on the bus to Georgia. When they got there, they found a cheap hotel and cleaned up themselves and had a good night's sleep. The lawyer was going to meet them and take them to the jail in the morning.

Mr. Spalding came the next morning and he took them to see Lizzie. Lizzie was surprised and very happy to see Abby and Teddy. She felt ashamed by being in jail and all, but she soon forgot that when Abby said, "Oh! Lizzie I'm so glad we found you, and that we could see you, how are you doing?" she asked.

"I'm fine, and so very happy to see you both. How did you find out about me?" Lizzie knew they paid no attention to the newspapers, nor did they buy any.

"A white reporter woman came to see us," said Teddy, "And she told us some of what had happened to you. Plus it was in the "Tattler" so everyone at home knows about you."

"How are my parents?" she asked

"I went to tell them I was coming to see you and they both send you their love," said Teddy, "They want you to know that they are very sorry to hear about your situation and wish there was something they could do to help you, but their prayers are with you."

Tears were coming down Lizzie's cheeks as Teddy told her about her parents.

Lizzie said, "I found out I was adopted, and that they were being paid to take care of me by someone named Doc. I also found out my mother was some Black maid who was sleeping with the Master's son. That's as much as my mother told me; so I do not know who my real parents are, and right now I really don't care," she said.

"You look beautiful, my little rascal," said Teddy changing the subject.

Lizzie smiled, "You still gonna call me that? I'm a big rascal now, and thank you both for coming to see me. I know it must cost you a lot of money." She just took in that Teddy's eye was covered.

"What happened to your eye, Teddy?" she asked. Teddy told her of the accident and that he needed an operation to fix it, "but I want to hear about you, what can we do for you?"

"Absolutely nothing, it seems that I have lawyers and what not, I know nothing, all I do is sit and wait for them to tell me what to do, but thanks for asking Teddy."

"You know that Abby and I believe in you, and we'll be here for you whatever it takes."

"Thanks, Teddy," Lizzie said softly.

She felt happy to know that her true friends would always be there for her.

Teddy and Abby promised to try to come to the trial if it was at all possible, to be there for her, and when she protested, they both told her to be quiet, "We'll make a way to be here even if is for one day," they promised.

It seemed the hour was up faster than they could imagine, but they were grateful for seeing her for themselves.

Teddy said, "I'm gonna be in God's face everyday asking him to help you now, so don't worry; He never turned me down yet, and I don't think He fittin to do so now, so relax and remember I love you, my little rascal."

Abby was crying so hard that she could only mutter, "luv ya."

CHAPTER 43

Joe called Sadie and told her he had to see her immediately. She was to get on a plane and meet him in Atlanta, and then they would take a car to a small town in Georgia. He could not tell her over the phone what his detective had just told him.

Joe met Sadie and they went to a coffee shop. He told her everything he knew. Sadie felt weak and started to cry. "Joe, let us hurry and get there, I want to see her."

When they got to Smithville, Joe booked them into a little hotel which was twenty miles away. He got in touch with the lawyer, explaining who he was and set up a meeting with him. Joe found out that Doc had hired the best lawyer, and that he had the backing of a good law firm to help Lizzie. He was happy, but he wanted to help his own daughter. He remembered Seff was a law student, and made arrangements for him to come as soon as he got a chance. Seff was sitting the bar examination in a few weeks. He and Sadie talked with the lawyer and wanted to see Lizzie. Ernie arranged the meeting.

Joe and Sadie sat across from a very sullen young woman. She was very beautiful, looked a lot like Sadie around the eyes and had her mouth. She looked like a lost soul. Sadie was praying all the time Joe was talking to her.

"There is a lot of explaining we have to do to you. Due to unforeseeable circumstances that were out of our hands, you and your sisters were lost to us. Sadie left after someone tried to murder her in a fire. She was badly burned, fighting for her life and could only manage with one child, which was Wendy Mae. Betty, you were sent to a relative of Doc's friend. You can understand that Sadie and I had no control over what happened to you. We are so sorry to find out what you went through. We will do our darnest to make it up to you, if you will let us," said Joe.

Sadie sat there speechless; tears were streaming down her cheeks. Lizzie looked from one to the other; she was taking in everything they said to her, but her mind was somewhere else. He said, "We are your parents, and we're here to help you." These two people who said they were her parents were not what she had expected. Her eyebrows narrowed; they were a strange couple; he was a very handsome, Caucasian, and she a gorgeous Negro. She kept looking at them, from one to the other, wondering what the hell was happening. Here she is in jail and now they come looking for her, are they crazy? They sent her away to strangers, allow her to be abused and never looked back for her. What did he say, "I thought you, your mother, and sisters were dead in a house fire. I just found your mother and your sister two years ago. I am still looking for your other sister, Mary Jane."

I have sisters, I am a triplet, and I have a younger brother. I have a family, a real family. Lizzie bit her lip to keep from crying. Suddenly, the woman spoke, "Betty, my baby I love you; I'm so sorry..." she stretched out her arms. It felt good to hear someone say that they loved her. She wanted to go into her arms, but she could not, not only because of the brevity of their acquaintance, but she could not allow herself to trust these people.

Lizzie was very thoughtful as she looked at these crazy people. She looked at her mother and did not take her gaze from her. She was searching, searching for something, but could not find anything. I do not know these strangers, why were they here? Are they here to torment me or prolong my suffering? If they loved me, why were they now coming to find me? It took them twenty one years. They were just like mom and dad. They did not really care about her. If they did, they would have found her a long time ago, and she would not have been in this predicament. Filled with sudden annoyance, Lizzie got up and signaled for the guard to take her back to her cell. She could not take it any longer and she did not want to break down in front of strangers.

Joe and Sadie watched in amazement as she looked at them before leaving; a look that Sadie will never forget- a look of deep hatred. As she passed by, Sadie reached out to touch her and

Lizzie stiffened her body. Sadie let her hand drop to her side. "God be with you Betty," Sadie said, and watched her walk slowly down the hall. Before Lizzie left the room she turned to Sadie and said, "Its Lizzie, my name is Elizabeth Edwards."

Lizzie thought to herself, this woman cannot even remember my name. Sadie felt as if a knife had sliced her through her heart. When she told Joe he brushed it off by saying, "Darling, she's hurting badly and she wants to hurt back, it just normal. Don't let it bother you too much."

When Lizzie got back to her cell she cried, and cried and could not stop crying. She wanted to talk to them but she couldn't, she wanted to be held, and be part of them but they were strangers. She wished mommy could have loved her, but she wasn't her real mommy. Her real mommy left her and ran with another sister, and left her to the mercies of those people. I hate them; I hate them all. I will never see them again.

* * * * *

A few weeks later, Lizzie had two more visitors, Seff and Bessie. She was happy to see the young woman and handsome young man who were her brother and sister. She wanted to go home with them and be free. The young man said, "Lizzie, we are so sorry for what you have gone through. I am a lawyer; I just passed the bar. I am going to personally assist your lawyer in whatever capacity he needs to get you free of this ridiculous charge. Joe, Duchess, Bessie and I will not desert you ever again, I promise."

Well, at least he knew that they deserted me. He seemed young, but at the same time, he seemed very sure of himself. He was a take charge person; she loved that. A flicker of a smile crossed her lips. Seff picked up on it and said, "Bessie and I were talking about how beautiful it is going to be when you get out of here and we can be together."

"You seem very sure that I will get off, can you promise me that?" she asked curiously.

Seff slapped his chest, "I make miracles happen, ask Bessie

here." They all laughed. She felt free and happy, and sad, and miserable all at once.

Then the girl spoke, "I remember you in my dreams, I always dream that you're always pulling my hair, and I'm crying," and they all laughed again. She was happy to see these young people, but they were free and she was in jail – get real. After a while, they got up to leave and promised to be there for her. As Bessie passed by, Lizzie wickedly reached up and pulled on her long silky hair. Taken aback, Bessie turned back and opened her arms and Lizzie went willingly into them. They laughed, and both started crying.

Seff said, "I'm sorry ladies, I cannot help the affect I have on women. Now, you both need to thank God for such a handsome brother, and just relax."

Lizzie and Bessie opened their arms and Seff came right in. Lizzie was very happy, and then Seff did a strange thing. He held her hands tightly and he spoke solemnly, "Father God, we thank you for finding our sister, Lizzie," and Bessie murmured, "Yes, Jesus"

Seff continued, "We are asking you to free her life and her soul from destruction. We know you love her dearly, please let her realize that we, her family, love her too. We have prayed and asked you to deliver her out of these horrific circumstances and send her home to us. We believe that you hear us and will answer our prayers, amen."

"Amen," murmured Bessie.

Lizzie went back to her cell a different person. She was somebody; she had a real mother, father, sister and brother. They all seemed so nice, even what Seff had called them, "Joe and Duchess." She smiled; her mother was a Duchess. That night she dreamt of being with her family and having a big party. For the first time in months, Lizzie had the most peaceful sleep, because she fell asleep with a smile on her face.

CHAPTER 44

J oe and Sarah and their two children had moved out of his mother's house. Mrs. Kettering had had a heart attack and she was in a weakened state. Nonetheless, Joe still moved out and left her. She went to the hospital and was there for a while then she was sent back home to recuperate. She was so miserable that she never kept a nurse for more than a few days. After a while, she had gone through so many nurses that it was becoming increasingly difficult to find someone who would take care of her for a long period of time.

As Joe and Sadie were in constant touch with each other, he told Sadie all that had transpired between him and his mother. Sadie told him, "I have forgiven her a long time ago after I got converted, and I hope you will find it in your heart to forgive her some day."

"Never," he said.

"You sound just like her," Sadie reminded him. "Anger and hatred only makes the soul sick. We don't need sick souls. Bessie will be having our first grandchild soon and I plan to come and spend some time with her when I get someone to take over the bookstore for me. I have a young girl who just loves books as much as I do. She's a college student, and I think she'll do fine."

"I do not think there is anyone in the whole wide world who likes books more than you do," said Joe. "Sometimes I thought you only liked me for my books." She could sense the smile in his voice.

"No, Joe I loved you because I could not understand how someone like you could want to love me as much as you do. I did not understand it, nor believed it for a long time, nonetheless, over the years I saw how much you loved me; you proved it to me over and over again. Now, I see true love never dies, we might not be together but we will always have love in our hearts for one another and our children."

*****

Bessie gave birth to a beautiful baby girl, whom she named Grace Ann. She was the most beautiful baby Sadie had seen, she told Joe who promised to come and see his grandchild that weekend.

"Could you ever imagine that we would be grandparents so soon?" he asked Sadie.

"I think I'll enjoy being a grandmother; I never had one and I miss the experience," Sadie stated. "I'll see you when you come to Bessie's."

After Sadie had been with Bessie for three months, Sadie and Joe were having a telephone conversation when he said suddenly in the conversation, "Well, I'm sure you'll be glad to know that your mother-in-law is getting just what she deserves. She has a problem keeping nurses to look after her. She's so mean that they come for as long as a week and then leave. I refuse to be bothered with her; she still has not shown any remorse for what she did to my family, and so I don't even go to see her. Let her sit there by herself and stew in her misery."

Sadie thought she should have been elated to hear how Mrs. Kettering was punishing for help. She had suffered a massive heart attack, had had surgery and was now home recuperating. She was confined to a wheel chair, and even with all her money she couldn't even pay for good help. No one wanted to be bothered with an old witch.

Sadie asked, "What about your sister, Lucy? Does she attend to her, or come see after her?"

"No way, they live in Florida, and so she comes for a little while and then she has to go home and take care of her own family. Plus she never got along with ma. She was a daddy's girl and ma did not take too kindly to that either. It's a long story as you know."

160

"That is so sad," Sadie said.

"What's sad?" asked Joe.

"It's sad that your mother, the grandmother of our children has no one to really take care of her; that's what's sad."

"You know, Joe, there are so many older people who live alone and don't have anyone who really cares for them. There are people who cannot afford to hire someone to come in and have to depend on neighbors or their church family to attend to them. But you know something? God always had a ram in the thicket."

"A what? What do you mean by that?"

"Well, when God told Abraham to take his only son, Isaac and sacrifice him, Abraham was going to do just that; when he raised the knife to sacrifice his son, God told him not to, but to look in the thicket and he would see a ram; he was to sacrifice that ram instead of Isaac."

"That's deep," blurted Joe.

"Yes, it is. Lots of older people who are poor and some of them disabled or handicapped, have to depend on the kindness of strangers for their livelihood. Others, although they have children, their own children, like your sister, Lucy, live far away with their families and find it hard to help. Most of the time the children are working and have their own lives; they cannot afford the time to help. It's really a dilemma."

"I see what you mean, Sadie, something's got to be done."

"That is why I am going to pray that God send someone who really cares for your mother to help her out in her time of need."

After Joe hung up the phone, Sadie sat and thought about what Joe had said for a long time afterwards. Bessie and little Gracie were doing fine and she was due to go back home soon any way. She decided to go to the Kettering house and visit for old time sake.

She called Paul to tell him that she was going to Mrs. Kettering.

"What the hell for?" he asked

Sadie was shocked; she never heard Paul react this way to anything she ever wanted to do. This was a side of him she did not know; and it angered her.

'Who the hell was he to tell her what to do?' She always felt something in her rise up when someone is opposing her. She has to ask the Holy Spirit to help her in this way, she reasoned.

She put on a smile and said sweetly, "Honey, I know you don't think I should be bothered with her, but she is the children's grandmother and she needs help right now."

"She can afford to pay for it, why do you think you have to save the world?" Paul snapped.

Sadie found herself reaching for his neck; instead she smiled, "Paul, I'm going to see what needs to be done and then I'll be home, take care of yourself," and Sadie hung up.

"Must I always have to fight for my right to do what I want to do, or what?" she asked herself. "Why can't people be considerate of one another?" Sadie packed and arranged to see Mrs. Kettering.

CHAPTER 45

She was amazed at being back there. It seemed as though everything had just stood still for a while, and now she was back. Her parents had died. She had found out from Joe who had enlightened her as to who had moved and who stayed. She also knew that her sister, Janie, had married and had two boys. Janie was also eight months pregnant.

Janie and Sadie did not really know each other. Janie was eight years old when Sadie left and there was no contact between them over the years. Sadie did not even try to find out how she was doing. There was no aching need to go back to that place. Most of the people who were there now were young people whom she did not know.

Sadie spent some quality time with her sister, Janie, and promised to help send her two nephews to college. She had some money now and Gracie has taught her to figure out things beyond her understanding. Now that Joe was back in the picture and that he was an accountant, he did not hesitate to help her in any way. She was able to set up funds for Janie and her family.

Janie was a beautiful young woman. Her husband, Amos and the two boys Obadiah and Rufus were beautiful children. They were polite and well mannered. Seff would love his cousins, and she smiled as she thought of this. However, she noticed that there was coldness in Janie, as she gave Sadie a perfunctory kiss. Sadie decided to ignore her request that she didn't need anything from Sadie.

"We're doing alright for ourselves," Janie said. "Amos works very hard down at the hardware store and I am a cook at the Elementary school in town."

Janie was thinking, Sadie never looked back to care about their mother who was very sick, after their father died. Everything was left for her to do while Sadie went off with her White man and forgot her own people. Sadie realized that Janie would never understand her relationship with Joe or what her life was like; or why she couldn't keep in touch. Sadie wanted to be angry with Janie, but she began to feel for this young woman who had a very hard life. Sadie resolved to help Janie in spite of herself and her two nephews.

Amos was a little more understanding, at least, he seemed genuinely pleased to see Sadie and hugged her and turned her around saying, "Let me look at you; Janie" he said, "I see where you get your good looks from. Your sister is absolutely gorgeous."

Janie just looked at them frowning. Amos apologized for his young wife; "Just give Janie some time; she'll get over it. But deep down inside, I know my Janie is glad to have her big sister back."

Later, that evening she called Paul, "How are you, doing?" she asked.

"Lonely and miserable without you, he replied. I'm sorry I was so insensitive, but I don't like the idea of you around Joe and his family," he said.

"A little jealous, eh?" Sadie snickered, "You don't have to worry, my heart belongs to you and only you; Joe is at home with his wife and children, remember he does not live here anymore."

'I love you Sadie and I need for you to hurry back," he said

"I love you too, Paul, and I will be back as soon as I can," she replied.

CHAPTER 46

S adie went up to the main house to visit. The people in the house were new. She wanted to see Mrs. Kettering and asked to go and see her. The nurse, a young girl went in to tell her and came back with the answer "no way." Sadie ignored her and went into the bedroom. Mrs. Kettering was in a wheelchair covered with a blanket. She looked up as she saw Sadie, "What the hell are you doing here? Get out!" she screamed.

"Now! Now! Is that the way to treat your daughter-in-law? I came to pay my respects to you" she said softly, "and how are you doing today?"

"None of your business," was the curt reply.

"I see your attitude has not changed, and that is so sad for me to look at you and not see any changes, Mrs. Kettering."

"What are you doing here? Joe and his wife have moved out," she stated.

"I know, Joe is in touch with me, and I have also met his lovely wife and children."

"At least he came to his senses before it was too late," she said

"What do you mean, came to his senses?" asked Sadie

"Well, I'm sure he didn't want to be married for life to a Nigger," she retorted.

Sadie felt all the old hatred rising up in her and she really wanted to wring her neck right now. Instead she said, "You know, Mrs. Kettering, Joe and I would still have been married if you had not interfered."

Sadie pulled up a chair next to Mrs. Kettering and sat down. Mrs. Kettering called for her nurse who seemed to disappear.

"Let me tell you," Sadie said; "I was very angry with you for a while, I even planned to come and do to you what you tried to do to me. I had it all written down in a book. I felt good to come and try to burn you up in a fire and watch you squirm and beg for mercy. I wanted to see you burn and to smell your flesh burn, and watch you experience the pain and suffering I went through; the surgeries I endured; and even now I walk with a limp. Why? Why? Mrs. Kettering just because I was Black? Your son loved me for who I was; not what color I was. He saw something in me that probably no one else could and he brought it out like nobody else could. Furthermore, he gave me three beautiful girls, triplets and a very handsome son.

So you see you have four Black grandchildren; do you hear me? Black grandchildren, but very beautiful Black grandchildren."

Sadie realized she had no fear of this woman. She was just an ordinary woman. She used to make her feel like someone from a different planet, but no more; she felt like an equal. I can stand up to her and tell her how I feel and not be afraid of repercussions. She felt wonderful and had a sense of freedom.

Mrs. Kettering was speechless for a while, then she said, "They are not my grandchildren; I would never accept them."

"Oh, you don't have to accept them – they could care less about you. They don't even know you exist." Sadie drew her chair closer to Mrs. Kettering who looked at her suspiciously.

"However," continued Sadie, "you met one of your grand-daughters, Bessie. Bessie and her husband just had a baby girl so now you are the great grandmother of another Black baby," and Sadie threw her head back and laughed.

Mrs. Kettering was as white as a sheet. She seemed scared and wondered what Sadie would do to her.

Aghast, Mrs. Kettering said, "Get out of my house and don't come back." Sadie got up slowly and came closer to Mrs. Kettering, she hovered over her for a while, then she stooped down and picked up the blanket that had fallen and gently covered Mrs. Kettering. She put her face close to hers, smiled and said, "I'll be seeing you soon."

CHAPTER 47

The next week Sadie showed up in the morning with a tray for Mrs. Kettering. She asked, "Where is my nurse?"

"I dismissed her and I will be taking care of you from now on. I have arranged to stay in one of the rooms here so that I can be close to you. You can ring your bell and I'll be here in a jiffy. I will go home on weekends, but I'll be here for you as long as you need me."

"I do not want you to take care of me. You have no right to fire my nurse," she protested. 'Go on back where you belong, and leave me alone."

"As a matter of fact, she was about to leave you. She could not stand your insults any longer. So let us set up some ground rules. No Nigger talk, no one is a Nigger. You treat me with respect and I will take care of you. I have some training from Gracie and from Doc. And from his doctors and nurses when he was sick; I know what to look for, and all that stuff.

Your doctor will come once a week, a nurse will come and check you out three times a week, and I will be your care giver for as long as you need me. You have nothing to say! I have cleared it with Joe and Lucy; they do not understand why I would want to help you, but I cannot in good faith stick around and not help you. Your husband, Mr. Kettering, God rest his soul was very good to my family, Joe is the love of my life and you have four beautiful grandchildren and one great-granddaughter. So let's get you back on the road to recovery, o.k.?"

CHAPTER 48

One day, while Sadie was busying taking care of Mrs. K., Amos came to tell her that Janie had given birth to a baby girl whom she named Lula Anne. Sadie was pleased more than she could say. It showed her that her little sister had forgiven her.

On one of her nostalgic days, Sadie decided to go to the area where she and Joe used to go and sit on a log. The log was still there, and she was surprised to see a couple of children sitting on the log. One little girl around ten years old was combing a younger girl's hair and she was corn rowing it so nicely that Sadie was amazed at the workmanship of this little angel. The work was intricate, delicate and yet there was a certain pattern emerging on the little girl's head. As Sadie looked at the other little girls in the yard, she could tell that their hairstyles were done by this young child. They all had beautiful hairstyles, yet everyone was different.

"Hi!" Sadie said as she drew nearer, "I love what you are doing with her hair; it looks beautiful and real p-r-e-t-t-y!"

The little girl smiled.

"What is your name?" Sadie asked

"Jessie, Ma'am"

"Well, Jessie, I wish I could do hair like you do. Have you been doing hair long?"

"Yes, Ma'am, I do everybody's children hair."

"Do you like doing hair?" enquired Sadie

"I just loves it," Jessie beamed as she pointed to one girl after another and said, "I did Rosie hair, and her sister, Mimi, and Penny too," and she smiled broadly.

Sadie was excited with her. This young girl had a gift and all she needed was someone to enhance it. It put her in remembrance of Joe helping her with her passion – reading. She resolved to help Jessie as much as she could.

"Would you like to do hair when you grow up? Sadie asked her.

"Oh! Yes, Ma'am" she beamed, "I really would."

"Okay" said Sadie. "I'll see what I can do to help you.

She sat there for a while, thinking of these children. There were about seven or eight of them running around and playing. It was ingenious what they were doing; they were making their own form of play and having fun with absolutely nothing much. One little girl was drawing in the ground. One little boy had an old bicycle tire and he was running after it, pushing it with a stick and he was going round and round an old tree with this tire. It seemed like he was having a world of fun. Her nephews were having fun with paper airplanes, and the other children were just running around and having fun.

Watching the children enjoy themselves, made the time go quickly. Finally, Sadie got up and went to the house.

CHAPTER 49

The next day Sadie ventured down to the old school house. It was a very old, dilapidated building and in dire need of repair. The six stairs leading to the building was rickety and seemed about to fall. The outside was weather beaten and there were broken panes in the windows.

The children she saw at the Ketterings did not attend school; with this in mind, she entered the classroom hesitantly. The woman who was behind the desk got up and smiled; she watched as Sadie advanced towards her. Sadie really did not expect to see anyone in the room because it was after school hours.

"Hi!" the woman smiled, as she came forward, extending her hand to Sadie.

"Come on in!" she invited Sadie.

"Thank you," said Sadie and introduced herself.

"Nice to meet you, I am Ms. Beatrice Donovan," she said, "What can I do for you?"

Sadie glanced around the room. There were six long benches and equally long desks; they were very old, and needed a good cleaning. It appeared as if three of them were in use.

Mrs. Donovan followed Sadie's gaze and repeated her question. Sadie nodded and smiled at the teacher.

"I was just wondering what I could do to help some children up on the Kettering farm? They seem so bright and talented, yet no one is even trying to help them. They do not go to school, just play and run wild. I see a lot of potential in them and I was wondering if I arranged with you, if you would be able to help them, even if it is one day a week, Ms. Donovan."

"Call me Bea, please. I will be more than happy to help. In fact, I live near the Ketterings' farm. Maybe I could go over there and see what I could do, or better yet, the children can come to my cottage and I'll set up something over there. Just let me think about it."

"Why can't they come here?" Sadie enquired.

Bea smiled and said, "I have seven children who come here regularly, but it is very difficult for us, not many supplies for anything, and it is very difficult for the parents who do send their children here; but we do the best with what we've got."

"I will arrange to pay you for helping them," said Sadie anxiously. She did not want to lose this good teacher who seemed so willing and able to help these children.

"No! No! No! You don't, I would be more than happy to help the children. I l-o-v-e teaching and my payment would be to see the expressions on their faces when they find out how exciting learning new things can be."

"I've experienced that feeling, and loved it." Sadie was so excited just remembering how she felt when she learned to read well.

"Oh! That's just marvelous and very good of you, Bea, but I will provide you with a budget to get them whatever they need to complete the learning experience, and I'll see what can be done with the building and furnishings."

Bea beamed proudly and could not contain her enthusiasm. This was wonderful.

Sadie told Bea about Jessie and what a fantastic job she was doing on the children who lived around her.

"I know of a hairdresser who can teach her, if Jessie would like to go to her, I can arrange it," Bea added.

"I will talk to Jessie's mother and hear what she has to say about that."

"Then it's settled," said Bea, reaching out to shake Sadie's hand. Instead Sadie pulled her to her chest and hugged her hard.

"Thank God for people like you Bea, you're a blessing to mankind. I really appreciate you." Tears were overflowing Sadie's eyes and ran down her cheeks.

Bea held her off, wiped the tears away and said, "They just need someone to motivate and encourage them by showing them love. That is what you are giving them. God will bless you greatly."

They embraced again, and Sadie left.

'What a wonderful woman,' Bea thought; 'she was so beautiful and sophisticated, and caring. What a combination? Where did she come from? Everyone knew the Ketterings, but they were Caucasians, she was not, but whoever she was thank God for her.'

Sadie called Joe and told him about the school situation and asked him for help. Joe promised he would. Two months later Joe had bought another building, not far from the old one, and he had ordered new school furnishings as well as supplies. Sadie was elated and thanked Joe for all his help.

"I did not mean for you to do all of that. I have some money from Grace and Doc and had intended to use that," Sadie explained.

"It doesn't matter, I felt good doing it for the children," Joe said. "If they are anything like you used to be, then I'll get my money's worth. Sadie, you would make any teacher proud." He hung up the phone and smiled to himself as he thought of Sadie as a child and her motivation to read everything she got her hands on.

CHAPTER 50

Sadie had stayed and worked with Mrs. K for about six months. During that time, Mrs. K was doing much better, she and Sadie had become friends; and most importantly she was a believer. Everyone admired the new Mrs. K and wondered how Sadie managed to make the changes in her. Sadie proudly told them that the Holy Spirit did work miracles.

Now, Sadie, Seff and Bessie went to see Mrs. Kettering who was slowly improving. It was a very good visit for the children and also their grandmother. She asked them about their lives, and seemed very interested in their well being. Once, while Sadie was helping her get ready for bed she said, "Sadie, would you forgive me?" She had tears in her eyes. "I don't know why I did it, my life was so miserable and nothing seemed to be going my way."

Sadie took her hand in hers and while looking into her eyes, said, "I have forgiven you, even before you asked, now just ask God to forgive you."

Sadie had really taken good care of Mrs. Kettering. Sadie changed her, fed her, took her outside to get fresh air, talked to her and most of all read to her from her Bible, and from historical novels which Mrs. K liked. She was amazed how well Sadie read and wanted to know where she learned to read so well. She also enjoyed listening to Sadie sing as she went about her work. As Sadie sat reading to her,

"Did the Doctor teach you?" she asked one day.

"No" Sadie stated, "I started in school here, but then Joe would bring me books and he would help me. I knew how to read better than most children my age who were in school, because I had a genuine desire to read. Joe understood that and he helped me as much as he could and that was the start of a very good relationship.

There was a flicker of a smile on Mrs. K's face.

"Why are you laughing?" asked Sadie.

"Nothing," answered Mrs. K. then she said, "When you started to read, you began to sound like a White person and that made Joe fall for you."

"No, he didn't, you just can't accept the fact that Joe loved me for who I am; he just fell in love with me, that's all, admit it."

"Say what you will, I know different," said Mrs. K and she laughed sarcastically.

"You may not believe me but Joe made me very happy; he loved me very much. I know you can't understand how a White man could love a Black woman, but he did. Only God knows why he did, but he sure knew how to love me and I loved him back; but you know what...because of his interfering mama we were separated nearly by death," as Sadie said this she looked right into Mrs. K'eyes. She thought she saw tears well up in her eyes.

Sadie found it was easier to talk to this woman who drove fear into her when she was a child. Now she seemed like what she was, a weak, old, sick woman. However, she was Joe's mother and her children's grandmother. They began to talk to each other daily now and it was if they had been friends for a long time. They talked like two educated adults. Sadie did not put up with her nonsense, and she realized that she could not get away with anything where Sadie was concerned. They spent a lot of time together, even after Sadie finished dressing her. The exchange between the two women became one like a daughter and a mother. After a while they were chatting like very old friends.

Sadie told her of the progress of the children in school. She listened intently and seemed interested in their well being. She even wanted to go the school to see the children and their teacher in action. Sadie made the arrangements. When Mrs. K left the schoolhouse she was wiping away the tears as they coursed down her cheeks.

Mrs. K had become a changed person. No longer was she disrespecting the help, she was not unpleasant to be near; she had a very nice nurse and Sadie checked in on her every week. Sadie and Mrs. K would have long talks and Sadie would fill her in on what was going on with Lizzie. She saw the newspapers, and one day she said to Sadie, "That Lizzie is a beauty; I think she takes after my side of the family. As a matter of fact she looks a lot like me."

Sadie laughed, "Whatever you say." Then she realized what it took for Mrs. Kettering to compare a Black person to her, a White person, even if the person was her granddaughter, and so Sadie, murmured, "Thank you, Mrs. K."

"No! Thank you, Sadie, for re-uniting me with my beautiful grandchildren. I really can say I love them and even begin to miss them when they leave, especially that Seff, he is a real charm. Do you know he reminds me of my husband when he was young?" and she smiled.

Sadie knew why God sent her here to look after Mrs. K. She had a job to do and she was sure going to do it. She talked to her about Jesus and how he died on the cross for her sins. How He was humiliated, beaten, and hung on a cross. His love for mankind and His determination to do his Father's will. She asked Mrs. K if she wanted to be a part of this family and she nodded. Sadie proceeded to lead her to Jesus.

CHAPTER 51

Mrs. K got excellent care and Sadie saw to it that she got
every thing that she needed and much more. Sadie had a
beautiful voice which Mrs. K. loved and sometimes she
would ask Sadie to sing for her. Sadie sang, and read the Bible telling all the stories of Jesus and his disciples. Mrs. K was impressed
by Sadie's knowledge of the Bible and her talk of the Holy Spirit.
Sadie also offered to take her to church on Sunday. Sadie made arrangements, and took her in her wheel chair to church. They both
enjoyed themselves tremendously.

Everyday, after that, they talked a little more, Sadie read the
Bible and they both sang the hymns of the church. Mrs. K found a
peace she never knew existed. It seemed as if she had just been
born and her life had just begun. She was happy, before this, she
just existed. She looked at Sadie with different eyes, and saw a
beautiful Black angel, who was intelligent, loving, compassionate
and kind. She could not believe that this beautiful, Black, young
woman had no ulterior motive when taking care of her. She
seemed to exude love and kindness, and a genuine sense of cama-
raderie. She was enjoying herself for the first time in her life. She
could let down her hair, or what's left of it, and not be criticized.

When Sadie announced to Mrs. K., "I think you are doing fine,
and well able to manage by yourself, so I'll be going back home,
but I'll check on you every week just to see how you are doing."

Mrs. K was sad to have to see Sadie go, but she knew that it
had to come to an end, after all, Sadie had a life of her own now
and it wasn't fair to have her time and energy tied up in her life.

CHAPTER 52

Sadie had gone back to Boston and Mrs. K. was doing fine. She missed Sadie more than she would like to admit. Sadie had brought a fire to the relationship, and took no nonsense from Mrs. K but she did it in love.

Sadie called Seff and Bessie and told them she was going to see Mrs. K in two months and wondered if they were free to come see their grandmother. Bessie came with the baby, and Mrs. K was holding the baby and talking to her as if she were an adult. Gracie Ann smiled a lot and played with her great-grandma. Seff talked to her and she was tickled. She said, "You remind me of your father, but somehow or the other I never got a chance to really know him. I just barked orders for him to carry through; we never had a relationship like your family."

"Utter nonsense," said Seff, "I cannot see you barking orders, M'Lady." They both laughed. Bessie took the baby from her and they chatted a little. Before he left, Seff promised to come again and take her for a ride by the countryside to smell the roses. He had a big exam coming up and he had to study for it. That weekend, Seff, Bessie and Sadie as well as Mrs. K prayed for peace and unity in the family. The grandchildren left and went about their ways, and Sadie went back home.

Seff sat the Bar exam and passed it. Joe decided to have a celebration for him. It was a lovely affair. Seff's grandmother was there, as well as his Aunt Lucy and her family; Joe, Sarah and their children, Duchess, Bessie and Gracie Ann. Paul flew in from Boston, as he said he would not miss this celebration for the world. The love of Seff's life was also there, Cindy Butler. Seff stood up to thank God for his family. He asked God to continue to guide them and to save their souls. Seff deliberately asked Joe and his

family if they wanted to accept Jesus now. He stated we are all believers and we do not want you and your family to be left out, but
the decision is yours. Sarah spoke for her family, "We are willing
to give our hearts to Jesus, Seff, if he would have us." Every one
joined hands and Seff prayed for the family.

Seff turned to his grandmother, bowed, and said, "M'lady what
was the name of your dear husband and my grandfather?"

She replied, "John Allan Kirkpatrick Kettering."

"Thank you," said Seff.

Turning to Cindy, he got on his knees and asked her to be his
wife. With tears in her eyes, Cindy got up and the two embraced
and kissed. It was a passionate kiss that had Bessie clearing her
throat. They broke loose, and Seff apologized, "Can't help my
charm."

Everyone was so happy for these young people. Usually, Seff
would have everyone in tears, laughing at his antics; but somehow
or other everyone knew he was dead serious about this proposal.
Seff then announced to Cindy, "My Queen, our first Prince will be
named John Allan Kirkpatrick Kettering, II."

Everyone clapped; Mrs. K had tears in her eyes, she looked at
Seff and whispered, "thank you Seff, God bless you."

Joe was pleased with his son and so he said lightheartedly, "I
need to tell you a thing or two before you get married.

"No need, Sir, Duchess taught me all I need to know about
love, marriage and life."

Joe was hurt, he began to question himself, and 'does he mean
that I was not there for him, or does he mean he doesn't need my
advice.' The more he thought about it, the more upset he got. He
was upset with Sadie, with his mother and with himself. So before
he could bust wide open and say something horrible, he got up
from the table and excused himself.

Sadie looked after him and realized what had happened. She
wanted to go after him and allay his fears, but she couldn't, if she
did Paul would be upset. She sat quietly while everyone else was
chatting and laughing. When Joe did not come back in a reasonable
time, she inched her way to Seff and whispered, "Joe's hurt by
your remarks, get to him."

Seff looked startled and tried to remember what he said, anyhow, if Duchess felt he should find Joe then that's what he'll do. He excused himself and set out to find Joe.

He was standing just outside the club, "What's up Dad, needing a little air?" said Seff.

"Yes, I needed some air," he replied. He also realized that Seff had called him Dad for the first time and he liked it. He really liked this young man and wished he had been with him while he grew.

"I'm sorry if I offended you back there, I really did not intend to, but Duchess has been such a force in my life that I tend to forget others. That's the effect that woman has on me. I told her she has to set me free" and he laughed. "I'm really sorry, Dad; forgive me?"

"Sure I do, I just feel so badly that I was not there for you while you were growing up. You're my oldest son and I'm very proud of you. I just wish I could have been there for you, that's all."

"Well, you're here now and that's all that matters," Seff said as he opened his arms to embrace his father. Joe could not resist, so he smiled as he hugged his son.

They walked back into the room with their arms around each other. Sadie; felt a modicum of relief, and smiled to herself.

CHAPTER 53

During the month leading up to Lizzie's trial, Joe took a leave of absence from his job, so he could devote his time working with the lawyers, and the publicity he wanted for the case. His boss was backing him for the media attention to the case. He told Sadie I want every newspaper, every radio station and television station carrying the news. Sadie began to protest, "They will have it out there what a whore she was and it will be devastating for her."

"I want her out of prison, and if that's what it takes, then so be it," he snapped.

Sadie agreed with him that the White population would like to sweep it all under the carpet and forget about it; then throw Lizzie in jail and forget about her. Joe was not about to let that happen to his little girl. Sadie knew from past experience, when Joe made up his mind to do something, nothing, absolutely nothing, was going to stop him. Right now, she was pulling at straws, and was just thankful to God that Joe was there to help her.

Joe enlisted the help of the newly formed NAACP chapter in Georgia. He invited a Civil Rights lawyer to be visible at the trial and he pulled out all the stops. Seff, the new lawyer worked feverishly with Lizzie's lawyers who were hired by Doc.

Seff told Joe, "This law firm is a very prestigious one and Lizzie is in good hands, plus she always has me," and he smiled as touched his father's shoulders.

"Thanks Seff, I needed to hear that," replied Joe.

CHAPTER 54

When the trial began, Lizzie's family was well represented. James came the first day of the big trial because Maggie did not come back to work. Joe and Sadie were seated in a room talking before they went into the courtroom, when James entered the room,

"Mr. Joe Kettering?" asked James

"Yes?" answered Joe, Looking at him anxiously.

"My name is James Henson," and he offered Joe his hand. "I run the newspaper here in town. However, I wanted to talk to you and your wife privately."

Joe turned to Sadie who nodded.

"I know that you are Lizzie's mother," he said to Sadie, "and you are her father, and I also know where your other daughter is." He let it sink in as they both looked at him expectantly. "I'm not sure she would want to meet you guys. It's a long story. She found out Lizzie was her sister and it threw her for a loop. Maybe we can talk about this later."

Sadie held onto her chest and took a seat abruptly. She bowed her head in her hands and sobbed quietly. Joe stood over her, then helped her to her feet.

"No!" both Joe and Sadie said together. Joe said to James, "Is there some place where we could have a meal or a drink? We do not have to be here until tomorrow."

James, Joe and Sadie went to a restaurant and sat talking about Maggie. James started, "I'm not going to hold back anything, but you have to go easy on her; she is in a mess right now. I don't know how much more she can take." When James finished telling them about Maggie, Joe said, "Oh, my God, the Klan!"

"Mr. Kettering, she's a mess right now," said James

"Call me Joe," said Joe

"And its Sadie for me," she smiled. "I would also like to meet her mother," said Sadie.

James said "I am going to arrange for you to meet her and let you know what she says."

"Oh! Please do," begged Sadie.

"How soon will we hear from you?" asked Joe.

"Give me until tomorrow."

James went over to Maggie's home and talked to Mrs. Ascott and Maggie. He told them every thing that went on and explained that Lizzie's family was out in full fashion and she should be there to see them. They seemed like very nice people who loved their daughter and were looking for the third child. He was so happy he could be of help. Mrs. Ascott was happy for Maggie; however, Maggie was deep in thought. She did not want anyone to know that she was a Negro; she did not want to associate with these people, whether they were nice or not. James loved everyone, so of course, they would be nice people. He just didn't understand. She didn't feel ready to meet them, yet she was curious to see what they looked like.

Sadie had bought some beautiful outfits for Lizzie to wear during the trial, and she looked so innocent in a pale, beige and blue skirt and blouse, and black patent leather pumps. She had her hair tied together with a light blue ribbon in a pony tail, and little wisps of hair by her ears. She was stunning and looked beautiful in whatever she put on.

Maggie and her mother entered the courtroom and took their seats. Maggie scanned the room looking for her biological mother and father.

Her heart was quickening, "I don't think I want to meet them" she whispered to her mother.

"Hush child, if you were my daughter I would want to meet you, so do not deprive them of the privilege of meeting their daughter. They are suffering enough."

"What about me? I have killed my father because of them."

"Now, now, don't go blaming them for something they don't

even know about. You're hurt and I understand, but it's not the end of your life, and stop saying you killed your father, because you didn't."

"That's what you think" she replied with a shrug of her shoulders.

CHAPTER 55

During the break, James came forward to Maggie and Mrs. Ascott; behind him were two people. James made the introductions, "Mrs. Ascott, Maggie this is Lizzie's father, Joe and her mother Sadie."

Mrs. Ascott extended her hand with a smile, "Oh! I am so pleased to finally meet you. I am so sorry for what you are going through with Lizzie."

"Thank you" said Joe and extended his hand.

"Thank you so much" said Sadie and opened both arms. Mrs. Ascott came willingly into them. Sadie had dealt with a lot of White people and she was no longer scared of them. It was either she accepted her or rejected her. It did not matter; however, she felt the warmth of this small, stocky woman. Sadie liked her. They all turned to wards Maggie, "How are you? Asked Joe.

"I'm fine, thank you" she replied.

"Listen," said Mrs. Ascott, "this is not the place for us to talk, please come to dinner this evening around seven; James will bring you."

Maggie looked at the woman who was supposed to be her mother. 'Gosh, she was really Black, there was no mistaking that. She looked very elegant, and her clothes were well made and expensive. She looked like an aristocratic Black woman. She looked like a clean Black woman. She did not look like the kind of Blacks that Maggie was accustomed to dealing with. She even smelled good; she had on some expensive perfume. She must be very rich. Mom and I did not look at all like we had any money; even Lizzie looked beautiful. Mom was in her floral dress which was pretty, and Maggie was in Jeans and a pink flowered shirt – she felt inadequate and cheap in front of these rich people, and for a moment she felt ashamed for herself and her mother. Then all of a sudden she heard her father's voice, "they are the scum of the earth and don't you forget it," Maggie smiled to herself and held her head up as she left the courtroom.

James was prompt and on time to pick up Joe and Sadie. He was a fine young man, and after idle chatter they arrived at the Ascotts' home. It was a modest little cottage, with the white fence and beautiful manicured lawn. Mrs. Ascott greeted them at the door, "Come in, come in" she smiled.

Maggie was in the background watching them from the living room. Mrs. Ascott ushered them into the room and they all sat down. James excused himself and stated he would be back in about two hours for them. Mrs. Ascott offered them something to drink and after a few minutes excused herself, saying, "I know you need to catch up."

Joe started in on Maggie, "My dear," he said, "I'm sorry to hear about your father's death, but I cannot believe how blessed we were to find you. Your whereabouts was going to be my next project, as soon as I had finished working on Lizzie's case."

Maggie flinched, "Project? I was a project, well whadda ya know?" She mimicked in her thoughts, outwardly, she just offered him a smile.

Joe was telling her about how she came to be adopted. "Doc felt it was too much for your mother to take all three girls, since she was in pain, and badly burned, she was going on a long journey to someone she didn't know and he felt that later on your mother can get the other two girls. Well, he was wrong and now we're all in a mess. Doc meant well, but he was wrong," Joe repeated. Maggie kept her eyes averted while he was speaking. She kept twisting her fingers in her lap. She kept remembering Doc crying and saying, "My Boo-Boo its Pop-Pop; I knew you'll come back Boo-Boo." He was right he did recognize me.

When Sadie spoke to Maggie, Maggie looked at her as if to say, "Who asked you to speak," then bowed her head and looked at the floor. She tried to shut out Sadie and did not want to hear from this Negro who called herself her mother.

Maggie closed her eyes for a moment and wished when she

185

opened them that Sadie would disappear and she would wake up from a bad dream. No such luck when she opened her eyes, and worse of all, Sadie was speaking to her, "I wondered about you every milestone, or every time Bessie did something spectacular, like getting a standing ovation at her piano recital, I wondered what you were doing right then." There were tears on Sadie's cheeks as she spoke to Maggie.

She spoke well, thought Maggie, like an educated White person, she had a very nice figure, was a clean, smooth Darkie. She really was exquisite. Maggie felt she could not hold a candle to Sadie. Sadie had class, she was dignified, she was educated and she seemed loving. Why didn't daddy meet these types of Blacks? She seemed like a real nice person, so why don't I like her?

Maggie ignored Sadie and turned to Joe, "you have remarried?"

"Yes," he said.

He knew what she was getting at. "I didn't know Sadie was alive. I would divorce my wife today and marry Sadie again if she would have me. I do love Sarah and my two young children, but Sadie will always be my first love and Sarah knows this. I did not marry Sarah until ten years after your supposed deaths."

Sadie interrupted, "The last time I saw you, I had just put you to bed at Doc's. You were running a high fever and coughing. Doc told me to allow you to stay over because he was going to check on you during the night."

Sadie smiled while tears trickled slowly down her cheeks, "He just wanted to keep you with him. You were his favorite although he denied it."

She wiped away the tears, and Maggie thought, "Oh Lord, here comes the mess, these people always like to make a spectacle of themselves."

However, Sadie continued, speaking softly, and lovingly, as if in a trance. Maggie realized that she was bringing to her memory that last night of the fire.

'Oh, my God, I can see why she's shedding tears; she lost her whole family and nearly died; forgive me God for being selfish,' Maggie thought sadly.

"He had bought you a puppy, named Sparky," continued Sadie, "do you remember Sparky? Sparky was lying at the foot of your bed that night. Bessie, Lizzie and you were all huddled in the bed together while I read you a story; then we sang your favorite song. Do you remember the song?" she asked Maggie.

Maggie shook her head and whispered, "No" She felt like crying herself, but she would not give into such undignified actions. She lifted her head, smiled although she felt like crying and running into this woman's arms, "No," she repeated, "I'm sorry."

"It was Little Bo Peep has lost her sheep," I gave you that song because you had a habit of finding out everything. You did not want to be left without a song, since Bessie had "Mary had a little Lamb." Bessie would suck her thumb and carry around a teddy bear in the other hand; that was her lamb. Lizzie's song was Jack and Jill. She was a tough one; she would jump on furniture for the hill then threw herself down laughing. She was a tough one that Lizzie was. When we were about to leave, you told me, "I love you mommy, and I asked how much? You would open your arms wide and say 'this much.' That was another of our favorite pastimes, then I would reply, 'I love you too Boo-Boo' Do you remember any of this?" Sadie asked.

"No" she whispered. She thought she remembered the "I love you Boo-Boo part" but she was not sure if she did or because everyone was talking about Boo-Boo; first there was Doc, then Ms. Ellie, now Sadie. She also remembered when she was little her mother telling her she had asked her to kiss her boo-boo when she had hurt her finger. Only Blacks used that word because she never heard it in the White community. However, she was not going to let Sadie know that she had remembered that one little piece of information. So she said, "I'm sorry, I don't remember, I really don't."

Mrs. Ascott served a delicious dinner of herb chicken, string beans, candied yams, homemade rolls, and she had ice cream sorbet for dessert. There was general chit-chat at the table, yet there was a sense of awkwardness. They talked about Lizzie's case. Joe told Maggie that Bessie and Seff will be attending the trial every day and she'll meet the rest of the family. She wasn't too thrilled.

Sadie was thoughtful as she looked at her eldest daughter- 'what a piece of work' she thought. I feel like I could wring her scrawny neck, and then she laughed softly. Every eye was on her. She cleared her throat and smiled sweetly.

In the car back to the hotel, Sadie asked James, "How long have you two been in love?"

James looked stunned, and then he smiled, "From the moment I saw her." When I asked you to tell me everything about her, you told us she was in love with a young man named John, what about him?"

"Maggie was going to break it off with him," James said sadly, "but when her father died and she found out that she was half Black she felt I would not want her and did not call it off. She felt John was the person her dad wanted for her and she was going to stay with John for her father's sake."

"She really must have loved her father" said Joe, feeling a tinge of jealousy.

"Yes, he loved Maggie and would have done anything for her, and it would have been alright if he wasn't the grand dragon of the KKK. That has really messed her up."

Sadie reddened. "What a horrible life to live,"

"Maggie doesn't think so, if you listen to her, her dad was the salt of the earth, and anyone who said anything against him became her enemy," James said tolerantly.

Sadie asked James, "How do you feel about me?"

"Oh! Maggie knows I do not judge a person by the color of their skin and she knew her father did not like me. She was hoping he would come around before we got married. Now I do not know what's happening, but I'm prepared to wait for her."

"Good for you," said Sadie. She liked this young man.

At the trial, Seff, Bessie, Sadie and Joe were all there. Seff and Bessie were also looking forward to meeting Maggie. Sadie looked for Maggie and did not see her. She became angry, "Why that little self centered bitch…"

"Is that you Sadie" a voice seemed to whisper in her ear; Sadie smiled to herself and kept her head straight ahead. She's just a piece of work that's all. Lord, you have to handle both your daughters, handle me and then handle Maggie, please. Sadie looked at Seff and felt proud. This young man so strong, so handsome, so loving, so dignified, so compassionate was her son; he loved her without question. Bessie with her sweet disposition was as loving a daughter as one can ask for. Joe sitting next to me – was the love of my life. Thank you God, Thank you for all that you have given me, and Paul, so loyal and patient. I am grateful, but I want it all, I want my two girls back. I want Lizzie out of jail and I want Maggie's friendship.

The doors opened and as Sadie glanced towards it, she was surprised to see a wheel chair being pushed. It was Mrs. K. Sadie smiled; Joe got up to take the wheel chair from Frank, her driver. After making sure she was alright, Joe returned to his seat beside Sadie. Lizzie looked back and wondered who the woman was. Then she figured it must have been daddy's mom because he got up to take care of her. She was happy to have a family. She never had a family before, and wanted so much to be a part of them. She liked Bessie and Seff, and loved Joe but Sadie was no fool and it doesn't seem as if she makes too much fun, yet everyone seemed to love her and worship the dirt she walked on. I want to be like Sadie. I admire her; that's where I get my spirit from; I am her daughter, and she loves me. Lizzie smiled to herself as she thought about these things. She was rudely brought back to reality as Mr. O'Reilly's voice broke through her revelry.

Lizzie looked around the courtroom and was surprised to see Teddy and Abby sitting together. When she made eye contact with them they smiled and held up clinched fingers indicating they were holding tight for her. Her heart was full, and tears of gratitude started to slowly make their way down her cheeks. She just let them flow. She felt loved by these people, her parents, her friends and family. "Thank you God," she whispered and she just let the tears flow and wash her anger from the past right out of her life.

In his closing statement, Mr. O'Reilly got up slowly and as he talked, he walked over to the jury, stood in front of them, and at times for effect, walking away and making lots of gestures with his hands. He pointed to Lizzie as he spoke about her, "And so you have here a very young child, adopted as a toddler into a family who abused her. As a teenager, she was pushed out into the mean world, no one to turn to, no where to go, jumped on a bus and ended up finally in a whore house. If that was not unfortunate enough and horrendous enough, she was paired with Mr. Richardson, a weird, psycho, sex maniac. We learned this from his sexual partner, and you have seen the doctor's reports of the fractures, broken bones, that she suffered at the hands of this gentleman.

My client, this young innocent child, scared out of her wits because of a previous bad experience; did not even know that she was going to have sex with a maniac. Thanks to the testimony of Ms. Greta, this young child should not have been sent to the room with Mr. Richardson, because everyone knew his sexual preferences. He liked to dominate his women, whip them, beat them, choke them, and whatever else turned him on. My client was desperate to stay on in that house because she had no where else to go. She decided that she would make enough money to split. She was also eager to please her madam, because she was threatened with expulsion the next time she messed up.

With this in mind, when Ms. Ellie, frantic and confused, and overwhelmed by the presence of this prominent man who came in unexpectedly and demanded to have someone service him, sent in the only person who did not know what a pervert Mr. Richardson was. Did anyone warn her of the hazards of being with him? No! No! She was just sent as a lamb to the slaughter. Well, she was not willing to be slaughtered and so she fought for her life. In doing so, while trying to protect herself, being panic stricken, she reached for something to protect herself and found the knife she had just used to pare an apple. She was protecting herself and so ladies and gentlemen of the jury you cannot in all good conscience rule any other way other than not guilty. It was pure self defense."

He walked back slowly to his seat and sat down.

Judge Richard Charlton Davis was a stern, but a fair person. Like every other judge in this town, he knew the victim. He however, could not stand abusive men, and most of all listening to the perverted way Richardson handled the whores was just too atrocious to him. It made him sick. Now this young, beautiful, child had to have the stigma of a murder rap on her name, what a shame he thought. He pounded his gavel and said, "Court is in recess for lunch. We'll meet back here at three o'clock."

Everyone got up, Joe took Sadie's arm, and they walked outside. Seff and Bessie followed. The lawyers and the family gathered into a room, while they sat talking, James came in bringing Maggie with him.

"Hi Joe, Hi Sadie" he said. Joe introduced Seff and Bessie.

"Glad to meet you," said James. "I'm sure Lizzie is happy to see some smiling faces" and he smiled. Joe took Maggie's hand and introduced her to Seff and Bessie.

"Maggie, this is your sister, Bessie and your younger brother, Seff."

Maggie smiled, but Seff reached out and took her in his arms and hugged her tightly. She was taken aback. He was a handsome young man with twinkling eyes, and a broad smile, sandy colored hair and a very fair complexion. You would have to guess that he was Black. Then Bessie looked her straight in the eyes, smiled and came forward to hug her. Maggie felt her self stiffening. This young Black girl was her sister. She did look a lot like her, but she was Black, not as black as Sadie but you can tell she was Black.

Bessie began to cry, "Oh Maggie I am so happy we found you. Now we can all be together again. Thank God."

Maggie smiled, and nodded as Bessie came forward to hug her. Maggie groaned inside, I have never really touched a Black person before, but she allowed a quick hug because all eyes had turned on her. Joe took her over to the woman in the wheelchair and said, "This is your grandmother, Maggie.

Mrs. K had been observing her and recognized herself in Maggie. She smiled to herself, and said to Maggie, "Come and visit me when you get the chance, Maggie I would like to get to know you."

Maggie jumped at the chance and said, "I certainly will. Thank you."

Mrs. K decided that whenever she could she had to set this one straight, especially where Sadie was concerned, and she was determined to let her see her evil attitude before it was too late.

CHAPTER 56

They had sandwiches brought in but somehow no one was in a mood to eat, so they chatted lightly. Before they went back into the court room, Joe got up and asked everyone to stand, "Let us pray," he said. They all joined hands forming a small circle and even Mr. Spaulding got up joined the circle between James and Maggie.

"Father God in Heaven, We come to you today, praising you and thanking you for blessings and mercy. You have restored our daughter, Maggie to us and we are grateful, we are asking for our daughter, Lizzie to also be restored to us. Please Lord; do not let her spend another day in this prison, just how you rescued Paul and Silas, we are asking for you to break the bars of this prison and set her free. She has been a victim of circumstances beyond her control. Forgive us, as parents who unknowingly made her feel uncared for, and unloved. This is your child, Lord, and we ask that you grant her the privilege of being with her family at this stage of her life. We know that there is a reason for everything that has happened and we thank you. Please grant our request, amen."

They all said, "Amen."

Maggie was amazed at her father; he was a cool guy and she liked him a lot. As they left the room, Bessie was looking at her, smiling at her, and was waiting to walk in beside her. Maggie grabbed James' arm, as Bessie turned away, but Seff grabbed her around the waist and said, "I need my big sister to take my hand" and she kissed his cheek and they held hands as they left the room. Sadie noticed the whole incident and whispered, "Thank you God for Seff."

Judge Davis sat on the bench and the jury filed in. Today was the day they would have the verdict. "Did the jury reach a verdict?" asked Judge Davis

"We have, your honor," the lead juror said.

"How say you?" asked the Judge.

"We, the jury, find the defendant, Elizabeth Edwards not guilty."

There was uproar. Joe, Sadie, Seff, Bessie hugged each other and then they tried to get to Lizzie and hugged her. They were crying and laughing. Joe, big, handsome, manly Joe was sobbing like a baby. Sadie held him in her arms and rocked him. She looked over at Seff who was doing the same with Lizzie. Lizzie was in shock. She did not know what was happening to her life. She was so confused but one thing was for sure she did not have to spend the rest of her life in prison. She did not see Teddy and Abby today at the trial and she realized how much it must have cost them to be there for her, and she was sure that Teddy had extended himself and not allow Abby to spend a penny. She smiled to herself, "they were beautiful people" she thought.

* * * * *

After all the paperwork was finished for Lizzie, Sadie took control of her family and decided that Lizzie should leave Georgia. Sadie explained to her that she can go back to Alabama and stay at the house. It was hers and that she, Sadie would go back with her and get her settled, or she could stay with Sadie until she decided what to do. Lizzie agreed to go to Alabama and get settled once and for all.

Everyone took off and went to Alabama with Lizzie, except Maggie. Joe stayed a couple of days and then left to go back to work and to his family. Sadie and her children sat and talked night after night, they got to know each other well. Lizzie decided she wanted her real name back, "Elizabeth Edwards has murderer on her name; she had a very hard and miserable life, I want to bury her and start over using my real name."

Seff assisted Lizzie in changing her name back to Betty Lou Kettering. Betty Lou was a little scared of Sadie and she still blamed her for leaving her behind; but Sadie was proving very hard to dislike, however, she could not call her "mother," at least, not yet. Nevertheless, she called Joe, "daddy." She loved her daddy, he was tall and handsome and he loved her dearly for the right reason. She did not have to prove anything to him and she was not afraid of him. As a matter fact, she felt very comfortable with him. In her young life, the men she dealt with were scum and she knew the difference when she looked at Seff and Joe. These were men, and were worth something. She was proud to be the sister and daughter of such great men. Her father and brother were what men were supposed to be like. They were not selfish, self-serving bastards. They were real men and they were her family. She knew she never would have any reason to be afraid of these two wonderful guys.

Bessie and Betty became close buddies very fast. Sadie caught them whispering and laughing like two young children. When asked what was going on, both said together, "nothing" and then they both burst out laughing at themselves. Later on, they were making arrangements for Gracie Anne to be christened and Betty was going to be one of the godmothers. Sadie looked at her two daughters and smiled.

Bessie and Seff left, and Sadie and Betty were alone. They went shopping for new furniture for Betty's bedroom and had it painted. She said she felt clean and never wanted to feel dirty again. Betty talked about her mother and father and wondered how they were. She wanted to see them but decided that it would have to wait until she can really forgive them for what they did to her.

Betty Lou wanted to be a nurse and so Sadie enlisted Joe and Seff to set her up for school. After all of this was done, Sadie left her and headed for home. She was in good hands with the people on Doc's estate, and everyone else was just a phone call away. Betty Lou could not wait to start her new, exciting life. Every thing had turned out just great for her, and she loved it.

CHAPTER 57

Sadie and Paul's wedding was in one week. Everything was set for the wedding and honeymoon. Maggie was the only one who had not responded to the invitation. Mrs. Ascott and Sadie had become friends and she would tell Sadie about Maggie and how she was feeling, which was always terrible. However, she had started back out to work, and that took her mind off of a lot of things. Mrs. Ascott did not like John, her boyfriend because he really was a bigot; he was brash, crude and a racist. He found out about Maggie and she was amazed that he still wanted to be seen with her. But nothing surprised Mrs. Ascott about John. He was trouble and never liked him for Maggie, but Edgar liked the young man, always saying, "Ah! Cool it Essie, that's what young men do."

She would have been amazed at what John's father was telling him. "You have a Nigger for a girlfriend, but a very rich Nigger, there's the difference. Marry her, and you've got it made. No one need know she's a Nigger. You'll have power, my boy, and enough money to do whatever you want. Don't let her get away."

Mr. Henson was thinking about his son's drug habit. John thought his father did not know about his habit but he did. Mr. Holiday could not wait to get rid of John and his nasty behavior. They were always fighting in the house and he had already threatened to kick him out. This was the chance he was looking for. He himself was in debt because of his wife's illness. He could use a little money. What a streak of luck. I hope he doesn't let her get away.

He said to John, "Yes, my son, grab her quickly before some city slicker comes to grab her up. She's worth it, yes! She's worth it."

His son was lazy and didn't like to work, so what else was he going to do? "If you have any sense you'll marry the Nigger. Ah! Hell, she's a good looking Nigger and anyhow, she can pass for white."

Mr. Holiday was laughing now, "My boy, you'll have a lot of Niggers waiting on you, left and right, so don't be a jackass; marry her as soon as you can."

John did not like the idea of marrying a Nigger but dad was right, she had a lot of money and no other way he would be making that kind of money, she was his ticket out of there.

CHAPTER 58

I t was a beautiful, Saturday afternoon, and it was Sadie's wedding day. Sadie was dressed in a beautiful off white, peau de soie, sheath dress, button hat, off-white pumps, carrying a white Bible with white carnations tied to it. She looked radiant as she walked down the aisle on the arm of Seff. Every one in the church was waiting for Seff's response when asked, "Who giveth this woman to be married?"

He replied, "This one I'm not giving away, but he can borrow her for a while, because I'll never give my mother, my queen away."

There was not a dry eye in the church. Bessie sang, "It's only the Beginning." Paul's two daughters were bridesmaids along with Bessie and Betty Lou. They looked lovely in light green/ white dresses.

Joe and his family attended the wedding. Mrs. K sent her congratulations but she had taken a turn for the worse and the doctor had advised her not to travel, but she told Sadie she would have liked to be there. She also told Sadie that Maggie had come to visit her and she spent the week telling her about racism and how it affects not only your body, and your soul, but then you miss out on all the friends and family you could have had fun with because of ignorance. I explained life to her how I know it and used myself as an example. I told her that her father never got a chance to redeem himself, but I thank God that I got the chance and whatever I can do to help some one else see the error of their evil ways, I will do it. I told her "your mother taught me how to live and love, and you will be hurting yourself if you miss out on getting to know your mother better, she's a wonderful person, take it from me. I wouldn't tell you this if I did not believe it myself. I don't know how much of it she bought; for she is a hard nut to crack, but I tried."

Sadie was happy at what she was hearing; she wondered if this was the same person she knew? It was amazing how prayer changed people. She said to Mrs. K,

"Thank you for trying, Mrs. K, I really appreciate you putting yourself on the line for me, thanks."

CHAPTER 59

Maggie flew to Boston for the wedding, but she did not want anyone to know she was there. She rented a car and was going to show up at the church and surprise them. The wedding was scheduled for four o'clock in the afternoon. She found out where the church was by taking a practice run on Friday. The church was in a Black neighborhood. She began to imagine all those Black people hanging around. Sadie was marrying a Black man. She met Paul at Lizzie's trial. He seemed nice, but he was still Black, though not as black as Sadie. She liked her sisters and Seff also her father, but Sadie was the one she had to get used to; and it was very hard to do. She reminded her so much of people she ought not to like. Good God why wasn't she White, or light skinned Black like Lizzie or even Bessie, then I could be proud of her.

On the afternoon of the wedding, Maggie got in her car and went to the church, it was after five o'clock. She parked in the parking lot which was crowded but stayed in her car contemplating whether she should come out or not. Just sit in the car and watch the bridal party from her car. She stayed as long as she could, but she could not bring herself to go into that church filled with all those Black people. She decided to go back to the hotel and call Sadie from there. Suddenly, the tears began to flow and Maggie could not contain herself. Tears were messing up her new outfit but she did not care, "Oh. God I tried, but I'm not ready."

She gunned the pedal and the car sped off; she traveled for just over two miles on the winding road; she wasn't familiar with the street and with tears running down her face, she reached for a tissue to blow her nose. As she sped down the winding road, tears were streaming down her face, and she could not focus properly on the road. As she turned the corner, she blew her nose into the tissue and for that split second lost control of her car and sped straight into the oncoming car head on. The crash was awfully loud and Maggie blacked out.

CHAPTER 60

As Sadie and Paul sat in the limousine headed for the reception, they were slowed by an accident on the way. Sadie and Paul prayed that whoever was in the accident was not badly hurt. Soon the road was cleared and they continued on their way.

Sadie and Paul left for Paris early the next morning.

In the meantime, Mrs. Ascott got a call from a hospital attendant that her daughter was in a serious car crash in Connecticut. She threw a couple of things in a bag and made arrangements for the next flight out of Georgia.

When she finally arrived at the hospital, and saw Maggie her heart sank. She was covered in bandages. "My baby, my baby" she whispered as she touched her daughter. "Don't you worry about a thing; mummy is here to take care of you."

Mrs. Ascott called Joe and told him after three days what had happened to Maggie. Joe was livid, "Why didn't you call me right away?" he asked.

"I didn't want to bother you," she replied.

"It's never a bother to see about my children," he said. "I'll take the next flight out."

When Joe arrived, Maggie was just a little bit better. She had a lot of broken bones, as a matter of fact she was plain lucky. She could have been killed in the crash. She had a lot of healing to do. Joe said he would tell Sadie just so she did not worry, also Seff and Bessie. They need to know what's going on with one another. Joe telephoned Seff and got the name of the hotel in Paris where Sadie was staying. Joe called Sadie and he got Paul. There was an awkward moment, when Paul answered the phone.

"Hi, Paul! This is so unorthodox, but Sadie will never forgive me. Maggie was in a car accident and is in the hospital"...

"Hold on Joe, here's Sadie." Sadie looked at Paul suspiciously.

"What the hell's going on?" she asked before taking the phone."

"Talk to Joe," he said.

"Hi Sadie, it seems I'm destined to be on both your honeymoons," he laughed.

"What's up Joe," she said, her heart beating faster.

"Well, I just wanted you to know that Maggie had an accident, she's alright though. It seems that she was coming to the wedding when she got into an accident. That was the accident we all saw on our way from the church to the wedding reception,"

"Oh, my God," whispered Sadie. "I have to come back."

"No!" said Joe, "If she needed you that badly I would let you know. Hang in there and enjoy your honeymoon. I will take care of things here until you get back. I just felt that you would want to know."

"You bet your life," she replied "or else, I would have been very upset if you did not let me know what was going on with anyone of my children. Thanks, Joe, say hello to Seff and Bessie for me and tell Maggie, I'll see her as soon as I get back."

Sadie sat on the bed with the phone in her hand. Paul came over and took the phone out of her hand. He put it on the hook, and held her in his arms, "You know something? I am a greedy man; one honeymoon is not enough for me; I want two."

She smiled, "You wicked thing, you."

He said, "Let's finish off our sightseeing for tomorrow and then let's leave the next morning. I'll make the arrangements."

"Are you serious?" She asked.

"Of course, I am. Do you thing if something had happened to one of my girls, I would not want to be there? Oh! Come on! Sadie, I want you to be happy." He kissed her cheek, then her neck, nestled his head between her breasts, "plus I want all your attention." They both laughed.

"Thank you, Paul for being so understanding. I'll make it up to you, I promise."

"Hey, I love you sweetie, and nothing must distract from that love, ever, plus I heard the honeymoon is better the second time around."

CHAPTER 61

When Sadie got back home, Mrs. Ascott had arranged for Maggie to be transferred to the hospital in Georgia. Sadie called Mrs. Ascott and made arrangements for a hotel near the hospital. When she went to see Maggie, Mrs. Ascott was seated by her bedside. She got up and welcomed Sadie, "Congratulations, my dear, I'm so sorry you had to cut your honeymoon short."

"That's o.k., I'm just sorry that Maggie had to be so broken up over my wedding," and she and Mrs. Ascott laughed. Maggie was silent.

She stared at Sadie as if to say," What are you doing here? My mother is here looking after me. I do not need you. Sadie looked her right in the eyes and said, "I'm sorry that you got into an accident. It must have been horrible for you."

"Thanks" said Maggie. "But you didn't have to rush back."

She turned to Mrs. Ascott, "What are the doctors saying about her condition?"

"Well, they have not said much to me" she replied.

"Did you ask them?" asked Sadie.

"Not really."

Sadie excused herself and went in search of the doctor. She was told that he was making his rounds. Sadie asked to speak with him when he was finished. Sadie was happy with her new confidence and how she was no longer afraid of White people. They were just ordinary people like her. To hell with the White skin; and she smiled to herself.

Dr. Allen Blessinger, a pudgy looking, slightly bald, middle aged man came into the room, walked right over to Mrs. Ascott and said, "You wanted me?"

Sadie walked over to him, and put her hand out, "my name is Mrs. Thomas. I am the one who wanted to find out about Maggie's condition."

He looked at her and then at Mrs. Ascott. Mrs. Ascott looked at Sadie and said nothing. He did not know what was gong on, but it seemed that Mrs. Ascott had given this woman permission to talk about her daughter.

"Well," he said, "May we go outside?" Once outside he said, "She's got a broken pelvis, many fractures, bruises, but we are taking tests because we are worried about her kidneys. It seems that she had been suffering a while and no one paid any attention to it. She is scheduled for dialysis as soon as we get the final results."

"What else could be done for her if dialysis does not work?"

"A transplant," he said looking at his hands. "One kidney is all she needs."

"Well, let's check out the members of her family first."

"Whoa! Whoa! It takes time, scheduling and personnel. It's not something that can be rushed; there are lots of tests and matches to be done..."

"You do what you have to do and I will line up whoever we can for testing." Then he asked, "And who are you?"

Sadie looked him right in the eye and stood tall and said, "I am her biological mother," then walked out of the room and returned to Maggie and Mrs. Ascott who was brushing Maggie's hair and singing to her.

Sadie looked at her daughter lying in the hospital bed all broken up, and prayed silently to God to save her. Maggie is so tormented that you could see it oozing out of her. Her children had suffered because of her. Why should they suffer? Joe and she had loved each other; they meant no harm to come to anyone. Here was Maggie; she was suffering because she tried to come to Sadie's wedding. She did care and was coming to the wedding after all. It meant something to Sadie. She had to call Joe and inform him of what was going on.

Joe was flabbergasted at the news, "Oh My God, what next?" he exclaimed.

"I know!" answered Sadie. "Well, there's not much we can do

other than have those who might be willing to give her a kidney be tested."

"Put my name down and let me know when; I'm available whenever it is possible. Hang in there Sadie; I'll be there as soon as I can get away."

"Thanks Joe"

After making some more phone calls, Sadie went back into the room and she decided to tell Mrs. Ascott and Maggie what the doctor had told her. Maggie began to cry and Sadie ached to put her arms around her and soothe her fears, but Mrs. Ascott was there treating her like a baby and comforting her.

Sadie continued, "The good news is, I have Joe, Seff, Bessie and myself to be tested to see if we match. I haven't talked to Lizzie yet, but if they find a match we are willing to give a kidney to you."

Maggie cried harder and bent her head down. She felt good that there were people willing to give up a kidney for her. Daddy would have done it, but she did not hear her mother offering to be tested.

That made her a little sad, but then she thought that her mother never did too much without daddy backing her. She was glad Sadie was here because she kept asking the nurses questions as they came in to tend to her. She was very knowledgeable about medical procedures, etc. Maggie was impressed. This was no ignorant Black woman. She knew what she wanted and went after it. Now when the doctor or nurse came into the room they addressed Sadie directly.

Sadie told Mrs. Ascott that it didn't make sense for both of them to be with Maggie; that they should take turns. One day, Maggie in conversation with Sadie asked her "How come you know so much about medicine?"

"Did you forget I lived with Doc? I also tended to him before he passed on and I also took care of your grandmother. I ask questions to find out what I need to do." Sadie looked deeply into Maggie's eyes and said, "I remember a little girl who was two years old, she used to walk around with me asking so many questions," and she looked at Maggie with a wicked twinkle in her eye, "this little girl never gave up until she got all the answers she needed, let me tell you this, sometimes I wished she would go away and not ask so many questions."

Sadie smiled as Maggie laughed softly. This woman was wearing her down, she was beginning to like her; she already admired her for her strength which her own mother was lacking. She reminded her of daddy.

"What else did she do?" Maggie asked smiling.

Sadie took her hand in hers, "Well, let me see... I remember her taking care of her younger sisters, always being helpful and attentive, wanting to do everything I was doing, so wherever I went, she accompanied me; and whatever I did, she wanted to do. We had lots of fun together."

Sadie laughed, "I remember when I taught Betty and Wendy their songs that you were annoyed and wanted your own song and you said indignantly, "I first, I sing first."

'You did not want to give up your rank of being the first born. You followed me around like a lost puppy, and loved to have your boo-boos kissed."

Here was that word again. "Where did I get that word from?"

"Boo-boo?" asked Sadie.

"Yes, I seem to hear it spoken but do not know much about it."

Sadie told her the story of how she fell and she offered to kiss her boo-boo. She told herself I knew it came from her, and for a moment, just a brief moment Maggie felt like a little girl again and Sadie was her mother. She had to take the images Sadie was putting in her head away. She knew exactly what Sadie was doing. Maggie drifted off, "Was that what I am doing now, want to have my boo-boos kissed only now it was my kidneys. Good Lord! What a mess. Sadie's voice brought her back,

"You always showed me how much you loved me," and here Sadie looked at her. "You would spread your arms wide and say to me, 'Mummy, I love you this much' and you said it so often in the day that now I look back and thank God that you said it so many times."

Sadie looked her straight in the eyes, and continued, "Because now it made up for your not being able to love me now. There was so much love in you then that you had to give it to me every chance you got. I appreciate that now. At the time it was a little annoying," she smiled, "but God always knows best."

Maggie withdrew her hand slowly from Sadie's and turned her back to her. Sadie relaxed and sat back in her chair, she did not see the silent tears stream down Maggie's cheeks. Maggie fell asleep, but before she did, she realized that she could close her eyes and see Sadie differently; she wasn't so black, she wasn't one of the people daddy hated, and if daddy were alive he would change his mind about Black people, especially Sadie, I know he would; she reasoned. With her eyes closed, she just heard her voice and she could put any color to the voice, it never was black. Here was a very beautiful, intelligent and sophisticated woman and she was her mother; however, whenever she opened her eyes, reality returned. Sadie was a very Black woman, and there was no escaping it.

CHAPTER 62

After testing, it was found that Sadie was a perfect match for Maggie's kidney. Although Sadie was scared of the operation, she decided to do it. Joe and Paul said they would be there for them. It was decided that since the best thing would be the transplant that they should go ahead and schedule it.

Sadie was terrified, but she knew she had to give her daughter a chance. Mrs. Ascott came over to her before the operation and said, "Thank you so much for helping Maggie; I do not know what I would have done without you, Sadie."

"Not to worry, just pray everything turns out alright," said Sadie.

"I certainly will," said Mrs. Ascott.

Seff, Bessie and Lizzie came that weekend as well as Joe and Paul. Sadie and Maggie had gone through the operation, and it was successful. They were both doing marvelously well.

As they recuperated together, they talked more and more about when Maggie was two years old. Everything seemed fine until young John came to see Maggie. He showed Sadie no respect and completely ignored her. One day as Joe was visiting; he came over to Joe and with outstretched hand said, "Hi, Mr. Kettering, my name is John Holiday."

Joe shook his hand and they began to talk. During the conversation, Joe detected what John was really like and he did not like it at all. Joe was saying, "I'm so glad Sadie was able to give Maggie a kidney. We were really blessed."

"Ah! Well. It's really no big deal. No offence but those people can endure anything."

"What do you mean by those people?" Joe eyed his suspiciously.

"You know what I mean? Niggers;" he whispered.

Joe jumped on him so fast and held him by the scruff of the neck pinning him against the wall. "Who the hell are you calling a Nigger? You little punk! Tell me who you calling a Nigger?"

"Stop, Daddy! Stop! Put him down, please," cried Maggie and she began to sob. "Please let him go."

Joe let him down and told him, "Get to hell out of here and don't let me see your ugly face around here again."

"Screw you, Nigger lover," shouted John and he scrambled his way down the hall.

Joe went to the nursing desk and told them never to give him entrance to Maggie's room ever. Sadie lay on her bed and smiled to herself. Maggie lay sobbing. When Joe came back Maggie said, "Why did you have to hit him?"

"I did not hit him and I am not going to let any of your damm people call your mother a Nigger, do you understand me?" He went over to her bed and stood over her. "There are no Niggers in this family. Think about it Maggie. No Niggers! We are what we are. Your mother, you and your sisters and brother are not Niggers; I will not allow anyone to disrespect my wife or children. Do I make myself clear?" His face was so near hers she cringed in fear.

Sadie whispered, "Joe, Joe, it's alright."

"No it's not alright. I don't want her or any of her scum friends calling you or anyone in this family Niggers. Even if she's my daughter; she's addressing herself when she allows it. I'm telling you I would have punched his teeth to the back of his head, if he didn't leave here."

"I'm sorry, daddy" she said. Sadie smiled to herself, this is the second time she called Joe, "daddy."

Joe walked out of the room to calm himself down. He passed Mrs. Ascott in the hall. She spoke to him and he just grunted. She wondered what was wrong and hurried in to see Maggie. Maggie was sobbing.

She hurried over, "What's wrong, darling? Tell me? What happened?"

Maggie began to sob harder. Mrs. Ascott looked over at Sadie. Sadie just shrugged her shoulders and then closed her eyes. She did not feel like being bothered with any of this.

All she wanted to do was get well and get out of this hospital. She was soon released and headed home to Paul. She had neglected her husband long enough. Maggie would be released soon.

When Maggie went home while recuperating she realized she missed Sadie more than anyone else. Sadie had told her so much about herself, her sisters, and her life with Doc that she felt as if she had grown up with Sadie.

James came by and it seemed he talked with her mother more than he talked with her. Mom liked him more than she liked John. Maggie reasoned that she was not going to let James into her life now. He deserved better.

One night while she was doing her exercises, James came again to visit. He had tried calling her but she never returned any of his calls. He pleaded with Maggie to talk to him and not shut him out like she was doing. She stated bluntly, "my life is in shambles now; I do not want to mess up your life as well."

"You cannot mess up my life. I love you, I do not care what you are; I love you, Maggie Ascott. I want you to be my wife. Please do not do this to us Maggie."

"I can't think straight now, please leave me alone and it would be better if you don't come back. Whatever is wrong with you? Do you want to marry a Black woman? Can you stand having people stare at you because you are White and sporting a Black wife?" she cried.

"Good gracious, Maggie come off it; look yourself in the mirror and come up with another excuse; if you don't want to be bothered just let me know."

He turned and walked out of her life.

CHAPTER 63

Maggie decided to call Sadie. Sadie was happy and surprised to hear from Maggie. "Hi, Sadie, how are you doing?"

"Why, I'm doing mighty fine. How about you?"

Maggie thought to herself. Sadie even sounded Caucasian over the phone. She did not speak like the Blacks she knew.

"I'm o.k." she replied.

"You sound down, what's wrong?"

"Oh! Nothing you can help me with."

"Try me; you might be surprised," Sadie replied. After being on the phone for a few minutes, Maggie had nothing much to say, so Sadie said, "I know you are a very troubled young woman, and I am asking God to help you. You must remember we serve a God who unites us; not divide us. Take care of yourself Maggie." She wanted to end with "I love you," but could not bring herself to say it.

Sadie ordered some roses and a book to be sent to Maggie. She got a call from Maggie soon afterwards. "Thanks for the flowers and book, Sadie. They're lovely."

"I'm glad you like them, which one is your favorite?"

A trick question, Maggie thought. Sadie had sent her every color rose possible. Yellow, red, pink, and white; "I love them all," said Maggie

"Good answer," said Sadie, "God made the roses and each has its own beauty, yet they are different. Now some people prefer pink roses, and that's fine while others prefer red, but there is no reason to hate the white or yellow rose. Do you understand, Maggie?"

"Yes, I do. I'm sorry if I made you feel uncomfortable."

"No, you didn't; at least not for my sake," Sadie replied and then she continued to speak.

"We serve a God who is bigger than racism. He doesn't want to divide his people, but to bring us together. He wants unity among his children, not division. We have to show God we love Him and His children of every color. God is bigger than you and me. We are one racially, emotionally, physically and spiritually in God's sight. He loves us.

I look back at my life and see that I had given birth to three beautiful girls of different colors, but they are of one mother and father and therefore one heritage. They are all different, yet your father and I love you all, every one of you. We love you and always will."

Sadie realized that she had gotten on her soap box with this young lady again, so she decided to say goodbye, before she said something she would later regret.

Maggie said, "I really don't want to make you uncomfortable around me,"

Sadie felt as if she were dismissing her again, and was about to say goodbye when Maggie said,

"I'm sorry that I can't love you the way you want, I'm sorry."

Sadie felt her heart softened, and so she replied, "That's alright, I have enough love in me to last a lifetime, be good to yourself" she said affectionately, and she hung up the phone.

Maggie always seemed to feel inadequate after speaking with Sadie. Sadie seemed to always say the appropriate things; she was so damm sure of herself. Maggie used to pride herself on her assertiveness, but compared to Sadie she had to take a back seat. It seemed as if she always had to try to prove herself to Sadie. Sadie was not intimidated by her in the least; even mommy loved her and sang her praises. Maggie thought Sadie would have been all over her trying to get her to love her and be her daughter, but surprisingly, she paid her no mind and that made her angry. However, everyone who knew her loved her, even Mrs. K. told Maggie a story she could not believe, yet she was Sadie's staunch supporter.

CHAPTER 64

Maggie and John decided to get married and her mother was very upset and begged her not to marry John. "Maggie, James loves you very much and you love him, why not give him a chance?"

"I don't want to talk about James. He's better off without me."

"And do you think John will make you happy? He's a racist like your father. You will not be able to have a relationship with Sadie and your siblings."

"I do not want to have a relationship with them, and don't you call daddy a racist."

"Be honest with yourself, Maggie. I loved Edgar but that was the way we were all brought up. Edgar was a member of the KKK, and he loved every moment of it. Everyone in town knew he belonged to the KKK, as well as his father before him, but they paid not attention to it. However, I have learned a lot from being around Sadie."

Maggie interrupted her; "I do not want to hear that woman's name in this house again. I'm happy she gave me her kidney and am very grateful, but she is not going to be a part of my life. John wants to marry me; he understands me, and will protect me from them."

"Yes, he will" replied her mother; he will keep you isolated and alone- what type of life is that for you?"

"It will have to do for now. I plan to find a job and continue my career, but we will move away from here."

"And how is he going to take care of you? He doesn't even have a steady job, but hangs around with the wrong kind of people making mischief. Is that what you want in a husband? Even your daddy had a steady job, and he would not have advised you to marry John now."

"I have some money now; I can use it to take care of us until he settles down."

"That's exactly what John wants - to use your money for his own means. Oh Maggie, sweetheart, I wish you can see him for what he is. He will make you miserable. Don't marry him, please."

Maggie turned and walked out of the room. Mom doesn't understand, John and daddy were all she had and John was like keeping a part of daddy alive. She had to marry him; end of discussion.

CHAPTER 65

Maggie and John had a very quiet wedding. Mrs. Ascott called Sadie and confided in her. Sadie told her to come out to visit her and to get away from the situation. She protested, but Sadie told her, "You have gone through too much in so short a time; you need to get away for a while. You are so welcome to stay here with us. Let us be able to catch up on things. I really would love to have you."

"Oh, I don't know," she protested.

"I'll make the arrangements when you let me know when a good time is for you."

Two weeks later Mrs. Ascott was at Sadie's. They had a wonderful time together. Sadie took her to the bookstore, then to her volunteer job at the hospital in the geriatric ward where she helped feed the elderly, comb their hair, take them out to the garden and read to them. Mrs. Ascott forgot all her problems when she was with Sadie.

"Sadie," she said, "slow down, my dear, how do you do it, you make me tired just looking at you," she said smiling. "I am enjoying myself. I've been with you to distribute food in the poor areas of the state, volunteer at the hospital, and work at the bookstore and still take care of your garden, your husband and his two beautiful daughters. You are just wonderful, Sadie; and I am glad you encouraged me to come stay with your family. I am having a wonderful time"

"I am truly blessed, and we enjoy having you," replied Sadie.

"Sadie, this is a whole new world to me. I never hung around Black folks before and was scared of them. I always thought of them as low class, thieves, servants or what not, as my husband would say 'the scum of the earth.' I put all Blacks in the same category, I'm so glad to see they are people just like me, with the same needs, likes and dislikes. I enjoyed the members of your church; they were so warm towards me; they made me feel so welcome. I will never forget this wonderful experience you have given to me."

"I'm glad you had this experience because it will enrich your life fully, goodbye, Essie;" and she and Sadie embraced before she boarded her plane for home.

CHAPTER 66

Maggie and John arranged to move into Doc's house. Lizzie called Sadie and told her what was happening. It was o.k. because the house was big enough for them to live together and yet be separate. Since she was entitled to the house with Lizzie there was nothing anyone could do.

John was in his element. He liked the fact that there were servants on the place and that they were so eager and willing to serve him. Maggie was there to tend to his sexual and financial needs. He bought himself a truck and some new clothes. He was riding high on the horse. This was living. He was happy. He just wished he could have gotten over the fact that Maggie, his wife was Black. When Maggie told him she was pregnant he told her to get rid of it.

"What? Why should I get rid of our baby?"

"You know exactly why; I do not want any Nigger children. Suppose the child comes out Black what will we do. We cannot take that chance, honey."

He tried putting his arms around her but she brushed him away.

"You'd better think again because I am not getting rid of my child."

"Who are you pushing, Nigger?" and he pulled his hand back and slapped her hard across the face. It stung Maggie and she ran from the room crying.

"Teach you who is boss around here."

Maggie was devastated. She had gone through so much to have this baby. The difficulty came because of her transplant. She had to be under doctors' care for the rest of her pregnancy.

She felt she needed someone to love her, and whom she could love without reservations, and this child she felt would be the answer; so to hell with John and his racist attitude. This was her child and no one was going to tell her different.

Maggie gives birth to a beautiful baby boy, David Edgar Holliday. David was a little cherry faced, cute little boy; he had reddish blonde hair and hazel eyes. He was gorgeous. She decided to name him after Doc.who had left her a home and some money to help herself, and Edgar after her beloved father.

Ms. Ellie and the other servants that Doc had paid to stay on in the home were very helpful to Maggie. Essie came and spent two weeks. Sadie stayed away and sent her flowers and spoke congratulations to her as well as Joe and the children.

When Essie returned home she called Sadie right away. "Sadie, how are you doing?" asked Essie."

"Fine and how are you? How are Maggie and the baby?"

"He's just beautiful, but Sadie, she's not happy. I know they've been fighting. He's nothing but a racist. He's worse than her father. He doesn't love Maggie and he would not even look at the baby. He told me he made sure the baby didn't look Black so people can condemn him. It's all about him and how he feels. He has no compassion for Maggie and the baby. What am I going to do, Sadie?"

"There's nothing you can do other than pray for them all."

CHAPTER 67

Betty Lou spent most of her time at school. When she got a break, she spent it with Bessie and her husband, David. They were a great couple and she loved her little niece, Gracie. She took her shopping and she and Bessie were quarrelling about Betty Lou spoiling Gracie.

"Gracie has everyone spoiling her, her grandparents, grandma Kellerman, uncle Seff and now you. Then you all go away and I have to bring her back down to earth." They laughed. Betty Lou loved being with Bessie; she had a gentle spirit; David was clearly a loving husband and father. Bessie tried introducing her to every single soldier she knew but Betty Lou was not interested.

"I'm just going to study for now. I enjoy it, I just want to finish school and start my nursing career."

Seff and Bessie were very close and so Betty Lou spoke with him every time he called to see how Bessie and her family were doing.

"Next year I am going back to school to become a teacher," said Bessie. "I had promised Auntie Grace that I would always fulfill my dreams."

"Who is Auntie Grace?" Asked Betty Lou.

"She was the most wonderful person, besides mom that I grew up with."

Bessie told Betty Lou all about Gracie and what she had done for them. "She filled in for mom whenever she could. Seff and I were like her own children. She loved us very much. She left me and Seff her home in Connecticut. Seff had bought his own home where he and Cindy are living; so as soon as David is ready we will go back to Connecticut to live in the house."

CHAPTER 68

Betty Lou invited everyone to her graduation. She also wrote her mom and dad and invited them. They did not show up; everyone else did and Betty Lou was extremely happy. Paul and Sadie, Joe and his family, Bessie and Seff were all there to help her celebrate and she was so grateful to them. She sent invitations to Abby and her husband, as well as Teddy and his wife. She didn't expect to see them, but just to let them know that she had not forgotten them. However, she was pleasantly surprised when Abby and Teddy showed up. Teddy as always hugged her and then Abby joined in. It was like old times, just the three of them together. They were all crying as everyone looked on.

Teddy was saying, "My little rascal, you done gone and tore up the schooling. A nurse! A good nurse! I know you showed them at that school that you could do it. I'm so, so proud of you, my little rascal; and he hugged her as if their world depended on that hug. They both realized this was the last time they would be so intimate.

She wished her mom and dad had come but they didn't. She did not even get a letter or card from them. It made her sad. After all that he had done to her, Betty Lou still loved her father.

Maggie was there in body but it was plain to see that she did not want to be a part of the celebration. However, little David was having the day of his life with so many people around him at the same time. He would run to Sadie and then to Joe. Joe got on his knees and gave him a piggy back ride. He told the children "My poor back is aching from all the piggy back rides I used to give you guys; Doc also, God rest his soul, had given you all lots of rides, especially you, Maggie he loved you a lot."

Maggie smiled. She did not mind Doc he was white and he was a doctor plus he did leave her money to make something of herself.

CHAPTER 69

About two months after the graduation, Sadie got a call from Betty Lou. She wasn't feeling well, thought she was coming down with something and decided to take few days off from work at the hospital.

"Did you see a doctor?" asked Sadie.

"Nope! I figure some rest will do, because I was working non-stop for the past month."

"You'd better go see a doctor, and I will come and stay with you for a while so you can recuperate.

"No!" Sadie you stay there with Paul and the children; they need you more than I do."

"The kids are in college and Paul doesn't really mind. He knows I do what I feel is right for me to do and he does not refute that. I do the same for him. So make an appointment or I will make it for you, nursie."

"OK, Sadie I will."

Betty Lou had caught a virus that was going around. She needed to take care of herself and get plenty of rest. Sadie came to stay with her. They sat and talked for hours and Betty was enjoying Sadie. Sadie was full of knowledge and Betty was very interested in what she had to say, and any way it made the time go by pleasantly.

One day, Betty said to Sadie, "You are something else."

"What do you mean by that?" asked Sadie.

"Here you are, a Black woman who seems so strong, caring and compassionate, even towards those who openly rebuke you; you seem as if you do not have a care in the world; I think I get my attitude from you," at this remark, they both laughed hysterically.

Sadie took Betty's hand in hers, "I'm truly sorry for what you went through. It was horrendous. I pray that you came out of this situation a different person. I see changes in you and I know that you are still hurting. Maybe when you get a chance you should go and see your parents. Try to forgive him for what he did to you and you will be able to move on with your life."

"You really think I should go see them?" Betty asked.

"Yes," said Sadie; "Only then can healing take place; go and close out that part of your life. There might even be some friends of yours who might just want to make sure that you are alright."

"I think that's a good idea, thanks mom."

Sadie smiled and whispered, "Thank you, Jesus."

"Sadie," whispered Betty, "How did you do it?"

"Do what?"

"You know? How were able to forgive people who wronged you so badly, like my grandmother?"

"Well," smiled Sadie as she came closer to Betty and took both of her hands in hers. "It was not easy, I killed her many times and in many ways," Sadie burst out laughing, and then suddenly she became deathly serious.

"Betty Lou, let me explain it to you this way. Just imagine we're all in a boat and it capsized, everyone else is trying to hold on to something to save them; I was able to get to land and save myself. What would anybody in my situation do?" she asked Betty

Betty shrugged her shoulders, "I don't know."

"Yes, you do, you find a way to save the others in the water, and that is exactly what I did. I had so much hatred in me and it was sinking me fast, so when the Holy Spirit brought me out, I had to go back and save those in the same situation like me."

Betty Lou reached up and grabbed Sadie and hugged her tightly, "I love you Sadie, and you're not only beautiful on the outside but on the inside as well. I want to be just like you when I go up," snickered Betty Lou.

"You are even better than I am, Betty, you are your own person and you have the Holy Spirit guiding you. You cannot ask for anything else. I love you too, baby." They held on to each other for a while and then Sadie said, "Look at you trying to make me into a cry-a-baby."

* * * * *

One day, as they sat during their daily chit- chat session, Betty Lou asked Sadie, "Tell me about my grandmother."

"Mrs. K?" Sadie asked

"No, your mother," replied Betty

Sadie looked shocked and surprised, and repeated, "My mother?"

"Yes," said Betty, "You had a mother, didn't you?"

"Yes, but, I can't remember anyone asking to know about her, or even me telling the children about her. I'm pleased that you asked."

Sadie clutched at her heart as if it was beating too fast, she never ever gave her mother much thought, and she felt ashamed for not thinking or talking about her.

"Well? Tell me about her," Betty Lou said as she sat back lazily in the chair, smiling up at Sadie.

Sadie returned the smile and sat opposite Betty Lou.

"Well, let me see," she drawled, digging deep in the recesses of her mind, to see what she remembered about her mother.

"She was a very clean woman; she always had on clean clothes and a spotless apron. She worked in the Kettering's kitchen as the head cook. She was a wonderful cook, and made many delicious meals for the family. She never went to school, never learned to read or write; she was a wonderful wife, and mother. She sewed our clothes, tended to us when we were sick, better than any doctor. Sadie looked off into the distance, "I never appreciated her; she never did the things I wanted to do, and she never encouraged me to do what I wanted. She was a very practical woman, though.

Now I see her in my girls, you all have her high cheek bones, and the shape of her eyes. It seems that she lives on in you girls.

Something else about her...I remember, she woke up early every single morning and she kneeled down and she would pray to God. I would hear her asking Him to 'bless my husband, and my two girls, and keep them healthy, and safe from all harm, and God please send your angels to keep them from going the wrong way.'

When my father got a stroke and died, she was just as calm as could be. She said that God was so good; He did not allow George, my daddy to suffer for too long. She was pleased and thanked God everyday for whatever she was going through. She said it was not good not thanking God for everything, because He could do whatever he wanted to do and we could do nothing about it." Sadie smiled as she remembered her mother telling her and her sister about God.

She said God was leading me and I was following- so as long as she doesn't take the lead everything will be alright." Sadie smiled.

"I now realize what she meant; her faith in God was so strong that no one could make her stray from this thinking."

Tears filled Sadie's eyes I never knew when she died, but my sister said she died of 'sugar.' I never mourned for her either;" after a moment, Sadie said, "thank you Betty for allowing me to open up this part of my life. I just locked it away and never opened it again. I was too ashamed of the way I ran off and left them to suffer the consequences of my action; knowing full well that Mrs. K must have hounded her day and night, trying to find out if she knew anything about my whereabouts. I could imagine her telling God every morning, 'please take care of my lil gyal, and keep her covered under your wings, and I will bless you for your goodness and kindness to me and mine."

Sadie sat there and cried, while Betty Lou got up and put her arms around her mother, "Granny, we both are mourning for you, and we ask you to forgive us, Amen."

CHAPTER 70

While she was in the house Sadie hardly saw Maggie. It seemed that she was keeping far away from her.

Betty said, "I don't like John and I think he beats Maggie. It's as if she feels she has to be beaten to be loved by him. He's a creep; nothing but a country bumpkin; he doesn't even like to see me play with David. They keep him all locked up with them, and he's not allowed to play with the other children, as if he'll turn dark like the Negroes on the grounds. Mom you have to do something to help her."

"Some people you can help but sometimes they are others you just have to leave alone. Now, let me read my favorite scripture for you and then you get some rest."

CHAPTER 71

That night Sadie could not sleep and so she went into the kitchen to make a pot of tea. She made the tea and was drinking some when the kitchen door opened and Maggie entered. She did not see Sadie sitting at the corner table having some tea. Sadie spoke, "Hi, Maggie, would you like some tea?"

Maggie spun around and Sadie saw the black eye. Sadie got up and went towards her, "Oh! My God, Maggie what happened?"

Maggie tightened her robe around her and said, "It's none of your business," as she tried to walk away from Sadie.

Sadie saw red, blue, green, and yellow. She grabbed Maggie by the scruff of her neck and jacked her up against the wall. "It is my business, you pitiful little snob. You think you're somebody! You are nothing! - Because you think of yourself as a nobody. You don't love yourself so you can't love anybody. Do you think anybody wants to be in your company?"

"Well let me tell you something! Sweetheart! Nobody wants to be in your company either, not even your own husband. I see him leaving every night and watch him come in during the wee hours of the morning, just to whip your ass and spend your money."

Sadie let her down and said, "Sit down and listen to some sense, child."

Maggie sat heavily in the chair and was watching this mad woman. She was crazy, the way she lifted her up, and then put her down.

"You may call this a marriage," Sadie began, "but a marriage is a covenant between two people. We go before God, friends and family and make all those promises. Some people make them knowing darn well that they would not keep them after the first argument. That's what your marriage is like. He's using you, because he doesn't like Black people and can't stand them; so now he's taking your money and living the life he wants at your expense and you are allowing him to knock you around like a piece of filth. Well, my dear, you don't have to like me one bit. I have enough love in me for the both of us. But I'll tell you one thing....

Your father never allowed me to feel inadequate. Through him I was able to grow and mature. The only person who ever made me feel inadequate was my mother and I understand that she was scared for me and did not want me to have any illusions about living better than what she envisioned for me.

Joe on the other hand, loved me, never made me feel sorry for myself; or feel less than a human being. I was everything to him; I was his breath, his life, his everything. To him I was his favorite flower, his favorite animal, his sweetest wine; you name it, whatever he liked I was always a part of it. I felt as if I could conquer the whole, wide world when I was with your father. He made me feel loved, so I now could return that love to him totally, and then when I had you kids the love flowed. I wasn't one to be jealous of my kids. You guys were loved by everyone on the grounds and Doc loved you all. By the way, I know you were always his favorite; and believe it or not; you were the only child of mine, I repeat, the only child of mine who kept following me around saying, "mom I love you this much. You never failed to tell me how much you loved me; sometimes it was ten to twelve times a day; now look at us; you detest me because I am Black, and because of that you are in turmoil; your hatred is eating at your soul, why? Because I have done nothing to you but give you love and a chance at life, not once, but twice.

I want you to know that I was never ashamed to show my face anywhere. I could do anything I wanted and Joe would encourage me to do more. Now that I am married to Paul, he is just as wonderful as Joe. I have been blessed to have the two most wonderful men on the face of the earth to fall in love with me. Paul encourages me to 'shout,'" Sadie laughed here, "he wants me to shout to the Lord, tell Him how much you love him, Sadie. Sometimes we would both shout and then fall down laughing. We become like children when we talk to our Father, God."

"Marriage, my dear is not silence. There must be communication – that is the key. We hesitate to speak the truth. No one wants to hear the truth. We suppress our opinions and concerns because we feel it might annoy our partner. We try to please our spouse and in doing so we kill off a piece of ourselves to please our spouse. This should not be; learn to be yourself, love yourself, be proud of who you are; and what you are.

We have to love ourselves before we can give that self to someone else. We have to be in touch with our feelings and own them; we cannot give away what we don't own.

Paul also told me "love the lord and let Him be your friend, your lover, your father, your mother, your everything. Appreciate Him and thank Him and give Him gifts and always serenade Him. When you do these things you learn to do them to your spouse. I was never allowed by any of my husbands to be stifled, or abused or hit."

Sadie looked Maggie right in the eye. "You are NOT what John says you are. You are a beautiful woman of God; a great creative work of love. Love between a man and woman who knew what they wanted and went after it. We made each other happy because we were happy with ourselves.

If you want to stay in a relationship that is not working for you and your son; if you want to be abused because you think less of yourself; if this is what you want, then go for it, but I do not have any pity for you. I refuse to waste my time on someone who does not feel they are worthwhile. You are actually saying to God, "I do not like how you made me, and so I am going to let this racist bastard beat the hell out of me; and use my money. Well, then go right ahead, my wanna-be white girl, and enjoy your life."

Sadie got up from the table and left her sitting there. Maggie put her head down on the table, and started sobbing loudly, "Sadie," she cried between sobs, "I'm pregnant again."

Sadie came back into the room, and walked slowly over to Maggie and started patting her shoulders, even then Maggie stiffened;

Sadie took her hands away and said, "I guess your husband doesn't want another Black child, does he?"

"No. He's scared the child will come out dark skinned and we are taking chances; but I cannot get rid of my baby, I will not."

"Stick to your guns and if you need my help in any way, just call on me."

Maggie sighed and said, "I wish I could."

Sadie looked at her for a moment then walked out the room.

That night when she went back to her room, Maggie fell on her knees and asked God to help her sort through her life, and that she wanted the relationship she had with Him when she was young and going to church, and reading the Word. She begged God to help her, and not to leave her by herself as she had no one she could trust.

CHAPTER 72

E arly the next morning, Sadie sat outside in the garden reading her Bible. There was crispness in the air this early September morning. However, she could tell it was going to be a balmy day, all hot and humid. So she liked to get up early and smell the freshness of the morning. She was reading the book of Romans, Chapter 10, and as she came to verse 16, "how do we get faith, by listening to the Word of God," as she was reading out loud, as she usually does, Sadie heard a vehicle entering the grounds. She looked up and recognized John's pick-up.

He came out of the pick-up and Sadie could see from his ungainly gait that he was intoxicated. He stumbled many times before even reaching the first stairs. Sadie felt sick to her stomach.

Her thoughts began to run wild and at the same time her emotions got fired up. She couldn't believe her thoughts, 'this son of a bitch comes in all hours of the morning and then wants to beat up on my child!' She had to control her thoughts. 'Whoa, there, be calm; God is in control,' she reminded herself. She calmed herself down and looked up as John staggered up the stairs. Just as he was about to put his right foot on the last stair, he tripped and fell flat on his face. Sadie did not know whether to laugh or cry. She sat there for a while and then when he did not attempt to get up, she got up and tried to help him up. As she got close to him, he reeked of liquor, and smoke. She bent over him and tried to help him up.

He groaned and looked at her, "What the hell are you doing, Nigger, get away from me! I can do it!"

He tried to get up but fell right back down on his face. Sadie smiled then and was about to walk away and leave him be, when he said, "give me a hand."

Sadie turned, looked at him on the ground for a while then decided to help him up. She put her arms around his back and tried to help him to sit up. He struggled, but finally was able to lift himself up. He sat heavily down again and simply said, "Shit!"

Sadie returned to her seat, picked up her Bible, but could not read another word. She looked out straight in front of her as he sat there looking at her suspiciously.

"What are you doing out here so early?" he asked slurring his words, while he massaged his legs as if he was trying to get them working again.

"Oh, it's a good time for me to read my Bible while it is quiet," she replied

"I guess you do this often," he looked at her sadly.

"No, just whenever I feel like; I usually like to have my quiet time at night."

There was a deathly silence between them after that; each with his own thoughts.

John thought bitterly about his life and hated the fact that Sadie had to see him in this condition. This was one of the reasons he came home at this hour, because no one was usually around to see him. 'Why the hell was she up? Of all the people in the house he had to run into her. He hated himself right now for allowing this woman whom he hated for messing up his life to see him in this condition.

He got up finally and was about to go into the house, when she said, "Why do you do it?"

He turned around and said, "Excuse me?"

"You heard me! Why do you drink yourself into a stupor and then take the risk of driving home?" Sadie paused then added, "Don't you care that you could cause an accident and probably kill yourself?"

"It's none of your freaking business," he said sourly.

Sadie looked him in the eye and said quietly, but firmly "You have a family, my daughter is your wife and I have a grandchild, they are my business!"

"You keep out of our lives, you hear! We want nothing to do with you, so get out our house! Go where you belong and leave us alone."

"Don't you worry, I'll be gone soon," she replied meekly

"Not soon enough for me," he retorted.

"You're married to my daughter! You made vows! Do you know that your marriage should be pure and honorable?"

Sadie sat back and looked at him with eyes of steel, "You need to call upon God to help you with your problems, let the Holy Spirit help you to become the great young man I know you are. Please, John, get a grip on your life before it's too late."

"You make me sick," he said angrily, "you make believe that you can stand me but you can't."

"That's where you're wrong," Sadie said evenly, "My God commanded me to love you."

"Love me? Don't go quoting scriptures to me, I grew up in church and not even my parents or my pastor care what happens to me, so why should you? You hate Caucasians because of what they did to you, so don't try to fool with me."

"If you remember the scriptures well, you'll remember that Jesus challenges us to love the ones who hurt us, to bless them, and do good to them. Therefore, I would not let the enemy get the better of me. I do care about you, whether you believe it or not." Sadie smiled sweetly.

John looked at her with such disdain, laughed loudly and went into the house.

Sadie left at the end of the week, and headed back to Paul.

* * * * *

Seven months later Maggie gives birth to a little girl – Sara Jane Holliday.

Sara Jane was a pretty brunette with a cherubic face, and light brown eyes. She was the delight of her mother. Maggie was very happy with her daughter. She was even freer with this baby than with David. Betty Lou was allowed to hold Sara and bond with the children more, since John stayed away a lot from the house since the birth of his daughter.

John was angry that Maggie wanted to keep her children. Children to him were a setback and Maggie spent all her time and a lot of money buying things for the children just like her father used to do for her. He felt she was spending money foolishly. Now since her daughter was born, she was getting stingy in giving him all the money he needed and he did not like it one bit. His drinking became more intense and his friends always wanted him to buy the drinks. He always had a lot of money to spend and his friends had become accustomed to having him spend money on them. Maggie kept harping on him about when he was going to get a job. She must be crazy; she had a lot of money and she wanted him to work to take care of her and her two children.

Now this Nigger bitch had brought another baby into the world and he was not having any part of this baby thing. Plus Nadine at the bar was good in bed and much better than his wife. The things Nadine did to him made his toes curl. Maggie, compared to Nadine, was a cold fish. There was no passion in their lovemaking. The only reason he made love to her was because he felt it was his duty. It was getting far and in-between now and it seemed as if it didn't matter to Maggie at all.

He thought he loved Maggie when they were young but he realized now that he didn't. Her father used to make him feel like a man, and he knew Mr. Ascott liked him for Maggie. Now Nadine was demanding more of his time and money. She liked nice things and she should have them; she was a good looking White girl, and she made him feel great. He sat looking at the baby crawling around the floor. She was a cute little thing always laughing and bobbing her head that he could not help liking her. She was eight months now and holding on to the chairs as she tried to walk. Drool was running down her chin as she struggled to get to another chair. She was fascinating to watch. For a moment, he forgot where he was; he smiled as he looked at her, she was a determined little gal, just like her mother. He got up and picked her up in his arms for the first time since she was born. She smiled and grabbed his shirt, before he put her in her crib.

He was surprised that he loved the feel of his little girl. There was something about a baby to make you feel rejuvenated, and that's just how he felt.

Maggie loved her children, David and Sara. John had never

spent time with them so he didn't quite know his feelings. He had taken the children to his parents and they did not pay too much attention to the children, because of Maggie, he figured. He was disappointed, and deeply hurt. Yet, his father was only interested in when he can write him a check from Maggie's money. John had given them over $5,000 to fix up their home, and for his dad to buy a new truck, but they were not interested in his children. Somehow or other that hurt him, and he resolved that he would not bring them back to see his parents any more.

CHAPTER 73

etty Lou called Sadie and told her how her trip back home to see her parents had gone. She was happy she went back. Her father was very sick and her mother was taking care of him. I engaged someone to come in and help her take care of daddy. She was happy to see me and could not help asking my forgiveness. I told her I forgive them both and she seemed happy to hear that from me. We talked about their future and I told her I will send her money every month.

My old girlfriend, Abby is married and working on her second child now. She's a cook in a cafeteria and her husband is a gardener. So I arranged for Abby to own her own cook shop, a nice little cozy place where I know she will get all the best customers, because she really can cook. She makes the best steaks, barbecue ribs, and her potato salad is delicious. Her sister will help her run the place and I know she'll do fine. I told her I will help her for a few months until she can really establish herself. She said I really was a good friend, and so she'll name it, "Best Friends Restaurant."

My old boyfriend, Teddy was the hardest to help. He is such a stubborn man that I had to promise I will never talk or see him again as long as I live before he would agree to my help. Before he came to see me in jail, he had an accident that affected his eyes, and he needs an operation to correct it. The operation is very costly and naturally he could not afford it. We consulted the doctor and I will arrange to pay for the operation over a period of two years. Teddy was the boy I had intended to marry when I was young, but after everything that happened and my moving to Alabama; he fell in love with a young lady and they were married two years ago. They are very happy together, and I like her for Teddy. He deserves someone special. Everyone seems to be happy and I am so glad to see that. Teddy's wife, Jennifer is expecting their first child and they are both ecstatic. If it is a girl, she'll name her Elizabeth; however, I am going to be the godmother whatever it is. I was so happy to be able to bring some joy into the lives of the people I love.

"Thanks to you, Sadie, for helping me come to the realization that forgiveness, and compassion should be a part of my life. I love you so much for it. I feel so good when I can make someone happy."

"You're welcome, my dear," said Sadie.

"My dad and I had a long talk and he apologized for his sexual misconduct towards me, saying that he was young, stupid, and always intoxicated; he claimed that he did not know what he was doing. He asked for my forgiveness and I remember what you said, mom, and so I forgive him. I feel good about myself now. Thank you for all the help you have given me. I am glad to know I have a mother who loves me; it's just a wonderful feeling. Thanks mawma."

Sadie loved the way Betty called her 'mawma,' she had the most sensuous voice and a southern drawl that made one feel loved.

"You're welcome Betty," Sadie said, "How did your mother feel about you changing your name back to Betty?"

"She agreed with me, she said that Lizzie only had a hard and miserable life and so we buried her," she giggled. "She told me I can start afresh, or re-start with Betty Lou."

"I am so glad you had a chance to do the things you did when you got back home, God will bless you for your caring attitude, and I love you very much for it," said Sadie.

"Why don't you come and spend the rest of your time off with us. We would love to have you," said Sadie.

"I might take you up on your offer. I feel I need to get away from this house for a while," replied Betty.

CHAPTER 74

Betty and Sadie had the most wonderful time together for her last week on vacation. They bonded even better than when Sadie came to visit her. They sat up late at night and chatted, Sadie took her to the bookstore – Betty loved romance novels, and she picked out a few to read when she got back home. "Mawma," she said to Sadie one evening while they sat on the front porch; "I feel terrible."

"Why?" asked Sadie anxiously.

"Because I'm trying so hard to feel about you like I feel about Ms.Edwards; I know she's not my real mother, but I still feel as if she's my mom; why is that? I feel disloyal to her when I even think of you as my mother; do you think that feeling will go away?"

"It may not, Betty and that's alright with me. Ms. Edwards was your mother for over fourteen years – your very formative years; she taught you everything that you know, whether you think she did or not, and it is going to be very hard to throw that away. Everything in your life was not bad, there must have been good times; don't dwell on the bad, think of the good and let that be your benchmark."

"But we never got along for a minute, it wasn't like we were close in any way; as a matter of fact I always thought she hated me," replied Betty.

"It doesn't matter; there is rarely a woman and her daughter who get along well for too long; especially when the child reaches teenage; deep in your heart she is still your mother; just continue to love her as much as you can; it would not hurt anybody. Love overflows – it can go from breast to breast and some; so don't let it bother you on my account. Just love me as much as you're able to and let it be, o.k.?"

238

Betty reached over and hugged Sadie hard; "I admire and love you more each time we're together. I'm so glad you found me; I still want to hate you and Bessie for leaving me behind, but Bessie is such a sweet child, I can't help but love her."

"Listen to you, 'she's such a sweet child,' what do you think you are, nothing but a child yourself," smiled Sadie and reached over to hug her daughter.

Betty Lou returned home and felt rejuvenated when she started to work. She was so glad to get away and rest up. She enjoyed Sadie and Paul so much and she even had fun with her step sisters, when they came home on the weekend. They got along marvelously well with Sadie. Betty Lou was glad for that. However, when she got back home things were very different. Maggie and John were at it again. It seemed Sara did not bring them any happiness at all. John was always drunk and was doing heroin. Betty Lou was worried about Maggie because she just locked herself away, and kept to herself.

CHAPTER 75

One night, John came in all drugged up and tried to make love to Maggie. They had been quarreling all week. She was not about to let him touch her. He disgusted her, he never intended to get a job, and was using up all her money as if there was no end to his needs. He slapped her when she told him to leave her alone. This was getting to be too much for her; he was always trying to hurt her, and the reason she felt was because she had the children. He didn't mind her, but he was scared down the line that the children would become Black. He was so ignorant, she wondered now what the hell did she see in him. She thought of James now, and how she had given him up to be with this bigot. She smiled to herself; imagine I am thinking like this.

"Daddy, oh daddy, what have you done to my mind," she whispered with great trepidation and remorse.

John came back into the bedroom and he was swaying in his drunken stupor. "Maggie when I ask you for sex, you better give it to me without question; and never, ever, say 'no' to me; do you understand?"

"You disgust me," she said and turned her back to him.

It seemed as if a fire was burning in Maggie, she swung around angrily. With one knee on the bed and balancing on her hands as she spread them on the bed, she practically screamed at him. "My mother told me that I should stop you from using all my money. I was a fool to think you understood me, and my feelings, you don't care for me, or, the children. My mother told me that I was living a lie, and that I should get real."

"Since when does your mother do all this talking with you, she never did talk to you that much anyway, only your father," said John.

"I said my mother! Not Mrs. Ascott! I mean Sadie. She's my

240

mother you know, yes, she's my mother and you know something else, I admire her, I think she's one first class woman. That woman has spunk, she has strength, and integrity, she has whatever it takes, and most of all she's got love. Something you don't have in any bone in your puny body."

"Why you little bitch, you dare talk about me in the same breath as that Nigger?"

"You forget that Nigger is my mother, yes, that Nigger is my mother, you hear me, my mother," and she shouted as loud as she could and finally she felt free, free, she began to laugh. She lay back down on the bed and began to laugh hysterically. He saw red, he put his knees on the bed and grabbed her to turn her over; she resisted, and he swung at her hitting her in the face and he kept on swinging. She sat up and picked up the bedside lamp and threw it at him; it stunned him and he was shocked. He looked at the blood streaming down his face, as the lamp cut him on the forehead. She had never raised her hand to him.

"What the hell? You stupid Nigger bitch, you dare raise your hand to me, I will show you who is boss in this house."

He left the room and came back in a terrible rage, this time he had a gun in his hand, she was acting crazy, she was still laughing and screaming to the top of her voice, "Yes, she's my mother and I love her this much," she yelled, at the same time she opened her arms and spread them wide, "Yes, this much," she said; he pointed the gun straight at Maggie and before she could say another word, he fired the gun three times, one straight between the eyes, and the rest into her body. He then dropped the gun to the floor and fell on his knees and began to weep. He was hurting, but he knew he had done something terrible. He had to leave but he was bleeding so terrible that he was afraid he would bleed to death.

"Oh my God, what have I done? What have I done?" He buried his head in the rumpled sheet which he pulled off the bed and wrapped it around his head. He got up and headed for the door. Once outside he got into his truck and drove off.

The next morning, when Betty Lou was having her coffee and reading the newspaper, Ms. Ellie came running into the kitchen, "Betty Lou! Betty Lou! Oh, my God! Come quickly!" Tears were streaming down her face and she was frantic.

"What's the matter?" asked Betty Lou

"It's Maggie, she's dead," Ms. Ellie replied

"What? Are you crazy?" asked Betty Lou

"No! I wish I was. There is blood all over the bedroom and she's as stiff as a board."

"Where are the children?" Asked Betty Lou.

"They are alright, I checked their room, and they are fine," replied Ms. Ellie.

Betty Lou followed Ms. Ellie into Maggie's quarters and felt faint when she surveyed the scene.

Maggie was lying on her back with her arms stretched out wide and her face a bloody mess. Betty could not take any more and ran from the room screaming.

"It's that bastard, John, he did it. We have to call the police. Oh God, her knees felt weak. She had seen so many dead people in her line of work, but this one brought back memories of the scene with Mr. Richardson, the cops, Ms. Greta, and she could not deal with it. She asked Ms. Ellie, "Please call the cops, and then call Sadie and Joe."

As they took Maggie's body away, draped in a black bag, Betty sat in a chair hugging herself and while rocking back and forth, she whispered, "I killed her! Oh my God! I killed her" repeatedly. Her stomach felt weak, her feet were like jelly, she could not stand up, and her eyes could not focus.

"Why is this happening again?" She asked herself, "Oh God Why? Why?"

The police officers were there asking Ms. Ellie questions, then they came over to her and asked her name. "I'm not going back to jail." She whispered, she looked up at him and said, "I don't know, I don't know, I don't know," she repeated over and over again. The other officer said, "We have enough from the housekeeper; she's in shock, leave her alone. We can always come back later." And they left her alone. Betty watched as the police bombarded the house and were securing evidence from the bedroom. She got up slowly and went to her bedroom and locked the door. She knew Ms. Ellie could handle everything.

CHAPTER 76

John did not know where to go, and then he decided to go to Nadine's home, maybe she could tell him what to do. He got to her place and woke her up; she let him in and asked, "What happened to you, you're bleeding?"

"My wife hit me with a lamp and busted my forehead," he replied

"What the hell did you do to her?" she asked

"What do you think I did, I shot the Nigger right between the eyes, that's what I did. No upstanding White man is going to take no shit from his Nigger wife."

"Are you telling the truth? Did you shoot her? Is she dead?" Asked Nadine frantically.

"I sure did," and then he passed out right there on her couch. Nadine was scared; if he had killed his wife she wanted nothing to do with murder, after all, he was good for the money but her life was not worth going to jail as an accessory to any murder conviction.

She called the cops and told them what he had told her and they said they would check it out and get back to her.

CHAPTER 77

S adie called Essie and told her what had happened. She was crying so hard on the phone that Sadie told her she would arrange for her to fly to Alabama. She thanked Sadie between sobs and then hung up the phone.

At the funeral, James was there and he covered the story for his local paper. He was crying unashamedly. Betty Lou was overwhelmed and Sadie had to hold her and console her. She felt as if she was going through the murder scene all over again. Sadie surveyed the scene and looked at everyone who was there, she saw Seff, his wife and children; Bessie, David and their two children, Joe, Sarah, and their children; Mrs. Ascott, Mrs. K who came in her wheelchair, and Paul, and his daughters. John's parents did not attend the funeral.

It was a very solemn and serious ceremony and the minister prayed for the soul of John whom he said was in such torment that he was under suicide watch. He told the reporter he loved his wife and children dearly but clearly did not know how to show that love and since he was under the influence of heroin it got the better of him.

Joe's head was bent and Sadie could actually hear his thoughts. "I should have killed that punk in the hospital and then this would not have happened."

"Poor Joe, he was so naive in a sense, he would not hurt anyone and could not see why these things happen in the world." Sadie sat with her thoughts rolling over in her head, she played back the tape of Maggie as a little girl, following her, and saying 'I love you mommy' also how Maggie always wanted her boo-boos kissed. Sadie smiled.

As they were viewing the body, Sadie suddenly and impulsively bent over and kissed the mark on her daughter's forehead, it was her boo-boo and she kissed it for the last time. In her mind, she saw Maggie smiling and saying, 'Thank you mommy, I love you this much and she extended her arms to show Sadie how much she loved her. Sadie looked at the body again and it seemed as if there was peace on her face. "Praise God" she whispered.

Mrs. K was crying softly and as Sadie came over to console her she kept saying, "I killed her, I killed her."

Sadie said, "hush, you did no such thing."

"Yes, I did, if I did not interfere in your life your children would have all been normal children living the good life."

"In your wildest dreams!" replied Sadie, "everything happens for a reason and only God is in control of our lives; we have no control, but we make choices. Maggie chose to marry John. Now, what did you have to do with that? We just have to praise God and give him the glory for everything that happens in our lives. He lets us go through, so that we can become strong, only then can we turn around and help encourage others who are going through the same things we have gone through."

Sadie pointed a finger at her, "you have no such power, so don't flatter yourself. That power belongs to God. No doubt, you allowed the enemy to use you; you choose to do evil, but God turned it out for our own good. Do you know months after the fire occurred, I was about to come after you and really murder you, now that would have been murder."

Sadie got up, patted her on the back, and kissed her cheek, "Don't you worry about a thing, just enjoy the rest of your life."

Neither of them knew that was the last time they would see each other alive.

CHAPTER 78

Betty Lou called Sadie, "Mawma, I have some good news, I persuaded Essie to come live with us and help me take care of the children. She didn't want to come, but I persuaded her that I needed her as much as the children. I told her Maggie would have wanted it this way. So she came and we are going to arrange for her to sell her house and settle here permanently. The children are happy to have her and I'm sure Maggie is resting in peace knowing we are taking care of her children. Oh, mom I miss her so much and we never even got along much, but she was there for me all during my trial and she was fighting for me as much as she could."

"I know dear, I know you and Essie will do a good job with the children," Sadie said encouragingly.

I will adopt the children so that John's family would not have a hold on them, or their inheritance."

"You have made some wise decisions, Betty, however, I want to hear more about you and Daniel, you know that handsome young intern? It's all nice to take care of others but never forget to take care of your own needs too, do you understand?"

"Yes ma'am," she replied.

"I will love to have Essie and the children here for the summer, and that will give you a chance to spend time with that young man of yours without any interruptions."

"Yes, ma'am" smiled Betty Lou.

"Sadie?"

"Yes, my dear, what is it?"

"I want you to know that I found this little agency, within the hospital compound that really work for young people, and I volunteer to work with them."

"What type of agency is it?"

"Well, they have a rape crisis hotline, teen pregnancy and sexual abuse counseling. Mawma when I had my first counseling session with one of the girls that was raped by her step-brother, I felt sick to my stomach. She was only eleven. When her mother found out what was going on she left the home to protect her daughter. After they left, I cried, and cried. I cried for her, for myself and for every other young child out there being abused. I have no more crying in me now."

"Oh, baby! I know how you felt but those young people are blessed to have you as a counselor, you understand what they have been through and you can lead them to a better life. God has really brought you a long way."

"Yes, He has and I am so grateful for what He's done and will never forget to thank Him as long as I live," Betty Lou replied.

"Alright now, let me get Essie on the phone to talk to you, bye Mawma."

Betty Lou put Essie on the phone to talk to Sadie'

"It's so wonderful of Betty Lou to ask me to be here, Sadie, I am really enjoying my grandchildren."

Sadie felt a little twinge, 'My grandchildren' and she found the old Sadie rising up again, but instead she turned her head upwards and said, "Thank you, Jesus."

As if she heard Sadie's thoughts, Essie corrected, "I mean our grandchildren, sorry Sadie."

"Oh, it's alright," replied Sadie. "I'm so glad you are there with Betty Lou because she sure can use the help."

"Do you want to hear something strange?" asked Essie.

"Uh huh" replied Sadie

"Well, yesterday I was out in the garden, just sitting and reading the newspaper when all of a sudden I remember something Maggie said to me when she was here and investigating Betty Lou's background."

"What did she say?" asked Sadie.

"She called home and while talking to me she said, 'Mom, I can see you in this garden sitting and enjoying the rest of your life here,' or something to that effect. Now I'm sitting right here and I intend to spend the rest of my life enjoying the scenery. Isn't that weird?'

"Not at all, even way back then her spirit showed her what was for you. Now you know that you made the right decision in moving there."

After some chit-chat they said their goodbyes and hung up the phone.

CHAPTER 79

Three months later Sadie got the news that Mrs. K had died. Sadie was summoned for the reading of her will, and was literally shocked to find out that Mrs. K left a small fortune for her. Sadie was pleased. She also left a letter which was read by the lawyers before everyone then it was given to Sadie.

In her letter she stated, "I took her life, her children's lives, and the man she loved. No amount of money can make up for it. Sadie had the sense to find God and come back to share Him with me and for that I am grateful. No one cared for me like she did. No one took the time to show me compassion. She understands forgiveness because she allowed the Holy Spirit to rule her life and not let her emotions control her like I did. I now understand why Joe loved her the way he did. I fell in love with her myself and with her God. I prayed for you all and I know God has answered my prayers. Make God the Master of your life, love Him with all your heart, and soul and then, only then, you will be able to treat others as they need to be treated. I love you all, and ask your forgiveness for anything that I have done to you, and Lord knows I have done plenty. God has forgiven me, and I hope you will too. I am no longer miserable but happy and content.

Sadie left that house for the last time with her head up high, not through the back door, not as a housemaid, not as a runaway, but as a wonderful, loving, rich, Black spirit. She could not wait to get back home to Paul. She knew he was waiting for her.

Before she got into the car, Joe caught up with her. He took her in his arms and kissed her lightly. He held her off and said, "Our son calls you Duchess, and I think I like it. Sadie you will always be my bride, every time I see a doorway I still imagine I'm carrying you over the threshold. Do you remember how much fun we used to have? Those were the happiest days of my life. I remember...."

She put a finger over his lips, "shhh...that's over with. We could never relive the past." Let's just live for the present. I will always have a special place in my heart for you and you for me. I know what's done is done and we have to move on. You now have a lovely wife and children and it is not good for her that you think of the past. I have Paul and so I have also a fresh start." They embraced once more and then she was gone.

Sadie used the money to help her sister, Janie and her family, invested in the school, donated some to a Heart Association, and split the rest among the children.

Lucy, Joe's sister tried her best to protest the last will of her mother; telling everyone that her mother hated Black people and most of all Sadie; so why should she leave most of her money to Sadie, a person she hated with all her heart. But Mrs. K, figured that some thing like this would happen and had her lawyers prepare to show that everything she did was ironclad and could not be changed for any reason, whatsoever.

Lucy soon found out she was fighting a losing battle and give up the fight. She resigned herself to the fact that her mother must have been brain washed by Sadie, while Sadie was taking care of her. She could not see her mother doing what she did, although she did see some changes in her for the better and that she was getting along better with Sadie. It was hard to know that your own mother left most of her money to a Nigger woman and her children, even if the children were your own brother's children.

She was left plenty, and would not have to want for anything; her husband was an upstanding lawyer and provided well for her and her children. So she decided to relax and leave things the way they were.

CHAPTER 80

Sadie did not go to John's trial; however she went to the sentencing. She was happy that she went. John took the stand and began to explain Maggie's strange behavior, he said, "She had gone crazy, she kept saying 'my mother, meaning her Nigger mother and she knew I did not like that woman,

'Yes,' she said, my mother loves me and I love her that much," she stretched her hands way out to show me how much she loved her mother, and then she laughed in my face. I couldn't deal with all that so I shot her, 'bang' right between the eyes. I am so sorry, because I realize that I loved Maggie and my children in my own way, and I miss them terribly, but I was so messed up with the drugs, I couldn't see straight.

When my parents found out that she was a Negro, they turned against her but only accepted her because of her money. That confused me, and left me vulnerable, I asked God to forgive me; you know, I met Maggie in church, you know. We sang in the church choir together; he smiled as he said this, "yes, we were two birds of a feather." I really loved her and she cared for me. It really didn't matter that she was a Negro; I knew her as a Caucasian and that's what she was to me. She never turned Black."

He bowed his head and started to sob, "I'm so sorry, Maggie, so sorry, I did love you." He was sobbing so hard that the Judge ordered him to sit down and have some water. There was not a dry eye in the courtroom.

Sadie's tears were for her own reason. Maggie did remember that Sadie was her mother and she died telling John that she loved her. Her heart was thumping so hard she had to put her hand on her chest to calm it down.

Sadie left the courtroom elated. So Maggie did love her. She smiled to herself. What a way to go; with arms outstretched, and at the top of her lungs, "I love you this much, Mommy." Sadie clenched her fist, lifted it up in the air, then brought it down, and yelled, "Yes! She died loving someone instead of hating them."

CHAPTER 81

About three years after John's sentencing, he was surprised when a guard came to tell him that he had a visitor. He was pleased and surprised; probably his parents had relented and come again to visit him. They had visited him twice after his sentence, and then his father complained that it was too long a drive for him. John was upset, he felt he had given him the money to buy the new pick-up he was driving; the least he could do was visit him once in a while. He soon got used to having no visitors.

He entered the visitors' area expectantly. He looked for his mom and dad and did not see them. He made his way over to the guard who told him he had a visitor, and asked, "I thought you said I had visitors, where are they"

"Visitor, and she's sitting in the corner over there," pointing to the far back of the room as he spoke.

John looked back there but could not make out who it was; he went closer and gasped, "What the hell are you doing here? You're the last person I expected to see here," he said ruefully.

"I came to see you. How are you doing, John? Sadie asked pleasantly.

"Not bad, not bad at all," he replied. "What's the problem?

"No problem at all. I came to have a little visit with you and to bring you up to date on the children. I also have some pictures; the guard is checking the envelope, then he'll give it to you."

He was happy, he longed to see or hear about his children but no one ever took the time to write him or inform him about them. His parents were not going to find out about the children because they were Black – and he realized that there was nothing he could do about that. Now, sitting in front of him was a woman he hated, but she took the time to visit him and to bring him news of his little ones.

The guard brought the pictures over to him and he was overwhelmed that tears ran down his cheeks. He did not make a move to wipe them, but inside he hated himself for being weak in front of Sadie. When he looked up she had tears on her cheeks too.

She was laughing now, and through the tears she told him about his beautiful, little girl.

"She reminds me so much of Maggie," she babbled, once while I was visiting she jumped into my lap, started to caress my cheeks and said, "I love you, Grandma, you're so pretty. Then she got up and threw her little arms around my neck, and laid her curly top upon my shoulder, and you know what John?"

"What?" he asked

"I melted, right there before my granddaughter, I cried like a baby. She wiped my tears and said, "Don't cry, cause I love you a lot, lot, lot."

John started crying all over again, just thinking about his children. He was missing out of so much in their lives. Oh, God, please forgive me," he begged and bent his head in his hands.

This woman always did something to him. He wanted to hate her but he couldn't.

She asked about prison life and how he was adapting, and promised to keep in touch with him as much as she could. He was surprised that he held a civil conversation with her without demeaning her or calling her names. It was a good visit.

Before she left, she promised him that she was going to take the children to see their grandparents soon.

"Don't bother yourself, they're not interested in them and will not accept them."

"Oh! That's okay, I want the children to know their grandparents; I'm taking them for their own sakes, not your parents'."

"Good luck to you, remember I told you so," and he gave her a weak smile.

He didn't know what to make of her visit, but he was elated. It felt good to have someone, anyone visit you. He didn't have to pretend he didn't care. Sadie saved his face this time; he wished secretly that she would come back again. He couldn't think of anyone else who would want to give him the time of day.

CHAPTER 82

Ompne day after visiting the bookstore, Sadie went for a walk. She was drawn to the little square where she used to go and sit on a bench. She smiled as she sat on the same bench she used to come and plot to kill Mrs. K. and wring her scrawny neck. She chuckled to herself as she remembered all the hate she had in her, and her plans to inflict hurt on Mrs. K. 'My, my, how times have changed- Mrs. K. had been reformed and is now in heaven with her Savior, and Sadie is the one who showed her the way. She was thankful to God for allowing her to be the one to do this. She just wanted to please God, and do His will.

She searched in her purse and found a little notebook, she took it out and wrote the date, then she wrote, Hello God, it's me again. Tomorrow is not promised to anyone, and so I am going to thank you for all that you have done for me. Just like Joseph in the Bible You had to get me away from my surroundings so that You could bless me. We both left under horrible situations, but You brought us out. Mrs. K. intended to kill me but You did not want me yet, You had too much work cut out for me, and I thank You for sparing my life. I hope I have fulfilled all Your wishes for me. I've been through the fire and the storms both with Lizzie and Maggie. I hated to bury my child, but her life was tormented by hate and racism. In the end, she turned to You for help and I know you never leave us or desert us, so I am thankful. I thank you for Mrs. K. how You turned her around and made her a much better person to everyone. I thank you for reuniting me with my sister and her family. There is still work to do, but I see the smile slowly creeping back on to her face when she sees me. I thank you for that. I thank you for putting Doc and Gracie in my life, for without them, I don't know what would have happened, but I guess you know. Now I must thank you for both my husbands, Lord, not one, but two (here Sadie laughed out loudly) wonderful men of God. What were you thinking of? I could not have asked for more. I thank you for my children and beautiful grandchildren. I have been richly blessed and I never want to appear ungrateful, so I am taking the time to write my thanks to you now. I love you lord. She signed her name, closed the book, put it back in her purse and sauntered off with a great big smile on her face. She remembered the last time she was here; now she was different, she felt liberated and free.

CHAPTER 83

I t is six years later and Sadie is standing at the mail box with a letter to be mailed to John Hopkins. She had visited him every year and planned to do so whenever she could. However, Sadie had also been corresponding with him, filling him in details of his two children and their successes. Today, she was sending another picture. He had written her back the first time she wrote him asking her to forgive him.

Sadie was finding it hard to go back to Georgia, and since Essie had to go back there, Sadie told her about her promise to John and asked Essie to take the children to see their grandparents.

Essie had reported to Sadie when she came back from Georgia what had happened when she took the two children to see John's parents. Sadie and Essie both had a good laugh when Essie told her that when John's mother saw the children she forgot what her husband had told her and hugged them so hard, they winced. Sara Jane went over to her grandfather who was sitting in his chair, trying hard to ignore them, and asked, "Can I give you a hug? It will make you smile." He could not resist a hug from such a pretty little girl. He picked her up in his arms and kissed her cheek. She was the cutest, baby girl in all the world and he fell in love instantly. Tears were running down his cheeks, and he made no move to wipe them away. Sara Jane took her hands and wiped his tears, and she said, "I'm so sorry I didn't mean to make you cry. Please don't you cry."

"Why?"

"Because I love you a lot, lot, lot."

Essie reported that Sara and her grandfather were good buddies now. On that first day, he unashamedly allowed a little Negro girl to kiss his face, while his wife and Essie looked on. He seemed a defeated but happy man.

CHAPTER 84

S adie stood with her hand on the mailbox, and smiled after imagining the scene. She was happy for the children. She was always counting her blessings.

Betty Lou had married Dr. Daniel Paige and had a four year old, boy, James; and a six month old girl, Helen, named after Sadie's mom. Sadie's heart was full. Betty had come full circle and she was a woman that Sadie loved and admired.

Sadie remembered her conversation, with Betty when Betty Lou was seven months pregnant with the second child, Sadie had asked her what names she had selected for the baby.

"If it is a girl, I'll call her Helen."

Sadie clutched her heart, 'why…that was my mother's name," Sadie said excitedly.

"I know," said Betty Lou, "Now she will live on in our little girl."

Tears were streaming down Sadie's cheeks as she looked at Betty Lou. Betty Lou opened her arms to receive her mother.

Sadie taking Betty's hands in hers, confessed to her

"Betty Lou, you have made me very proud of you. I longed for one of my children to really love me, and God answered my prayer. Don't get me wrong, Bessie and Seff loves me very much, but there is a connection between me and you; something that I can't put my finger on."

"Bessie has her Aunty Grace, and Maggie had Essie, I had always wanted a mother so badly, so when I got you, I didn't want to ever let you go. I guess when I went to live with my family, I had to give up who I was …Betty Lou. I became Elizabeth and had to bury Betty Lou fast. I never knew what was going on. I had a new family and never realized what had happened to the old one. I had to survive and do it fast, I did not know what was happening to me, and I could not ask the questions that were formed in my mind.

I decided to give them all the love I had and hoped they would return it to me – my father did, my mom did not want me, and so she tried hard to ignore me, and my brother couldn't care less. So, all I had was my father's love and I took it with all that was in me, never realizing how twisted his love was.

I think of Maggie and what she might have gone through those first years with the Ascotts. She adapted easily because they both loved her and she wanted to be loved so badly that she became all that they wanted her to be – a beautiful white princess. She must have felt she was in a dream before - because the people she loved had all disappeared as if in a cloud of smoke, 'poof' and you're gone. It must have been very confusing for her. Poor Maggie."

"I will never let you go now that I've found you, my darling."

"I want you to know I couldn't stand you when I first saw you," Betty said smiling as she remembered her jailhouse visit.

"I felt it," Sadie said. However, I'm so glad we two are so close, I just love it."

"I love it too."

CHAPTER 85

S adie was content. Seff, his wife and their two children were doing fine; Bessie, David and their two girls also were great; Paul's oldest daughter had married and the younger one was about to graduate college. Life had been good to her. She still had the book store, and went in a couple days a week to keep up with the new books sales. She didn't have to work, as she was a wealthy woman now. She lived a normal life and was always looking for ways to help young Black women to educate themselves in whatever way they wanted. She also volunteered at the hospital twice a week in the well-baby section, where she could help young mothers with their babies. Life was wonderful, and she never forgot to thank God every day for what He had done for her. He was just so wonderful to her and her family that she had to pinch herself every now and again to make sure she was not dreaming.

Before Sadie headed back to the house, she sat in a chair in her rose garden; it was a beautiful afternoon in late July, the air was dry and hot. She fanned herself with her hand as she began to think over her life. Here she was in Connecticut living as Sadie. She had decided to keep her new name, because she reasoned that Lula Mae died in that fire; and Sadie was born out of it. Sadie had a good life and a life worth living. God had a work for her to do and that is why he allowed her to have a name change, like he did with Abram and Saul.

Lula Mae could not have done the things Sadie had to do. What Mrs. K meant to be bad turned out to be good. She thought of how 'all things work together for good to them that love the Lord.' I really have to thank the Holy Spirit for being present in my life; and thank Him for using me the way He did. How he used me to bring White folks to Christ and used White folks to spread their riches to help me and children all over the world, as Sadie contributed heavily to research.

She sat in her garden and surveyed the whole scene. This was a beautiful place to be, all the flowers blend their hue, and God's world was just marvelous to survey.

She went over the midnight of her life, when she had to run to save her life and her children's. It was God's order for her to move, as He rescued her from tragedy. It was just like if she were looking at a photo album, and as she turned the pages her life spilled out before her.

"Whew! What a life," she whispered.

She turned the pages and remembered Joe and his promises, their failures in bringing up their children. They also had victories, Betty Lou being released from prison; but also the tragic death of Maggie. However, as time passed, all these unpleasant memories fade away from us and after a while, they will just become a blur. "Thank You, God, we have become unified in our strength to serve and please God.

"All the children you have given me serve You, and I thank You for that."

She sat quietly for a while, and just closed her eyes; deep in her heart she was praising God and thanking Him for her life. She started to tell God how she had appreciated all the people he put in her life, beginning from her parents, it was a roller-coaster life but nonetheless, a life that grew from humble beginnings to a life of substantial wealth. Help me to use this gift in the right way, show me where to spend this money so that it will do the most good, and I will obey Your lead.

CHAPTER 86

After spending some time on this bench in her garden, Sadie got up with a pleasant smile on her face, she headed for the house.

She raised her hands in the air, and shouted, "Thank you God for your great love and mercy to me and my children, I love you, Lord with all my heart. I know you are a sovereign God, and you will rule my life forever."

Before reaching for the doorknob, she glanced back out in the garden, recalling her precious thoughts. She opened the door in front of her, then closed the door behind her, she rested against the closed door for a moment with her eyes closed. Sadie opened her eyes and smiled to herself as she headed for the stairs and the sanctuary of her bedroom. As she entered the bedroom a peace like nothing she ever experienced fell upon her, as she stretched her lithe body on the bed.

"Thank you Jesus," she whispered before closing her eyes for a well deserved nap.

Printed in the United States
134999LV00003B/9/P